Capricious
A Texan Tale of Love and Magic
by Julie Cox

Circlet Press, Inc.
Cambridge, MA

Contents

Chapter One

A satyr and a merrow burst through the door to the back office of Allison's Café in each other's arms. The satyr kicked the door closed behind him, picked the merrow up, and set her on the desk, a steel counter long ago commandeered from the kitchen. She wrapped her thighs around his hips, letting her waitressing skirt hike up high. He kissed her fiercely, the practiced kiss of someone who knew exactly how the other person kissed, how she liked to be touched—lips against her ears and her neck, hands cupping her breasts and then moving under her shirt and bra to stroke her hard nipples. His cock throbbed against the front of his jeans, and she unzipped his pants, pushed his boxers far enough down to get her hand around his cock, and began stroking him.

"Christ, girl," he gasped, "you're cutting right to the chase today, huh?"

"I don't have long," she said. "I gotta get back to the floor and keep an eye on things. Maybe we'll have time for foreplay another day. But today, baby, I want you to take me like crazy. No pretense, no long work-up." She reached up and grabbed his horns behind his head, soliciting a soft sound of want; she clearly knew exactly what that did to him. "We both know what we want, a fast and furious fuck before heading back into the fray. I been thinking about how I was gonna fuck you since you walked in." He gasped when she pressed against his cock. "I took my panties off before I called you back here."

His cock against her bare, slick pussy, he needed no further encouragement. He slid his hands underneath her rump and entered her in one smooth motion. She cried out, a wonderful noise, and moved against him as he thrust into her, giving her all his length in each stroke. With each thrust she made the most delightful noises in his ear, her pussy squeezing tight. She was so hot around him—he loved how she felt, how wet she got, the silky texture of her skin. Her clit was positioned so that he rubbed against it with every motion. Not all women were built like that; she was lucky. Still, she slid a hand between them, pressed her clit harder against his thrusting cock, and her legs shook, the pleasure sending tremors through her already.

He sped up, harder, listening with rapt pleasure as she gasped repeatedly and bit his shoulder to stifle her cries, her body shaking as she came. He didn't give her long to recover. He unbuttoned her shirt partway, roughly brought her breasts out above the fabric, and ducked his head to suck her nipples. He drew out of her and flicked her clit gently between his fingers until he felt her starting to move again, wriggling with want, with the absence of him. He took a condom out of the drawer where she kept them and slipped it on, well practiced, with one hand. Turning her around, he pushed her down against the desk.

"Oh man!" she said, and he felt her jolt, the steel cold against her breasts, but she didn't pull away. He kicked her legs apart, held her against the desk, and rammed into her. She yelled, her body bucking with pleasure, raising her hips to take in more of him. He had her, thoroughly and vigorously, and she reveled in being had. She called his name, asked for more, thrust back against him. He gave her more.

When she came this time, her juices ran down her legs, and her voice was ragged, spent. He came hard, his body rocked with pleasure, and his knees threatened to buckle. Only when she was quiet again, relaxing under his hands, did he reluctantly pull out of her. She stood, a languid, loopy smile on her face.

"Hell, you're good," she said. "I needed, so much, to get fucked like that. Thank you, Luke."

"Thank you," he said, kissing her. "You have no idea how much lustful energy you put out. I won't have to go to a strip club for a month. That being the equivalent of satyr Hot Pockets, the dinner of last resort."

"Glad to be helpful," she said, retrieving the panties she had discarded earlier and rebuttoning her shirt. She fished a box of sanitary hand towels out of her desk and handed them to him. "The breasts-on-cold-counter thing was pretty damn cool."

"What can I say, I was inspired."

"I'm gonna go clean up," she said, starting clumsily toward the bathroom. "And Luke?"

He raised his eyebrows.

"You get low on magic again, you just give me a call, you hear? Just don't mention it to Sally Wilson."

He bowed his head low, though his brow furrowed with incomprehension. "As your majesty commands."

"I ain't a queen anymore; that was a past life. Now, I'm just a normal merrow running a diner and occasionally fucking this hot satyr friend of mine when we both need it."

"The charming lives we lead," he said.

When he walked out of the office, several people in the diner stared; a couple looked distinctly away. Orson just smirked at Luke from below his substantial mustache.

"So things went well, I take it."

"I thought that office was soundproofed," Luke said. He wasn't embarrassed at all, just surprised.

"Not soundproof enough, evidently. But I can tell you this, all these boys in here now, they're gonna be coming back. Allison's sex life don't exactly hurt her business."

"So I'm a feature," Luke said cheerfully, picking up his hat and leaving a handful of cash on the table as a tip for their waitress, who was blushing furiously and not looking at them.

Orson looked down at the table. "She didn't even buy you lunch?"

"Oh, she fed me."

"Not what I asked."

"Orson," Luke said with a sigh, "you just don't get women, do you?"

"No, and neither do you."

"Luckily, I don't need to, because they get me," Luke said.

Orson shook his head. "Just don't tell Sally you occasionally bang Allison."

"You're the second person in five minutes to give me that advice. What's Sally got to do with it? We ain't dating."

Orson rolled his eyes and held the door open for Luke. "If you don't know, then never mind."

"Like you got any more insight than I do." They braced themselves against the desert wind and headed out to Luke's truck.

Chapter Two

The red pickup truck kicked up a wake of dust as it sped down FM 190. On either side of the snaking two-lane asphalt, the West Texas landscape stretched wide and lonely, a flat scrub-brush plain dotted with mesquite and nettle, fringed with jutting mountains on every side of the horizon but east. Dark yellow dust covered everything, including the two men inside the truck.

Luke pulled a pack of Camels from his shirt pocket and passed it to Orson. "Light me one, will you?"

"Sure." Orson lit one for Luke and one for himself and rolled the passenger-side window down. It stuck partway down and refused to budge.

"Roll the window back up!" Luke said. "You're letting in dust."

Orson ran a hand across the dash and came up with an ochre-smeared palm. "Oh no, what will the help think."

"Fine. Have no standards." Luke leaned forward over the steering wheel and squinted. "What's that in the road?"

Orson leaned forward too. A white shape gleamed against the gray asphalt, far up the road. As flat as the land was, they had a long time to watch it grow larger. Finally Orson said, "Goat."

"It's not a goat. It's little."

"Baby goat."

"It's flat."

"Dead baby goat."

Luke scowled. "You want it to be a goat. You want to see me uncomfortable."

Orson reached over and patted the large set of ridged horns on Luke's head. "You know, satyr-boy, it's OK to admit you have a thing for goats."

"One, get your hands off my horns. You know what that does to me, and unless you been holding out on me all these years, neither of us wants that. Two, it's like monkeys for you. They're relatives."

"I hate fuckin' monkeys."

"Then why don't you stop?"

They laughed, short and nervous, watching the white shape grow larger. Finally they were upon it, and Luke stopped the truck and got out. A blue-ticked dog with a stub tail jumped out of the back of the truck and followed him.

"Sootie, get back in the truck."

She wagged her tail and grinned. Luke rolled his eyes and turned, allowing her to be present. She followed him as he walked to the white shape and knelt down.

"Well, it's a goat all right," Orson said.

"It's flat," Luke said, equally puzzled. The white kid sprawled in the road was, quite literally, skin and bones. Luke stubbed his cigarette out on the asphalt, took a knife out of his boot, and poked at a wound in the kid's chest.

"Don't touch it!"

Luke rolled his eyes. "Chill out. Look at this—no blood, no wounds except these puncture marks on its chest." Luke's eyes grew wide.

"Oh no," Orson said, "it's not a chupacabra."

"But it fits! A nice-looking young kid like this, dead for no reason I can see, with no wounds except frickin' vampire-looking fang marks and no blood—it's been exsanguinated!"

"Whatever that means. The chupacabra doesn't exist."

Luke put the knife back in his boot and stood. "You're a Tuatha Dé Danann. Your best friend is a satyr. You live in a border town that borders more than Mexico. How in the wide world can you say anything doesn't exist?"

"Just because I've seen some extraordinary things doesn't mean I've tilted my head and let my brain run out my ears to make room for any nonsense folk dream up. Like some people." He raised his eyebrows significantly, and Luke ignored it.

As they walked back to the car, Luke shook his head, a gesture made more emphatic by his horns. "You're a skeptical fae.

Remarkable. Sootie, get in the back. The back! Stupid dog—there you go, good girl."

They rolled around the body of the goat and drove toward town in silence. Finally Orson broke it. "I bet it's one of YC Wilson's goats. Better tell him. He might be looking for it."

"Oh yeah—I bet it was one of his Saanens. Pity that. I'm gonna tell more than Wilson, though. I'm gonna tell the council."

Orson laughed. "What, so the fairy princess can mock you?"

"Cormick's a good guy."

"He's more sarcastic than me, and that's just caustic."

"I'm well acquainted with sarcasm, thanks."

"Jeez, Luke, don't tell the council there's a chupacabra loose, they already think you're a nut. And in this town, that's saying something."

Luke set his jaw and stared down the road. "We'll see."

Orson was at the bar when Luke found him that evening. Luke slid onto the barstool next to him and, without preamble, said, "I told Wilson, and we're gonna set up a watch tonight."

"Oh yeah?"

Luke nodded. From across the bar a booming voice called, "Luke, you want a beer?"

"No thanks, Dad, I'm good," Luke answered. To Orson, he continued in a conspiratorial tone, "No matter what I think it is, something got ahold of one of his goats, so we're going to stake out the kid pen. Tomorrow morning Sal's going to go driving around in her four-wheeler, see if she can see anything."

Orson sighed. "Who's on watch?"

"Just me and Glen."

"Glen the goblin's in on this?" Orson groaned. "Just don't give him a gun."

"Hey, Glen's a good shot. And that donkey was just fine."

"Because he was using bird shot! And the donkey was wearing an orange 'don't shoot me' vest! God, no wonder people hate hunting season around here, if people like Glen are given free rein with a gun."

Luke shook his head. "Come up to the house tomorrow, I'll tell you if anything happens."

Orson sighed. "Fine. Good luck."

Chapter Three

Late that night or early the next morning, Luke sat in the bed of his truck, staring out across a pen of goats. They were startlingly white in the moonlight, almost shimmering. Earlier they had been noisy and boisterous, the deep bleats of the nannies mixing in with the sweet baby-bleats of their kids, occasionally punctuated with the deep-throated bleat of the billy. Now they were still and quiet, asleep except for the billy, who dozed standing up. The nannies and kids slept piled up next to each other with their heads laid across each other's backs, giving the impression of a great lumpy snowfield in the middle of the desert.

He hopped down out of the truck and paced around it to get his blood moving. It would be all too easy to fall asleep. The billy goat opened his eyes and watched Luke suspiciously. Luke grinned at him.

"Jealous of the horns or something? You know a bigger billy when you see one, don't you?" he asked the goat, who stared balefully at him. Luke stretched; with a twist of his head he popped his neck, which was constantly a little sore. He once thought he'd get used to the weight of the horns. Not so much, it seemed. He reached down to the tips of his toes—well, his hooves. He squinted at his feet for a minute, playfully throwing the mental switches that changed what he saw from what everyone could see to what other myth-folk saw, like opening one eye and then the other. Camera one, camera two. Steel-toed work boots below battered jeans, split hooves with soft buckskin-and-black fur. He pitied the true fae, like Orson and Cormick, who didn't have anything more than a vaguely otherworldly aura to differentiate them from ordinary people. It was fun having this other physical self so few could see. Plus, he had a hell of a headbutt. He tossed his horns and snorted. Just let that goatsucker try and take on this billy goat, he thought. Everyone knew what happened to monsters who took on billy goats who were too big. Especially gruff ones. And Luke considered himself gruff.

"Luke?"

Luke jumped, shaken from his thoughts, and looked over his shoulder. Wilson's daughter, Sally, stood there in a Pink Floyd T-shirt, striped pink-and-white boxers, and cowboy boots. As always, around her shimmered the vague impression of feathers and light. He didn't know what she was—she didn't talk about it—but whatever it was, it seemed happy. And avian. Luke grinned.

"Hey, Sal. Nice jammies."

"I'm comfy, so shut up." She climbed into the bed of the truck, and Luke joined her. "How's it going out here?"

"My phone ran out of juice, so a little boring, can't play solitaire, but all's well with the herd."

Sally nodded. "Real freaky what happened with that kid. Thanks for coming out."

"No problem. You been over to see Glen at the milking shed?"

"Yeah, he hasn't seen anything either." She stretched and looked up at the stars, a dazzling display of milky starlight against the velvet black sky. "Sure is a nice night."

Luke was not looking at the sky. "Sure is." He smiled. "You know, Sal, seems a shame to waste this semiprivate truck...."

Sally laughed. "In your dreams, satyr. Like I'm going to bang your hairy ass in your truck out by the goat pen."

"Don't sound like a bad plan to me," he purred.

Sally rolled her eyes. She picked up his cigarettes, lit one and fished herself a Dr. Pepper out of the little cooler in the truck. "I have bed hair, no makeup, I smell like death because I never did get to take my shower tonight. Why is it you choose these moments to be amorous?"

Luke shrugged. "You're your real self. Your daddy know you're smoking again?"

"Huh. That's almost sweet. And no, he doesn't. And he isn't

going to, is he?" she said, smiling, and blew out a thin stream of smoke like a tea kettle.

"I dunno, that depends," Luke said.

"On what?"

"On how good of friends we are," he said, circling an arm around her waist.

She smacked his hand and laughed. "Like I'd give it up to keep a cigarette from my dad."

"I was kinda hoping you'd be giving it up because you're after my sweet body," he said, running his hands down his chest in a playful Madonna-"Vogue" way.

Sally laughed. "Did you know that capricious comes from the same root as goats' scientific name? Caprine?"

"Of course I knew that. How could I not know that? Everyone knows that. And capri pants, which better display my nice, shiny hooves. Also related to Capri Sun, as in sweet and juicy."

Sally rolled her eyes. "You satyrs. Is there nothing you wouldn't jump?"

"Honey, I wouldn't jump you 'cause I'm a satyr. I'd jump you 'cause you're a sweet little thing."

"And I'm hot."

"And you're hot," he agreed.

She tousled his hair. "You know, you're strangely refreshing, Luke. I always know exactly where I stand with you. Other guys try to be my friends because they want to get in my pants. You want to get in my pants because you're my friend. The problem is, you have lots of friends."

Luke tilted his head. "That's most elegantly put."

Sally groaned and stubbed out the cigarette. "Yeah, it's what passes for elegant around here. Good night, Luke."

"G'night, Sal. You get bored, you know where I am."

"And will know where to avoid, then. Don't shoot anything that isn't a chupacabra."

"Aye-aye, Captain." He smiled, watching her leave.

Chapter Four

Luke watched the sky lighten and the world wake up. When the goats were bleating and the kids playing, he got into the cab of his truck and drove to Wilson's house. There hadn't been so much as a coyote all night.

He stomped the dust off his boots before giving a perfunctory knock on the frame of the door and letting himself in. He stopped halfway through the doorway. Sally was on the couch with her mother, Georgia, sobbing. Wilson stood behind them, awkwardly patting Sally's shoulder. He looked up at Luke and waved him in.

"Sally's cat was killed last night over by the chicken coop," he said softly. He led Luke into the kitchen and poured him a cup of coffee. "Same as that kid—puncture wounds on the chest, no blood."

Luke stared into his coffee for a moment and took a long drink. "Shit. Which cat?"

"Wormy."

"Christ, something killed Wormy? He was part bobcat! He took out a fox last winter."

Wilson nodded. "So... it was something mean."

Luke and Wilson exchanged looks loaded with worry, amazement, and a little bit of fear.

Sally got up off the couch, leaving her mother's embrace for Luke's. He handed his coffee to Wilson and wrapped his arms around Sally, the previous night's playful advances forgotten. She cried quietly against his shoulder while he stroked her hair and tried very hard not to think about what her shampoo smelled like. Finally she stood up straight and wiped her nose with a crumpled tissue. "Sorry," she said.

"Naw, naw," he crooned. He took a handkerchief out of his pocket and wiped her cheek. "You got cause to cry, don't apologize."

"Thank you for coming out and trying to help us." She smiled and chuckled through her sniffles. "What kind of a person still carries a handkerchief, anyway?"

Luke smiled back. "A very old one."

"Ha, you're not that much older than me."

"You know what I mean. Old souls, we are." He retrieved his coffee and leaned against the counter. "So what now? Glen will be here in a minute, I figure."

Wilson nodded. "I'm gonna contact animal control, see what they can do." He gave Luke a significant look. "Is there anyone I should ask for up there?"

Luke regarded Wilson carefully. As Sally's father, Wilson knew she was different, and he knew her friends were different. There had been too many extraordinary circumstances over the years, too many magical accidents, to leave a sharp man like him entirely in the dark. To his credit, he had never asked them directly to explain what they were. Still, to give him a name would be to give over the identity of one more member of their very secret group, the supposedly fictional creatures who lived in and around Fox Pass.

"I'll call," Sally said.

So there it was. Wilson nodded and went to find the telephone. Luke sighed. "Your dad's gonna be pissed."

Sally nodded and turned to retreat to her bedroom. Over her shoulder, she said, "Let him be."

When Luke got home, Orson was sitting on his porch. Luke was startled at first but then remembered he'd told him to come over. He parked under the big soapberry tree and walked up the steps to the sagging porch. His place was small, but it was as neat as he could make it, which meant that all the half-broken but conceivably useful junk was in the shed instead of in the yard. The house was tiny and in need of paint, but it was sound, and that was about all Luke cared about.

Sootie's stub tail wagged as she wriggled impatiently, waiting for him to notice her. Saul, a large white dog, lay in the shade near Luke's chickens and goats. This animal, unlike Sootie, took little notice of Luke or his comings and goings. Between the two, Luke preferred Sootie, but Saul was undoubtedly the more useful, keeping watch day and night over the other animals.

"Hey," Luke said.

"Hey," Orson answered, his brows knit in an expression of concern at Luke's dour manner.

Luke related the events of the previous evening to Orson, who nodded thoughtfully. When he finished, he sighed and looked at the dog. "Yes, I see you, Sootie. How're you, girl?"

Sootie vaulted up at him, grinning and wagging with her whole back end. Luke managed to unlock the door around her and motioned to Orson. "You comin' in?"

"Naw, I'd better get on." But he sat on the porch still, looking out across the yard.

Luke sighed. There was no car in the yard; he wondered how Orson had gotten to his house in the first place. He opened the door, and Sootie ran in, straight to the pantry where her food was. "Come on," Luke coaxed. "I been up all night and I'd rather have company for breakfast than be alone with my brain. And I can tell you about Sally's pajamas."

Orson relented. "All right. You realize that you're more interested in Sally's pajamas than in banging Allison, right?"

Luke gave him a strange look. "What? Both those things are interesting. I figure you don't want the details of me having sex with Allison. Besides, she's not romantically interested in me. We're friends with benefits, and happily neither of us is seriously interested in the other. Sally, now, that's a different story."

Orson looked unconvinced.

"And if you stick around while I take a nap, you can come with me to the hardware store, give me a hand. I'll buy you a beer afterward. Or get Dad to give you one." Which would conveniently put them half a mile from Orson's trailer.

"Sure, I can do that." He came inside.

Luke shook his head as he locked the door behind him.

Sometimes it was a pain in the ass, making it sound like Orson was doing him a favor when it was Luke doing the favors. But if that was the price of Orson's friendship, it was a small price to pay in the long run.

Chapter Five

Sunday night was council night. Luke didn't normally go, and Orson usually sat in the back and said nothing, arms folded across his round chest. Tonight, Luke, Orson, and Sally took the front row.

Council night in Fox Pass, Texas, was a sight to behold. It appeared to the human eye to be any ordinary city council meeting, though heavily attended and held quite more often than any other. The eyes of a magical creature saw things differently.

The crowd was a melting pot of mythology. A golem and an ifrit discussed livestock codes in one corner. A group of Irish fae, mostly from the same family, argued among themselves. A giant boar, a dripping-wet horse, a jackalope, and two armored women listened politely to a sea serpent who had passionate but wholly unworkable ideas about damming the Rio Grande. At a table at the front of the room were seven people—six representatives from the far-flung districts surrounding Fox Pass and the "mayor" of their secret community. The representatives were equally outlandish: a deer woman, a man with skin composed of leaves, another man with a grinning brown face and backward feet. A gorgon looked bored at the end of the table, nodding to a monologuing centaur. A large and bloody wolf sat next to the myth community's mayor, a young man named Cormick; she looked at him with something like admiration, something like hunger. The mayor himself appeared to be perfectly human.

Allison was there too, looking in her otherworldly self as if she'd just stepped out of a shower, with a sort of slick-wet shimmer to her. Her hair was tangled with twines of seaweed, and when she raised her hand to wave to Luke and Orson, translucent webbing stretched between her fingers. Seeing Sally with them, she smiled and turned quickly away. Luke started toward her, but Orson stepped on his foot, stopping him in his tracks.

"What?" Luke said.

"Trust me."

At last, Cormick banged a gavel to call the meeting to order. When this had no effect whatsoever, he sighed, stood up, and yelled, "Hey, shut up!"

After several more minutes of diminishing squabbling, all the creatures were finally seated, if not perfectly quiet. Having apparently waited as long as he could stand, Cormick said, "OK, that's enough already. We've got a lot of ground to cover, so let's keep this going at a good clip, all right?" He turned to the wolf— the secretary—who read the agenda and, as Cormick wanted, kept the meeting going quickly.

"OK," Cormick said when they'd reached the end of official business, "we've got a few other things to go over that aren't on the agenda. Anyone surprised? No? Figured. We've got a delegate here from the national council in New York—"

The crowd went into an uproar. Cormick gave it a minute and then put both fingers in his mouth and whistled. "Hey!" he barked. "Shut the fuck up and listen!"

"Or you'll what?" a troll demanded from the back.

"Or I'll get really annoyed!" Cormick said, eliciting a handful of chuckles. "Give me a break, Alan, OK? Christ. He's here because Fox Pass is a border town, and, according to them, something big came through the border a few nights ago."

This had the curious effect of hushing the crowd. Nothing came through the borders without everyone in Fox Pass knowing about it, and yet some northerner claimed to know more about it than they did.

"So they sent us a guy to deal with it," Cormick said. "He's a German beast, though most of you will probably know his type best from Washington Irving's 'The Legend of Sleepy Hollow.'"

"They sent us a headless horseman?" someone cried.

"I thought that was Tim Burton," the secretary said.

Cormick closed his eyes, visibly pained. "Yeah, they sent us a headless horseman, who would eat Tim Burton for high tea if given half a chance. He seems like a nice enough guy, so give him a break. I know we've had problems with the council in the past. I know how a lot of you feel about them and that some of you have even talked about secession. Trust me, that idea is a dozen kinds of bad. They give us protection; they run the courts. So we're going to do everything we can to be accommodating to this guy. Okeydokey?"

Luke raised his hand. "Cormick, I—"

"Hey, horns and hooves, is it pertinent to this exact subject?"

Luke nodded vigorously. "Absolutely it is."

"Amazing. Go ahead, then."

Luke stood and told the council about the dead baby goat, the stakeout, and Sally's dead cat. He left out the part about thinking the culprit was a chupacabra.

Cormick nodded. "I'll let him know. Thanks for the info, Luke."

Luke sat. "So this is bigger than just us," he said softly.

"And isn't likely a chupacabra," Orson added, hopeful.

"We'll see," Luke said. "In any case, we need to figure out a way to keep tabs on this new guy."

"I'm kind of hoping he'll be helpful in tracking down whatever it was," Sally said.

Luke raised an eyebrow. "Either that, or he is what we've been hunting."

Sally was about to argue when Cormick stood up, talking. "—like you all to meet him before we go home to our respective caves, aeries, bogs, trailer parks, and condos. So try to look more like a dignified assembly and less like a Wild Hunt, OK?" He said this last with a note of hopelessness and sat.

The side door opened, and Glen the goblin motioned for an unseen figure to come in. A man dressed in black, complete with black hair and black eyes, walked into the room. Luke heard Sally say, "Ohhhh...." He scowled. He was unprepared for Sally to find this outsider attractive, though he had to admit the man was strikingly handsome, with his salon-cut hair, delicately pointed sideburns, straight white teeth, and white-collar hands. He was tall, sleek, well built and carried with him a sense of gravity.

He also carried with him, in his magical form, his own skull.

"Behold the world's ultimate goth," Luke muttered to Orson, who suppressed a chuckle.

"Cormick's just jealous he can't be as metro as that guy," Orson said.

"I didn't even know you knew the word metro."

Sally shushed them. "Shut up," she said, "I can't hear myself fantasize."

"Oh," Luke said, "it is so on."

Cormick spoke to the stranger, who then turned to the assembled mythological creatures. He cleared his throat. "I'm... not one for making speeches," he said in a voice remarkably free of any accent, "but your mayor has asked.... My name is August Waterford, and as you've surely been told, and can tell, I'm not from around here." The female portion of the crowd laughed lightly. "I've been told you have a problem, and I hope I can be of assistance to you. That's all." He sat in a chair that Glen had produced from some unseen corner.

"Cormick, you've made a friend!" Luke cried out.

Cormick winced. "Well, that didn't take long. August, he refers to the fact that I was the only person in this town with clean fingernails until you showed up."

"Hey!" Sally cried.

"The only man."

"Better."

"So forgive the ignorant peasants if they tease you," Cormick said.

"Please stop apologizing for us," Orson said, standing up. "I've had enough of being insulted by my own mayor. Mr. Waterford, it's nice to meet you. I hope you have a pleasant stay and are back on the road as soon as possible." With a withering look at Cormick, he turned and strode out of the room. Luke and Sally followed him, shrugging at each other.

Outside, Orson paced in front of Luke's truck, talking quickly and angrily to himself. Sally muttered her good-byes and headed toward her own car while Luke took out his cigarettes, lighting one for him and one for Orson. After a few minutes of stewing and smoking, they climbed into the truck. Luke pulled out of the parking lot in silence. It was only when they were on the road that Luke spoke.

"We've got to get that chupacabra, or whatever it is, out of here fast, and not just for my sake or for Sally's animals."

Orson nodded. "Whatever it is, it's dead."

"Glad to hear you're really on board now."

"Are you kidding? It's a matter of pride now." With a dark look, he added, "Sometimes pride is all we've got left."

Chapter Six

There was little time for chupacabra hunting during the week. Luke was up before dawn, as he normally was, to feed and water the animals, gather the eggs, milk the goats, check on a broody hen, weed the vegetable garden, spray the peach trees, and make note of the thousand little chores that needed to be done. The list rattled through his head on his way to work. Fix the fence posts that were rotting off at the bottom. Get the bees out of the shed— after building a beehive for them to go into. Take down the dead bois d'arc. Get the deadwood out of the trees near the house. Trim the goats' hooves. Treat the chickens for lice and mites. Get more diatomaceous earth to deworm the chickens. Deworm the goats. Take the dogs in for their shots. Dogs....

He looked up at the rearview mirror. There was Sootie, grinning ecstatically at him from the back of the truck.

"Son of a bitch!" he said, scowling. He considered pulling over and yelling at her, but to what end? He thought about going back, but he was almost to work. He shook his head and banged his horns against the headrest. Sootie'd just have to stay with Sally for the day. Her place was close enough to the construction site where Luke worked.

When he pulled into Sally's drive, he was surprised to see an unfamiliar black motorcycle under the carport next to Wilson's tractor. He took a second look at it—the bike only looked like a motorcycle to human eyes. He was actually looking at a massive black warhorse. He could guess who the animal belonged to. The horse eyed him as he passed it on his way to the house, its eyes blazing red, and he eyed the horse right back. He almost ran into a post, he was so concerned with the horse.

When Sally came to the door, she looked annoyed. August Waterford was on her couch, in crisp blue jeans that hadn't seen the dust of a single day's labor. His shirt was still black. He and Luke regarded each other coolly.

"Nice ride," Luke said.

"Thanks," August said. He motioned to Luke's horns. "Nice rack."

Luke smiled in spite of himself. "Thanks."

"So that makes you a...."

"Satyr." Luke moved around the couch so his hooves could be seen.

"Oh. That's... Greek?"

Luke shrugged. "Mediterranean. On my mom's side, anyway." He suddenly remembered he wasn't supposed to be friendly with the horseman and turned to Sally. "Sootie hitched a ride in my truck today. I wanted to see if she could stay here while I was at work."

Sally nodded. "Sure thing. I'll look after her." She was still holding the door open.

Luke pretended not to notice and leaned against the wall. "Anything happen last night?"

"No. Glen, Orson, and Dad were out patrolling most of the night. I'm going to be out tonight, as well as August and Mom."

Luke raised his eyebrows. "You be careful."

"Thanks for that. I can take care of myself."

"Don't I know it."

"Good-bye, Luke."

Luke called Sootie inside and patted her. "You take good care of Sally here, you understand?" he told the dog, who listened with rapt attention. "Don't let her out of your sight. Even if she tells you to go on."

"Bye, Luke."

"She's already ate, but I thought I might drop by at lunch—"

"Luke!"

"Fine, fine." He went out the door and scowled his way back to the truck, an image of Sally jumping that awful August guy forming in his head.

He couldn't get it out of his head all day. First he pictured them on Sally's couch, right where they had been when he left—August surprised but willing, Sally enthusiastic, brazen. She'd been wearing little cutoff jean shorts that hugged her ass and a spaghetti-strap shirt that could slide right off her shoulders. He hadn't seen bra straps. Had she even been wearing a bra? He wasn't sure if it was a good thing that he couldn't remember. He'd been so taken up with worrying about August that he hadn't gotten a good look at her breasts. Surely that was a bad sign, when he, the satyr, didn't notice breasts, behind a bra or not.

She'd been barefoot, as usual, her hair held back from her face with little bitty clips shaped like butterflies. His mind worked against him, and he got a mental flash of Sally delicately removing one of the little clips and seizing it onto August's nipple, eliciting a gasp from him. She'd like how he looked, his head thrown back, salon-perfect hair splayed over the couch pillows and her grandmother's afghan. Would she have the gall to take him right there, in the same living room where Luke had comforted her over her dead cat so recently? Or would she take him elsewhere?

Which was not a helpful line of thinking, because his obsessed train of thought went spiraling out in all kinds of directions. The barn, for a literal roll in the hay, where he could fuck her from behind as she clung to the hitching post in the lazy, warm sunlight. The kitchen, where he could lift her up and lay her on the island. Her bedroom, the same room and headboard she'd had all her life, his cock in her pussy, in her mouth, and her writhing against him, asking for more....

By midday Luke was half-mad with lust, unable to exorcise the image of Sally and August from his mind. He thought about going to see Allison, but he didn't want to fuck her when he was thinking of someone else; that would be an insult to his friend. He decided to take care of matters himself, and at lunch, he drove his truck to a secluded area, ostensibly to grab a bite to eat. Food was not what was on his mind. He'd been hard off and on for hours, and he was rock stiff as he took his cock out of his pants. He wet his hand with spit and stroked up and down, giving in to the image of August fucking his girl. Sally wanting sex, arching like a cat in heat, desire destroying her control and her poise, her pussy aching like a bruise.

That was what it was, he knew all at once as he thrust into his hand, body bucking. He wanted her to feel the same chaotic lust he felt. He wanted to bust down her reserve, make her show him that she felt it too. Because he could feel the lust in her, leaking from the seams of her carefully maintained facade. She might seem in control to everyone else, but satyrs knew lust; it had a color, a taste, that was unmistakable. As he came, moaning Sally's name, he was sure she wanted him, followed him with her eyes, dreamed of him in the dark and in the light. That surety would not remain, would falter the longer he let it sit, but for a moment, he was sure of himself.

Chapter Seven

Luke picked Sootie up from Sally's, which amounted to the front door of the house opening, Sootie running out, and the door slamming shut. He frowned at that, and his assurance that Sally really did want him, and not August, wilted. He turned from the asphalt highway to the concrete road running up the mountain, to the gravel street he lived on, to the deeply rutted dirt drive of his house, to his usual parking spot under the soapberry. Bone-weary, he climbed the steps to the porch.

He sat in a sagging folding chair made of crisscrossing vinyl, reminding himself to try to fix the few straps that were broken. Duct tape ought to do it. He pulled over the sand-filled coffee can that served as an ashtray and lit a cigarette. It hurt to think. He was sweaty and filthy from the construction site, angry and frustrated with Sally. He wondered why, exactly, he was so possessive all of a sudden. It wasn't like he had any kind of a stake on her, but he had begun to think of her as his. He dropped his head into his hands and growled. Sally never dated; she wasn't into anyone, that he could remember. Somehow he'd always assumed that if she had the inclination to be with anyone, why, he was a natural choice. For the first time he had to admit that she may have already considered the option carefully and dismissed it. His self-assurance from before evaporated.

Why? That was the question. Luke was vain enough to consider himself good looking, in a good ol' boy sort of way. He had the lean, ropy muscles that hard labor gave a man. Sally liked his horns. She even claimed to like his hooves. He wasn't as clean as Cormick or August, but that was because he worked all the time. A woman ought to like a man who was sweaty and dirty because he'd worked his ass off all day. It wasn't like he didn't bathe when he had the chance.

He looked around his little piece of property. It was a peaceful evening, one of those quiet times of day when the light caught just right in the wind chimes and the hummingbird feeders to make the whole place feel more magical than it was. And with Luke around, things were magical. He smiled at the cottonwood seeds floating like tiny fairies across the lawn. They might make him sneeze, but they were lovely. The chickens were in the front along with the two dairy goats and their kids. Saul, the big white dog that watched over the livestock, dozed in the shade until Sootie ran over and started climbing on him. He tried to maintain an aura of peace and dignity but finally gave in and rolled her over to wrestle.

Yup, it was a good place, Luke reaffirmed to himself. Some folks had tried to buy it several years back. He'd given them an unqualified no. The trees were tall and thick, and the livestock and vegetables flourished. At the moment the half-acre vegetable garden overflowed with tomatoes, cucumbers, and okra. In the fall there would be lettuce, pumpkins, and peas. With the vegetables, milk, eggs, kids, and chicks, he hardly ever had to buy more than basic staples like flour and sugar at the store. And the extra was good money. Not a lot, but well earned. He was proud to be self-sufficient. And he was proud that it wasn't just the spring a little higher up the mountain that made his little patch of land productive. It was Luke, too—that satyr core that embodied ripeness, lush forests, fertility. Drunk on the fruit of the earth. Of course, he had to throw some pretty wild parties to keep up the magical energy he sank into the place, soak up the lust-energy from others, but that was a hell of a lot of fun, too.

Satisfied that his home, his life, and his own self ought to be sufficient for any lucky girl, Luke and his ego settled deeper into his chair. He hooked his horns over the back, crossed his hooves, and closed his eyes, listening to the drone of the cicadas and the happy clucks of the chickens. Let Sally have her stupid fancy city guy with his soft hands and luxurious hair. She was the one missing out. He wriggled in frustration. If it had been Friday, he would have driven down to Del Rio—hell, maybe even as far as

San Antonio—gotten drunk, and found himself some obliging young thing all too eager to take him to bed. In fact, that's what he'd do this weekend, chupacabra or no. If Sally didn't want him, he'd find someone who did, even if it was just for a night. But as he drifted off, he couldn't help thinking about her still.

His dream would have highly offended Sally. He found her by the spring, barefoot in a thin, sleeveless white shirt and boxers, much like she'd worn the night Luke kept watch over the goats. Her nipples stood out against the soft cotton, and the strap of her shirt fell from her shoulder. Her toes trailed in the cool water. Luke knelt next to her. She smiled at him and lay back, stretching, and the loose boxers clung to the curve between her legs. Luke felt blood rush to his cock, and he moved to cover her. But she giggled, leaped up, and danced away from him. He followed.

She slid down the embankment to the clear water of the pond. His logical mind—what there was of it—tried to argue that wild pond water wouldn't be clear, but he pushed that thought away when she stood up in her wet shirt. Her breasts stood out plainly now, and her expression urged him to action. He kicked off his boots and slid down into the water with her, jeans and all. He touched his hands to her waist, slid them up her sides to her breasts. He bent his head to suck her nipples through her shirt, first one, then the other, and she writhed in the water, knotting her fingers through his hair. Lifting her shirt, he played his tongue over her nipples, feeling her breasts with both hands. He took her shirt off the rest of the way and cast it aside to float in the water.

When he moved to kiss her mouth, she slid away from him with a coy smile and lifted herself up out of the water. Her boxers slid off behind her. Her bottom was round and smooth, and she looked over her shoulder to watch him. He ran his hand up the back of her thigh and cupped her ass as he had her breasts. He was rock hard now, his cock straining against the zippered front of his jeans. He reached a hand between her legs, and she moved away from him yet again, up the bank to a flat, mossy rock. She stretched out, luxuriously, almost feline. The sun broke through above them and shone on her bronze skin. Luke thought he could almost see an aura of feathers.

Determined not to let her move away this time, he caught her by the ankles. She jumped and pulled, laughing, but he didn't let her go. He moved up between her legs. By dream logic, he had lost his usual jeans, that human attire, and was now simply a satyr, the wild creature he really was, hooves, horns, and all. He pinned Sally against the stone and began stroking against her clit with his cock.

Any play at resistance was gone now. Sally arched her back and wrapped her legs around Luke, moving in rhythm to rub herself against him. She felt so good, so hot and wet, up and down his shaft. She pressed against him with great fervor, almost feverish, with pressure he wasn't sure he could stand. Then, suddenly, she let go and flipped onto all fours. She raised her hips and pressed against him, clearly intending to envelope him. He put a hand on her back and laid his legs against hers. His other hand slipped down to her clit and began rubbing her in circles and strokes. He slid the head of his cock into her, just barely—then out, then barely in, then out. She cried out, her body bucking, asking for him.

"Do you want me?" he asked, rolling his hips to dip in and out of her rapidly.

"Yes! Oh God yes, Luke, fuck me!"

He'd thought to tease her, but he couldn't stand it anymore. He pushed his cock inside of her, the whole length in, feeling a sudden enveloping warmth and tightness. She yelled for more. He began thrusting, giving her all he could, as hard and as fast as he could. She was so wet, so slick, and the dream seemed to go on and on. She came and then came again, her body clenching upon him in bliss.

She rose up and turned, pushing him onto the stone. She was rough, and his head rang for a moment as she mounted him. Then Sally was riding up and down on him, taking in his whole length with each thrust, pressing her hand against her clit as she fucked him, her breasts bouncing. At last he came, deep inside her, and she shimmered again in the sunlight, going in and out of focus.

There again was that impression of feathers. No, not just an impression. Plumage blossomed on her skin and talons on her hands. A scream—no, that was his scream, as her talons landed on his chest—

He woke and realized it wasn't him screaming. Something out in the yard screamed for him.

Chapter Eight

Luke grabbed the shotgun that was always right inside the door and was off the porch before he realized it was full dark, with only the waning gibbous moon lighting the scene before him. The screams in the yard were garbled, inhuman, but easy enough to pinpoint. Saul wrestled with a creature in the moonlight, his bright white fur streaked with something darker. Luke raised the gun.

"Saul, move!" he yelled.

The dog was hurled through the air at him. He sidestepped and brought the gun to his shoulder again. He fired and only afterward realized what he had shot at. Spikes, claws, and wrinkled, slick skin like a mange-ridden dog. He'd shot at a chupacabra. He was sure of it.

What he wasn't sure of was whether or not he'd hit it. There was blood all over the ground, but a lot of it was the dog's. He turned slowly, looking for the chupacabra, and stared into a blue-tinged landscape that was achingly familiar yet terrifying.

The chupacabra landed on his back with all four feet worth of claws. Luke screamed and threw himself against a tree. The beast's grip loosened, and he bucked, flinging it up onto his horns. He butted against the tree and heard a crack. He hoped it was a chupacabra skull and not the tree or his own horns. Luke tossed his head, and the beast went flying. He crouched in the grass for long minutes, listening and waiting. Nothing.

Saul whimpered. Luke went over to the dog and tried to pick him up with one arm. The dog weighed more than a hundred pounds, and Luke had to half drag him to the pickup. But Saul wasn't the only one he was worried about.

"Sootie!" Luke screamed.

He opened the door to the truck, threw the shotgun onto the seat, and hauled Saul onto the floorboard. He stopped for a moment and looked out into the night. "Sootie!" he cried again, and his voice cracked. He called out for her again and again, his heart breaking. He felt suddenly weak, like his own legs wouldn't hold him up. The gouges in his back burned as if they'd been doused in alcohol. The hair on his neck stood up. He held his breath for a long moment, listening. Something was breathing nearby. It wasn't the dog.

Luke backed into the cab and shut the door. He was relieved to find he still had his keys in his pocket. He started the engine and pulled out of his parking spot.

The back window of the cab exploded inward in a shower of glass. Luke grabbed the gun off the seat and fired blind out the window. When he looked, half turned in his seat, he didn't see anything. Either he'd hit it and knocked it away... or it was on top of the cab.

Luke gunned the engine and made it almost to the end of the drive before he hit the brake. The truck skidded hard as it hit the potholes, and the chupacabra flew off the top of the cab and into the passion flower vine by the mailbox. Luke raced out the front gate, over the cattle guard and roared down the road toward town.

⁂

He didn't see or hear Sally when she came in, as he was sitting on the edge of the hospital bed, staring out the window. The first he knew of her was her arms around his neck, carefully avoiding the bandages on his back. She held him, and he cried all over again, shaking in terror and grief.

Saul had died before Luke could reach the veterinarian, so he turned the car around and went to the hospital instead. The doctors, after examining his wounds, blood loss, dead dog, and mauled truck, had declared it a puma attack. Everyone at the hospital looked at Luke with something like dumbfounded amazement. Luke agreed with the sentiment, though for different reasons.

Orson arrived after Sally, trembling with rage and vowing

revenge in surprisingly flowery and epic language. August and Cormick arrived at the same time, followed shortly by all kinds of other citizens of Fox Pass whom Luke had no interest in seeing at three in the morning. Everyone wanted to know the same thing— how to kill the creature that had attacked him. Theories were put forth, including traps, hunts, bigger dogs, armored dogs, and vorpal blades. Glen proposed that last bit, and the room grew quiet while Cormick ascertained that no, the goblin did not in fact possess a vorpal blade. He had just read about them, which astounded everyone. They hadn't known he could read.

"It's simple," August said.

The assembled magical creatures turned to look at the headless horseman, who leaned against the windowsill, his skull sitting on the rattling air conditioner beside him.

"You hunt it the same way you hunt anything else, by anticipating it," August continued.

"You can't anticipate a foe if you don't know anything about it," Orson growled.

"But we do already know enough about it. We know it's nocturnal. It's small but powerful. It's a predator. And we know what it hunts." He looked at Luke. "Goats, and whatever gets in its way."

"I'm not a goat," Luke said.

"Something thinks you are."

Luke tilted his head. "You got a theory?"

"I've been looking into the border violation. As you surely already know, the reason Fox Pass is such a well guarded gate is that it is a very thin gate. It's easy to go through this world and into the next if you have the keys. But because there are so many of you here, it's hard for strangers to get through. Your own magic does that. But you know that, I'm sorry, I'm just tired and repeating to myself what I've found today. With Leo the centaur's help, of course."

Luke saw most of the people in the room exchange uneasy glances. They clearly hadn't known.

"So if what came through—which we have to assume was the creature that attacked you—"

"The chupacabra," Luke said.

"Right. We'll call it that until we know for sure. If the chupacabra came through without anyone knowing about it, without any magical triggers going off, that means that someone who is already a part of Fox Pass let it in. Not only that, someone summoned it to the gate and guided it through."

Luke felt the room turn cold. "Are you sure?" he said softly.

"Beyond any thread of doubt."

His guts seemed to turn to water. Looking at the faces around him, he was pretty sure it was a common feeling. Before he could say anything, Orson spoke for him.

"All of you get the fuck out," Orson said. He directed a troll named Alan, who happened to be a cop, to take everyone who had heard August's theory down to the station and repeat to them over and over that they were not to tell anyone else the story until they were so sick of it that they could almost convince themselves they hadn't heard anything. Cormick turned pale and excused himself to compile some lists. August and Orson said they would go to Luke's place and see what the damage was. It was only as the room emptied that Luke realized Allison was there, and she gave him a smile as she exited, leaving him alone with Sally.

When everyone else was gone, Luke put his hand on Sally's.

"I had a dream about you," he said, "while sleeping out on the porch before all this happened. It was nice."

"I bet it was," she said, without a trace of sarcasm. After a few quiet minutes, she climbed onto the bed and curled up next to him. It was some time before he slept, and even then, he was troubled with dreams. Only Sally's quiet voice, telling him it was OK, kept him from slipping into nightmares.

Chapter Nine

Luke was released from the hospital after thirty-nine stitches, a dizzying amount of medication, and a blood transfusion. He took one look at his truck, with the back window shattered and the seats soaked with blood, and called for a tow. Sally drove him to his house in her car.

Orson and August were on the porch when they arrived, and Orson came down to meet them. "Your chickens are fine," he said as Luke got out of the car, wincing with every movement. "Apparently chupacabras don't like fowl."

Luke nodded. "And the rest?" He saw a freshly turned patch of earth beside the porch and for a terrible moment imagined Sootie down in the hole, still and dead. He breathed out, realizing the hole was too small for a dog.

"You lost a kid," Orson said. "That spotted doeling. Sorry about that."

Luke scowled. "Damn. She would've brought a good price too."

"We haven't found Sootie or the other goats."

Luke nodded. "No news is good news," he said, though he secretly didn't think so.

Sally wanted him to go inside, but Luke insisted on walking the perimeter of his property, calling for his dog. It hurt the longer he walked, and he was a good way away from the house when he realized he was going to have to sit down and rest before he tried to go back. He was angry about that, angry about Saul and the doeling, angry about everything. He shook his horns and sent a fresh wave of agony down his back. Breathing hard, he sat and waited for the pain to pass. Sally helped him get to his feet when he was ready.

On a whim, he put two fingers in his mouth and whistled loud. He waited. He was about to turn back toward the house when he heard a distant bark.

Hope rose like a tide in Luke's chest. He whistled again and again as the barking grew closer. The four missing goats came over a rise and down a tiny path little more than a rabbit run, and behind them, Sootie.

Luke fell to his knees and cried out in relief. Sootie ran up to him, and Sally stopped her before she bowled over her injured master. He hugged his dog, rubbed her fur, and buried his nose in her neck. "Oh God, you stink!" he said, but he didn't care. He hadn't realized how much he loved her, how much it would have hurt to have lost her.

When they got back to the house, Luke called in to work. His boss was miffed at his absence but quickly changed his tune to disbelief, then astonishment, at the puma attack tale that Luke spun. He insisted on sending someone over with some food (presumably also to see if Luke was telling the truth). He also added the very comforting comment, "Wow, at least you didn't get hurt at work!"

Sitting at the kitchen table, Luke bitched about having to lose two weeks of work. Finally August, who had not yet seemed to notice the barely concealed looks of dislike Luke kept giving him, said, "Look, I know it's lost money, but at least you get a vacation of sorts, right?"

Luke gave him an openly baleful glare. "Do you have any idea how close to the edge most of us are out here? I just lost not only two weeks of work but also an expensive, well trained dog and a doeling that would have netted a couple of hundred dollars. I have to come up with my insurance deductible plus twenty percent of the hospital bill. I almost refused the transfusion because I knew how much it would cost. Thank God I have insurance at all! When I find that chupacabra, the first thing I'm gonna do is punch his lights out. The second thing I'm gonna do is take his wallet."

August chuckled but stopped when no one else laughed. With a furrowed brow he said, "Isn't there someone in the local myth-community who could help you out with some of it? Up in New York we all share the burden of something like this."

Luke huffed. "Blood from a stone, man. No one else has

anything to give. I go broke, I lose the place, I might could find a couch to land on."

"You would have a couch," Sally and Orson said as one, looking offended.

"What I'm trying to say is," Luke said, "all of us are constantly at the point of losing it all. It's a party when someone's caught up on their mortgage. Tax season rolls around it's like Christmas, because no one here makes enough to pay income tax. We get those checks and suddenly the world's a little brighter, the wolf a little farther from the door."

August still looked skeptical. "But there are programs—"

Luke stood, his expression stormy. "Don't you come in my house and tell me about how there's help out there, how the government can come in and give me someone else's money. I ain't takin' someone else's money. Just because it comes from Washington doesn't make it free, or right. Ain't no such thing as a free lunch. This pitiful little wreck of a house, these old, worn clothes, that torn-up truck? It's fuckin' mine. Ain't no one given me anything, and I didn't need anyone but myself to get where I am. So fuckin' smoke that," he snarled and stomped off to his bedroom. He would have slammed the door, but there wasn't a door, just a curtain hung on a length of twine. Still, he did his best to snap it sharply across the doorway.

Through the thin fabric, Luke saw August turn toward Sally and Orson. "Does his accent always get that thick when he gets mad?" he heard August whisper.

Sally nodded.

"He's a loon," August said.

Sally closed the few steps between them and slapped August across the face. "Don't you dare speak about him," she warned. "He's one of the best there is."

August bowed his head in acquiescence and left them in peace.

❦

Luke wasn't entirely right when he said that it was all on him. Sally came to the house every few days to gather ripe vegetables and took them back to her parents' house, where her mother would exclaim how fine they were and insist on paying Luke more for them than she would pay at Walmart, which was the standard by which she priced all things. Orson found a trailer somewhere and hauled the goats and chickens down to Wilson's. He and Luke's father buried Saul by the side of the soapberry tree. When Luke's mother saw the bloodstains in the truck she cried all over again. Then she and one of her more stoic friends got after the truck with a steam cleaner and its very bulky attachments. Orson found a back window for the truck at a junkyard in San Antonio. He also found a man who knew how to install truck windows and happened to need his kitchen repainted. The scratches in the top of the truck would have to stay, though Orson painted over them with some highly unattractive rust preventative. Luke was touched beyond words when they gave him back his truck, fixed as well as it could be for thirty-seven dollars.

He spent three weeks, not two, on various couches before he returned to work. It turned out that back injuries made every movement hurt, even when that movement ought to have nothing to do with his back. He found to his puzzled amusement that he was told where to go rather than having to search for a safe harbor himself. The myth-folk seemed to have decided that the best way to keep their resident satyr safe was to pass him around. Should the chupacabra come looking for him, it would at least have a long way to walk before it caught up to where Luke actually was. Luke liked to think that as damaged as the beast must have been, it wouldn't be going anywhere for a while.

Luke decided early on that the best houses were the ones with women in them. When men lived alone, they made do. When they lived with women, they still made do, but the women made it look good. Women, as the gatherers to men's hunters, seemed to produce the most amazing finds. He was at Sally's house, being served his own vegetables by her mother, when Sally came in with a big grin. "Luke!" she said. "You'll never guess! No, I'm positive, you never really would guess. Stop guessing! OK, really, shut up. I found you a bedroom door!"

Luke clapped his mouth shut. She was right, he would never have guessed that.

"I took the measurements of the doorframe last time I was up there and kept them in this notebook I got in the glove box of the car. So I was driving home and saw this perfectly good door out by the street. So I stopped and measured it—yes, with the tape measure in the glove box—and it's like a quarter inch tall, but you can shave it down, right? Great! I'll go get it."

Luke hobbled out to the porch and watched, amazed, as Sally pulled a door with a hole kicked through it out of her car's hatchback.

"Daddy, can you fix this?" she called to Wilson, who had joined Luke on the porch.

"I figure so," he said with a laugh.

Luke shook his head, amazed. "Sal, you went dumpster diving for me! Why didn't you just say how you felt, baby?"

Wilson clapped Luke on the shoulder. "I don't want no illegitimate grandkids," he said before going back into the house.

Luke stared after him. "Shouldn't it be, like, illegal for you to even say things like that?" he said. But he smiled to himself.

Chapter Ten

Luke had vaguely hoped that in short order, August would be happily packed up and shunted off as far northeast as he could go without running into the ocean. But his hopes were dashed. The headless horseman was still hanging around three weeks later, followed everywhere he went by impressed female gazes (and the occasional appreciative male gaze) and an ominous black horse.

And Cormick, apparently. Luke met them at Whataburger at Cormick's request to talk about, as Cormick put it, their "pointy pest problem." When Luke had argued, Cormick offered to treat. Luke acquiesced.

It was more jarring than usual, standing in the winding line before the single Whataburger cashier, to be in the company of a headless horseman who carried his skull (which looked like a motorcycle helmet to the normals) under his arm and the myth-community mayor, with his pointed ears and distinctly glittery aura. Luke stamped his hoof. He ought to be used to such juxtapositions.

"What do you want, August? OK. Number two with a Coke. Luke? Yeah, make that two." Cormick looked at the menu as if he hadn't had ten minutes in line to consider his options. "I'll have the number seven deluxe with cheese, no pickles or onions, dry. A Dr. Pepper with no ice, please." He paid, their food appeared shortly, and they went to their table.

As Cormick distributed the food he said, "August's been compiling a lot of information lately, and I've been helping out as best I can. I mean, I'm not the investigator on the case."

"I'm not a detective," August said. "I'm just a hunter."

"Right. But you've still got quite a mind for intelligence."

August shrugged, but he seemed pleased.

"So what we've come up with is mostly more of what August

talked to us all about the night you were attacked. Who it might have been, motives, means, and such. It's complicated as hell. There aren't that many myth-folk around here who don't like you, and those who don't like you don't have the means to do what it would take to get a chupacabra here. Because I don't know if you know this, but those bastards are really hard to get. See, they don't have two appearances like we do. They look like themselves to any and everybody. You know why? Get this. Because there are enough people in the world who believe in them that they don't have to wear a disguise. In fact, they can't! Fascinating stuff. Son of a bitch, pickles and ice. I'll be right back." Cormick broke off his monologue to storm the front counter and demand his food fixed.

August smiled at Cormick's back. "He's quite a character."

Luke laughed. "Yeah, you got that right. He's touchy, but he's good at what he does. Even if he offends half the town when doing it." He hesitated a moment before continuing. "Sometimes I think he's so grouchy because he doesn't like it here much. I think he'd be a lot happier in a big city, like where you are. But he's too independently minded to get much closer to National."

He heard Cormick telling the teenage counter clerk, "It's already cold when it comes out of the soda machine. Ice just makes it watered down and flat. I don't want ice."

August raised an eyebrow. "There's more to New York than New York City, you know. I live adjacent to a national park. You think I could keep that horse in the city? He'd go nuts, and so would I."

Luke sniffed. "And here I took you for a city boy. Can I ask, what's with the black?"

"Hard to mismatch black. I'm color-blind."

"Ha!" Luke laughed. "Imagine that."

From the counter, he overheard, "But there's pickle juice on it already. Whole other sandwich, please. I can taste the juice!" Luke and August both laughed.

"Bet you'll be ready to see this place in your rearview," Luke said.

August was quiet for a moment. "It's not the place so much I mind. I just don't like having my character judged by my looks. Up north I'm not nearly so unusual looking. It's disconcerting, being stared at."

Luke had the decency to feel abashed. He reminded himself that his dislike of August had less to do with the man's looks and more to do with how Sally liked those looks.

August must have been eavesdropping on Luke's internal monologue, because he said, "By the way, what exactly is Sally? It's readily apparent she's a big bird, but she doesn't look like a Roc or a Firebird. Air elemental?"

"You know, I never asked. I think she explained once at a party, but I don't remember now. I figure if she wants to talk about it she'll bring it up."

"You're not curious?"

Luke shrugged. "I like to think of it as respectful."

"I swear," Cormick said as he sat back down, unwrapping his much improved burger and taking a sip of his iceless drink, "you'd think I was being unreasonable."

"Not unreasonable," Luke said, winking at August. "Just... prissy."

"Iamnotprissy!" Cormick hissed. "I am not flaming, or feminine, or delightfully quirky. I just like things how I like them, and there is nothing wrong with that."

"We wouldn't expect any less of you, princess." Luke grinned.

"Luke, I...." He looked up at the ceiling, composing himself, and smiled thin and vicious. "Cut it out, goat-boy. You're baiting me."

"I am. Sorry, my liege."

Cormick gave August an apologetic look. "It's not easy being the reincarnation of a fairy princess around these assholes."

"I can imagine," August said with notable restraint. He looked at Cormick and asked, "Are you gay?"

"What?" Cormick said.

"Are you gay? Just curious."

"What would make you think I am?"

"A lot of myth-folk who have been incarnated as both males

and females are more inclined toward experimentation, or at least are more open minded, having known what it's like on the other side of things."

"No! Having once been a woman does not make me gay!" The conversations around them stopped as people strained to listen to what Cormick was saying. His face flushed, and he dropped his voice to a whisper. "I am not gay. I wish people would stop jumping to that conclusion!"

"Sorry. You sound like you have something against gay people," August observed.

"I'm sorry to interrupt this fantastic conversation," Luke said, "but can we talk about me now? Or more specifically, why you asked me here? You guys can flirt later."

August smiled significantly, and Cormick growled. "Fine," Cormick said. "We asked you here to make sure you don't have any enemies we don't know about. Look. We made a list of all the people who theoretically could have done this. We mixed those names up with a bunch of people who couldn't, just so you don't end up with a list of names of people you would like to take out."

"Thanks for the vote of confidence," Luke muttered.

"We want you to take a look at the list and see if any names pop out at you."

Luke nodded and took the piece of paper August handed over. He scanned the list. "Joe Tabor... Max Cunningham... Sarah Lenny... I dated Sarah in high school, but she dumped me for a trumpet player. I heard she's got four kids now, that true?"

"Five," Cormick corrected.

"Good grief. All right then, Hank Richardson... I hit his car two years ago outside the hardware store. He's a cranky soul, but surely not that cranky. I mean, my insurance paid it, and we haven't seen each other since, except on council nights. Paula Mitchells and my mom hate each other's guts. Something about their Brownie troops. Who the hell knows. She's a nice lady otherwise, though. She waves to me when I pass her house and she's outside. Alice Harding... Neil McKenzie... Michelle Trents, she's the bell choir director, you got balls even putting her on this list. Surprised she didn't drop dead of embarrassment in the supermarket without ever knowing quite why. Oooh, Brent can do something like this? That shit, he never told me about it."

"You guys get on OK?" Cormick said.

"Oh yeah, we're all right. He had a thing for Sally a few years back. She got real creeped out by him, and we stopped hanging out so much, on account of Sally usually being with me. But I see him at work; he's on the same team with me now. Good fellow, decent carpenter. We've got an ongoing game of chess in the boss's trailer on site. I think he's gonna win."

Cormick raised his eyebrows. "You play chess?"

"A guy can't have layers? I was on my high school team. Look, Cormick, I can excuse August thinking that because I've got a nearly incomprehensible southern accent, I'm also stupid. But you? You ought to know better. You know I got a degree from A&M, much good as it does me in construction. You seen me and Orson work out shit all the time, building and fixing things. Why're you still surprised when I demonstrate I got brains?"

Cormick looked a little sad. "Sorry, Luke. I think it's because... you don't always use them."

"Excuse me?"

"I know you're smart. Hell, you're smarter than me. So what the heck are you doing in Fox Pass? Get the hell out, man! Sell the house, sell the animals, take your dog, and run and never look back. Go put your horticulture degree to work. What are you staying for?"

Luke stared across the table, and after a moment Cormick slumped and said, "OK. I know."

August said, "I'm missing something, and I think I'm happier that way."

Luke nodded. "You are." He stood and passed them the paper. "I got no kill-worthy beef with anyone on that list. Sorry." He looked down at Cormick. "So if it's so bad, what are you still doing here?"

Cormick smiled sadly. "I have my own anchors too. See you, man."

"Yeah. See you." Luke walked out to his truck.

Chapter Eleven

Luke was relieved to be back at work. Though his back still itched and ached, his wounds were healing well, and he could do light labor without straining the stitches. What the doctor meant by "light labor" was probably not what Luke or his boss interpreted it to mean. Brent, a tinker creature from a long-lost underground land and a framer for the same construction company, was particularly concerned about Luke's wounds, being more aware of what had happened than their very human coworkers. He came to help whenever he saw Luke doing something too strenuous, which was often.

The nights were more tense. To his shame, Luke had not yet worked up the courage to go back home at night. Every noise made him jump, especially since he couldn't attribute any noises to goats, chickens, or dogs, all of which were now housed elsewhere. By nightfall, he always found himself packing up and heading out, and he only relaxed when he got inside someone else's house, usually Orson's.

"It ain't fair," he said to Orson one night. Luke lay with Sootie on his feet and his horns hooked over the end of the couch, happy to be healed enough to rest on his back again. "I got memories spanning back past the Roman Empire. Bits and pieces, you know, they never come through intact, not for any of us. But I know I faced worse stuff. I lived in Haiti in the 1800s, for Christ's sake. I been through wars, plagues, childbirth. Why can't I shake this terror of a hairless, spiny rat?"

"Precisely because he's what you haven't seen before," Orson said. "He's new. Folks like us, we don't like new. But the whole world's new now."

"Don't I know it. It's not all bad. Phones have gotten really cool. And I really, really, really like modern medicine."

Orson grinned under his bushy mustache. "Tell me about it. I might not even mind being reincarnated as a woman next go round, if it keeps up. Pain-free childbirth is on the horizon."

"Dunno about that, but it's at least a helluva lot better than birthing while chewing on a damn root."

"I am immensely pleased to say that if that has ever happened to me, I don't remember it."

Luke shuddered. "I remember it."

Orson stretched and said, "Back to the chupacabra, now. You can't go on forever sleeping on couches. You're going to have to go back home. But as long as that animal is out there, you're not going to be comfortable at home. You're not safe. If it knows where you are, you're in danger. It's obviously not afraid to break windows."

Luke shuddered. He hadn't thought about the chupacabra coming in through one of his windows. Now he had a brand new fear to add to the list. "I can't go on like this. We've got to catch it and kill it," he said.

"And how do we do that?"

Luke thought for a moment. "August said we hunt it like any other animal. We know what it wants—me. So we can predict it. All we have to do is elicit the response we want."

Orson grinned, and for the first time in a long time Luke could plainly see the bloodthirsty Tuatha Dé Danann underneath Orson's dignified exterior. "And then... we kill it."

❧

A plan was proposed. It was modified, tweaked, stomped, rebuilt, and at last accepted by most parties. It went into effect a week later, when Luke declared himself all but completely healed. Sally was mad. That didn't change the plan.

She wasn't the only one to think that taking the fight to the chupacabra was a flawed plan. The evening of the hunt, Luke sat on the porch with Orson, August, Glen, and Cormick, discussing the layout of Luke's property, positioning, and tactics. The unexpected hum and crackle of a car coming up his dirt-and-gravel drive made Luke jump, but he relaxed when he recognized Allison's beige Escort.

"Hey, guys," she said as she got out. While she addressed the group, her eyes stayed on Luke. Orson, Cormick, and August muttered a collective greeting.

"Hey, darlin'," Luke said, greeting her with a one-armed hug; the other arm cradled his shotgun.

"I hear you boys are going hunting tonight," she said.

"That's the plan."

Allison took a deep breath, nodding. "Can I talk to you inside?" She hooked her thumb over her shoulder toward the house.

"Sure thing." Luke handed the shotgun off to Orson and followed Allison up the steps and through the door, closing it before Sootie could scoot inside behind him. The door had hardly clicked before Allison went up on the tips of her toes and kissed him. It wasn't the needful, lusting kind of kiss they'd shared in the back room of her restaurant recently. Her kisses now were full of affection, concern, and fear. Luke kissed her back, feeling the lust-energy rising in her, feeling it fuel his own fires.

He slid his hands beneath the edges of her shirt, feeling the soft skin of her waist, just above her jeans. His labor-hardened hands traced over the faint scars of her own labor, barely there stretch marks low on her belly from her one pregnancy, long ago. That baby was grown now, and Luke closed his eyes as he remembered what it had felt like to hold Allison's baby in high school, to play with him as a small child, to take him to games and movies as a teenager. Luke hadn't seen her boy since he'd left home two years ago. Ever since Garret had figured out Luke was his mother's friend with benefits, their relationship had been strained. Luke hoped that with time, it would heal. He remembered staying in the hospital with Allison when they'd taken her ovaries, her uterus, to stop the spread of tiny, malignant spots, and her hair and her hope fell away. Someday, she said every few years, it would come back, but so far, it hadn't.

Luke had shared so much with Allison, so much of her life. If things had been different, if she'd been inclined to tie herself permanently to anyone, if he'd felt just a little more strongly for her— but there was no sense in dwelling on it. They could not be anything other than what they were. Their shared history seemed to swirl around them and tie them together, amplifying the magic they summoned up between them.

She pulled him to his room, backing up, and he let her. He closed the door—the one Sally had pulled out of a dumpster for him, the one her father had fixed for him, the one he and Brent had hung on new hinges in the doorframe. At the same time, he closed a mental door on any sort of guilt. Sally was the future. Allison was the present.

Chapter Twelve

Allison knelt on his unmade bed and pulled off her shirt. Her white, lacy bra showed off her lightly tanned skin. Luke whistled. "You don't waste any time, do you, girl? You ain't got customers to get back to today, you know."

"I know," she said. "But you have to hunt. And I don't want to lose my nerve. C'mon, satyr-boy—"

"Lose your nerve?" He cupped her face in one hand and ran the pad of his thumb over her cheek. She was just starting to show crow's-feet and laugh lines. She bore her age well. It made her all the more interesting to look at. "What on earth would you need nerve for, to bed me, of all people? Surely you got over being shy about having me by now."

Allison bit her lip, suddenly looking much more like the young woman she'd been when she and Luke had known each other in school. Luke held back a flood of memories and folded his arms across his chest.

"Luke," she said, "everybody in town knows you might die tonight. And if you do, I don't want to be haunted by the idea that if you'd had a boost, maybe you'd have made it through."

Luke tapped his thumb against his arm, thinking. "So... you're here to give me a top off? I figured that was part and parcel. But Ali, I ain't never operated on charity, not in money and not in magical energy." A terrible thought occurred to him. "If you don't actually want me—"

"It's not charity," she said. "It's freely given. And more than a top off. I want you to take all you can stand. I want to help you however I can. And if I lose you, I'll know I did everything I could, and I'll have tonight to remember."

Luke thought about that one a moment. "I suppose I can see your point of view. You realize me draining you like that is going to give you a hangover from hell, right? For a week. Can't do it if you can't spend the next day or two in bed. And I won't ever do it again, from you. I make a habit of it, I could kill you."

"Understood. You and Sally haven't confirmed your relationship, have you?"

"Naw, we're still dancing around each other like a couple of damn teenagers at a sock hop."

Allison laughed, the loud, barking laugh of the unexpectedly amused. "Never thought a satyr could play shy. She wants you, you know. She wanted you all those years she got strung along by Mr. Big Shot up in, what was it, Washington state?"

"Oregon. Poor girl, ain't fair to hold on to a long-distance romance for so long and then get dumped by text. Guess I'd be gun-shy too if it happened to me."

Allison reached out and took Luke by the upper arms, pulling him toward the bed. "You, sir? Will never be gun-shy. You don't have the memory for it." She guided his hands to her breasts. "Now fuck me because we both want it. Because I want to give you the magical energy of an electrocuted stag. Because I'm horny as hell and need a cock in me." The magical energy around her shimmered, and her skin glistened. Her hair tangled as if it was underwater. The sea-folk magic that was part of her soul reached out like tendrils and curled around him. "Because I might drown in lust for you if you don't."

Luke laid her down on his twin-size bed, with its cheap sheets and the quilt made by his grandmother. He peeled off their clothes, pressed his body against hers with a kind of slow deliberation. He drank her in, little by little, making her want it. And she did. She wrapped her legs around him, rubbing herself against his cock, but he wouldn't let her take him yet. He slid lower and worked her with his tongue, calling up many lifetimes of memories to give her as much pleasure as he could. Almost. Right to the edge and not over. He didn't want her to come yet. Luke knew Allison, knew how much she loved to be penetrated. He teased her with his tongue, moving in and out of her, knowing it would not satisfy her. He felt the magic in her well up like a spring, pushing against the bounds of the earth to spill forth.

When she was clutching the sheets, gasping incoherently, her legs shaking on either side of him, he mounted her. He was in full satyr form, soaking up waves of lust magic, and she cackled evilly at the sight of his horns, knowing full well what it meant. He was bigger as his myth-folk self. She moaned as he slid into her folds, filled her, had her. She was so tight around him. He almost couldn't get all of his cock into her, he filled her so entirely.

Allison ran her fingernails hard down his back, to his ass, to where his fur started a little way down his thighs. Her hands were damp. Iridescent scales glittered like leaf-thin pearls along the skin of her arms, across her breasts, on her high cheekbones. She couldn't truly take her myth-folk form, but her merrow magic pressed at the edges of reality as she summoned up all the magic she could reach. Luke felt her pour that magic into him, digging for more, more, and thrusting it into him again, and again, and again, fucking him with raw magic. He felt almost waterlogged, saturated, and still she took him and fed him. He could feel her reaching her limits, and he increased his pace, the force of his thrusts. They came together, so deep and hard that Luke was afraid he'd pass out. Spots of color danced in front of his eyes as his body convulsed, spilling his seed into her. It felt so good, so unbelievably good, to come inside her. Allison was the only one he'd ever done that with. He buried his cries in her breasts. She let her voice fly wild.

When they left the house, the rest of the assembled crew didn't meet their eyes. Allison got into her car without saying good-bye. No sense in embarrassing the other men. Luke watched her leave and then turned to the others. His body fairly hummed with magical energy. He'd have to let some of it off that night, whether he wanted to or not.

"I'm ready," he said. "Let's go kill something dangerous."

Chapter Thirteen

Dawn and dusk were special times to the myth-folk, both in Fox Pass, Texas, and elsewhere. They were the in-between times—not quite day, not quite night. The myth-folk were almost mortal and almost eternal, not entirely human and not entirely magical, so their magic flickered a little brighter at sunrise and sunset, as if sensing a kinship with the changing light.

It was easiest to see the true forms of the myth-folk at these times. Luke, nearly glowing with his own satyr magic, could hardly be missed. His horns felt heavy and solid, sweeping back over his skull, and his cloven hooves raked the gravel. The warm, sage-scented wind ruffled his fawn-and-black fur. August, on the other hand, was a spectral vision, a black hole more notable for his absence of light than for anything that emanated from him. He felt like a cold spot in the earth, a ghost. Only the skull under his arm and the red fire of his horse's eyes would remain visible as the night closed in. Glen lurked in his shadow, a knobbly skinned creature with thin limbs and a frog-thick belly, eyes bulging and teeth jutting from his mouth at odd angles.

The two true fae looked long and lean, willowy even in their strength. It was plain why Cormick led the myth-folk. He radiated royalty in his true form, a spiderweb-thin circlet of light around his brow almost like a halo. His long ears tapered to points, and his almond-shaped eyes were dark and glittering. Orson looked like his lord's hound—vicious, dangerous, all glinting teeth and sinewy muscle, a wild thing barely restrained.

Luke grinned. "Well, ain't we a vision. Let's go hunting."

The woods around a satyr's home are not like ordinary woods, and though Luke led the group himself, the other myth-folk found it difficult to keep up. Mesquite leaves covered deep, abrupt dips in the red-rock landscape; briar patches and cactus spines caught and snagged at their clothes and skin, actively pulling them back. Yucca stabbed at their knees, and the pebbles on the ground slid like marbles. It was no place for a horse. August would not be without his mount, and he soon agreed to scout along the edge of the mesquite thicket, in the dry creek bed, in case their prey should leave the trees to run.

The paths the chupacabra had been following were faint, but they were there. The woods seemed to cry out to Luke, alerting him to the invader: a bit of skin caught on a mesquite thorn, a half track preserved in dried mud. They traveled through the dark hollows to a spit of rock jutting out from the hillside, which afforded a view of Luke's house down below. Luke clambered to the tip of the rock, saw the house, and curled his lip.

"It's been watching me," he said.

"It's watching now," Orson said. His gun was aimed farther up the hill, where shadows and a chill wind threw off the lingering heat of the day. He looked for all the world like a pointer, Luke thought, his whole body stiff and concentrated toward his prey, pointing with his weapon instead of his nose. Luke slid back down the rock and crept forward. Cormick stayed behind Orson, covering their backs, and Glen between them. They moved forward in that formation for many tense minutes, crossing the creek and a large patch of prickly pear, to a natural depression in the rocky terrain. Luke smelled the nest before he saw it. The ground sank away, and a gaping hole yawned there, recently dug out. It was surrounded by dung and the carcasses of small animals, not devoured but drained—sucked dry, judging from the puncture wounds.

"One of these days," Cormick said, "someone's going to draw the parallel between chupacabras and vampires. And then chupacabras will be sex symbols, too."

"Everything's a sex symbol, you look hard enough," Orson growled.

"Well hell," Luke said, "let's skip straight to making them sparkle." He set down his backpack and pulled out a road flare. He lit it, took a few steps to the side, and threw the flare down the den's entrance.

The darkness exploded with screams. Four adult chupacabras bounded out of the den, followed by scurrying mounds of young. Orson fired twice in rapid succession, sending two rounds of buckshot into the mass of them. Then he turned the shotgun around like a club and went after the closest one, giving up range for speed. Cormick fired once and then drew his knife as the fray became too complex in the dim light to fire safely. Glen met the largest creature face to face, both of them hissing and displaying mouthfuls of wicked teeth. They toppled over each other, Glen clawing for its throat and the chupacabra scrabbling for Glen's soft underbelly.

Luke bludgeoned one chupacabra after another, throwing his horns forward and sideways. He kicked, hooves lashing with inhuman speed, and a midsize chupacabra fell to the ground, its skull caved in. Teeth sank into Luke's arms, and claws lacerated his back, reopening his previously healed wounds. He cried out in fury and bucked, throwing the chupacabra on his back to the ground. He grabbed fistfuls of earth and howled, an unearthly sound that reverberated through the trees like a banshee's cry. His magic ripped through him, into the earth, twisting like the roots of a tree clawing its way into rock. The earth answered him. Great tendrils of root and stone rose up in spires and curled around them, fast and heavy. Cormick, Orson, and Glen managed to get out, squeezing past the bruising fingers of rock, but no chupacabra was allowed to leave the earthen whirlpool. They were dragged down, screaming, their mouths and throats choked with sand and stone, their ankles bound with tendril roots as tight as slipknot steel, biting into their flesh and pulling them down, down, into the earth to their deaths. The spires fell, crashing into them, pulverizing their bones and soft flesh, until no sound came anymore.

Chapter Fourteen

After the chupacabras were dead, the dust settled slowly and reluctantly, as if it relished the sudden burst of activity and yearned for more. Only stray pebbles dribbled down the cliff, which was now unrecognizable. Luke stood and shook himself, sending a new cloud of dust into the air. His magic spent, he was a weary, sag-eyed version of himself. Orson caught him before he fell and looped his arm around Luke's waist, draping Luke's arm over his broad shoulders.

"Lean on me," he said.

"Like usual."

"That was one hell of a show."

"What can I say, Allison is a demon in the sack."

"Let me see your back," Cormick said, ripping the remains of Luke's tattered T-shirt off. Glen moaned empathetically behind him, and for a moment Luke had a vision of another trip to the hospital, another round of disability and sleeping on couches. Then Cormick said, "Stars above, Glen, it's just blood. Stop being so dramatic. Put your head between your knees." Luke felt cool fingers on his back, exploring the new wounds. "Phew, you're lucky. These are little more than scratches. I don't think you'll even need stitches. A few places the old wounds are unhappy about the new ones, but you'll be fine, soon as we get you bandaged up. I'll be surprised if you miss a single day of work."

"Well hallelujah!" Luke said, grinning over his shoulder at Cormick. "I've played as much Tetris as I can stand for one lifetime."

"What happened?" August said as his horse pushed through the nettles and underbrush. "I heard crashing and felt a burst of magic—"

"Luke went off on them," Cormick said with a lopsided grin.

"Damn fool animals took on a satyr on his own turf."

"I couldn't have done what I did anywhere else," Luke said. "Might not ever be able to do it again, actually. I feel as drained as a kitchen sink. And I couldn't have done it before Allison, uh, charged me up. I'm gonna have to find someone else to fill me up at least a little before long. Allison will be asleep all night and most of the day, I imagine—I took a lot out of her."

"How does it work?" August said.

"How does what work?"

"Charging your magic. A talisman? A ritual?"

Luke laughed. "I'm a satyr, what do you think? I feed on lust. Someone gets horny around me, I get a boost."

August swung off his horse, strode forward, and kissed Luke. Luke was startled and made a high-pitched squeak of protest, but the lust-magic seeping into him soothed his soul, like water on cracked earth. He relaxed into the kiss, reminding himself that it was just for the purpose of magic. He didn't have to want it or enjoy it to get something out of it. Only those around him had to want it. He tried to forget who he was kissing. What he was kissing. In his myth-folk form, he'd be kissing air—August's real head was a skull under his arm. Luke focused on the mortal part of August, which was at least palatable. He parted his lips, letting August's tongue dip in and out of his mouth. August tasted like tea and smelled like horse and leather and earth.

Luke breathed in deep, surprised to like the way August smelled. He'd expected an expensive cologne, or aftershave, or hair product, not a natural scent so close to his own heart. His body responded, much to his chagrin. He didn't want August to touch him, and he wanted even less to enjoy that touch, even when it was necessary. Still, pleasure rippled through him like a warm wind. It was possible that he was feeling someone else's pleasure, not his own. His magic didn't always work like that, but occasionally it did, especially when he was unwilling. The magic didn't like to be denied.

As soon as he had strength enough to stand on his own, he put his hands on August's chest and broke off the kiss. August's hands had found his waist, and he didn't want them to find anything else. He cleared his throat and looked down at his feet. They looked like human feet now, in the full dark, not a satyr's cloven hooves. "Uh. Thanks."

August looked him up and down, a nearly sinister smile tugging at one corner of his mouth. "My pleasure," he murmured, turning to mount his horse.

"How'd you know that I'd let you do that? I haven't been with a dude in years, I don't exactly talk about it much." Somewhere in the dark nearby, Orson snorted.

"I didn't. Until you let me."

Luke chuckled. "Bastard." He walked ahead of the horse and rider back down the path toward his house, leaving Cormick to relate the details of the fight to August. Glen stuck close to Luke's side, the way Sootie did when she was feeling particularly vulnerable or especially protective. He wondered which way Glen was feeling after such a night.

The walk back was easier, the forest seeming to part before the party. But then, the forest was more Luke's now than it had ever been before, down past its roots, to the heart of the mountain. Luke was refreshed, able enough to function until he had a chance to recharge fully. The thing was, though, he was pretty sure the magical energy he'd soaked up hadn't come from August, if the ghost was even capable of producing the sort of life-filled energy on which Luke subsisted. He doubted it. No, the magic he'd soaked up had the distinct flavor of lustful fae.

Chapter Fifteen

Sally's hands moved over Luke's bare back as she clucked over the new scratches there. Her hands felt warm and soft, and Luke's eyelids drooped. He was glad she was looking at his back and not at his lap. Then again, from the way a steady trickle of magical energy was making its way into him, maybe she would not have disapproved. The conversation kept him from inquiring too closely.

"Does it really have to be Flintstones Band-Aids?"

"Sorry, it's all Mama had in the medicine cabinet." What Sally referred to as a medicine cabinet was actually a laundry detergent bucket at their feet, overflowing with every kind of item conceivably useful in a medicinal fashion.

"Eight boxes of Flintstones, huh?"

"She must've found them on sale some year back." She put her hand on his side to steady herself, and he shivered. "Your poor back.... Does it hurt you much?"

"Naw," Luke lied, taking the opportunity to be big and tough. "It stung at first, but I'm fine."

"Well, don't you go overdoing it at work, all right? Some of your old wounds look like they'd really like to open up again. They might be closed, but they're not strong. I'd hate for you to need more stitches. You're gonna have scars from the first ones as it is."

"Yeah," Luke said. "But how's the saying go? Something like, pain is ephemeral, glory is eternal, and chicks dig scars." He looked over his shoulder and grinned at her, but then his smile fell. "Hey, what's the matter? You look glum all of a sudden."

Sally smiled, but it was terribly forced. "Nothing." He didn't have to press with more than a raised eyebrow before she said, "I just heard about how you kicked the chupacabras' butts with the earth itself, and I know that must've taken a lot of magic. You must've gotten it somewhere. And you must have refueled after. Just not sure what to think about it is all."

"You don't like that I have to be around, if not necessarily involved in, a lot of sex to have magical energy to work with."

"Glad it's not me." She took the wrappings off another Band-Aid, this one sporting Bamm-Bamm. "I mean, that has to soak up magic like that." She stuck the bandage on him and added the wrapper to the growing pile of trash on the coffee table.

"Why? It's not so bad. There are worse fates."

"To not have a choice? Doesn't sound like it would be much fun after a while."

"Hey now," Luke said, turning around. "I have a choice, it's just my choices are more limited. I could choose not to practice magic at all. I could be monogamous like that. But I'd be hamstringing myself. And like I said, I don't have to be involved in the action, necessarily. It's just more effective."

"How often do you get an invitation and turn it down?" She let his silence answer for him. "To choose between having relationships and having a life?" She swept the wrappers into the trash can, keeping her eyes and hands busy. "Not much of a choice."

"It's not as black and white as that, if both parties are flexible."

"Flexible. There's a dangerous term. People are complicated, you know? What kind of flexible are you talking about?"

"Well, for starters, I was drained as hell after I killed the chupacabras. I needed a shot of magic. So August kissed me."

Sally clearly struggled to keep her expression blank. "Did he. Wow. Um. OK, I have to admit, I'm sorry I missed that." She looked off over Luke's shoulder, biting her lip, and he could almost see her filing that image away for later. "But it wasn't your idea, was it? You don't even like August."

"I guess maybe he's not so bad. Hey," he said, putting a hand on her arm, "look at me, will you?"

She stopped working and looked at him, resigned. "Sorry. I just get protective of you is all."

He breathed in and out for a moment before he said, "Protective or jealous?"

Sally stood, dumping Band-Aids out of her lap and onto the floor. The little trickle of magic that tasted of longing and warmth turned electric, prickling and stiff. Inwardly Luke groaned. He'd seen her shut down like this before, the pendulum swinging wildly from nearly giving in to him to slamming the door in his face. Here we go, he thought, bracing himself.

"Luke Shepherdson! Do you really think I'd hitch my wagon to a man who couldn't be faithful to me? You got another think coming, boy! If you weren't all scabbed up and grubby from fighting a den of monsters I'd kick you right out my front door!" She snatched up the trash can, swept a few remaining bits into it, and went to the kitchen.

Luke stood up and winced, having moved wrong and tweaked the scratches in his back. "Sally, c'mon! You think I don't know what you want? I soak up magical energy generated by the lust of other people. I know when someone's turned on."

"Oh yeah?" she said, dumping the trash into the big white can in the kitchen. "Can you tell when they're pissed too? Or do I have to demonstrate that another way?" She flipped him off and started gathering dishes in the sink, flustered enough to do housework.

Luke followed her into the kitchen. He stepped up next to her at the sink, watching her fill it with hot water and suds. She kept her gaze resolutely on the dishes. He traced a hand down her back, and she jumped. She didn't pull back or slap his arm away.

"I get that you're mad," he said. "I also get that you really liked watching me take my shirt off so you could doctor my back, and you liked thinking about me kissing August. I get that you're jealous. Now in return, can you get that maybe it's possible, in the right situation, to be in love with one person *and* fulfill the demands of magic in a way that both parties would be happy with?"

Sally didn't say anything. She sprayed him full in the face with the sink hose and stormed out the front door.

><

Sally did not attend the next council meeting in Fox Pass, and Luke was happy for it. He told, in a triumphant fashion akin to that of a revivalist preacher, how the fight had gone down with the chupacabras. He praised Orson and Cormick, Glen, and even August for their part in the fight.

"You left one out," Brent said from the back.

"What's that?" Luke said.

"Whoever it is pumped you up with magic."

There were a couple of catcalls and a round of laughter. Luke smiled and waved dismissively. "Is that what we're calling it now? Forget it, I'm a man of great discretion."

"Since when?" someone called, to more laughter.

"The point is," Cormick said, coming to Luke's rescue, "the chupacabras are dead. Turns out being a goatsucker is dangerous when the goat in question is Luke, our resident billy goat gruff!" After a round of applause, Cormick turned to August. "So, will you be leaving us, August, now that the threat is past?"

"No," August said, the only dour face in the room. "We still don't know who let them in, why, or if all of them are truly dead. Who says there was just one den?" This apparently had not occurred to everyone, and there was some uncomfortable shuffling of feet. August stood. "I don't want anyone to lower their guard yet. We have a long road ahead of us still."

Chapter Sixteen

"So then she sprayed me with the sink hose and left, all in a huff."

Orson laughed, and Luke scowled. "You really don't know anything about women, do you?" Orson said.

"I know plenty," Luke said, slouching back into his couch with a petulant expression on his face and a beer set on his stomach.

"Psh, whatever. You've been soaking in your satyr magic too long to remember what it's like to be a normal man. Sally don't want to be seduced, Luke. She wants to be romanced. There's a difference. And because it's Sally, what she finds romantic is gonna be different than most girls."

"Well, why don't you just tell me what she wants, since you're suddenly the expert."

Orson stroked his mustache while he thought. He picked up the TV remote and muted the football game they were watching before turning toward Luke, fingers steepled. "Some girls fantasize about a beautiful man, faraway adventures, grand romantic gestures, obsessive pursuit, expensive gifts. But the most romantic thing you could do for Sally would be to show up with a sensible ring, a big bunch of wildflowers, your toolbox, your health insurance card, a copy of your credit report, and your most recent pay stub."

Luke stared at Orson with a growing fire in his throat. "You saying Sally's a gold digger?"

"Far from it. I'm just saying she has control of her heart where most girls don't. She's not going to fall for you just because she wants you, Luke. And she does, I think we can all agree on that. But remember, she got left high and dry by a man who strung her along for years. Sally wants someone she knows will be able to take care of her, will be there for her. She wants babies and security and someone who's got her back. You know as well as I do that when a woman has children, she's exposing herself to a shit ton more danger than the man is. Motherhood is the most expensive occupation in the world, and it's not just the expense of the children that makes it so. By showing Sally you can and will look after her, you're saying the most romantic thing of all: that you're man enough to shoulder the terrible burden and wondrous joy of a family, with her."

"I could do that," Luke said.

"Not if you're banging other chicks. Because you might end up with babies from those women. Most basic, reasonable cause for jealousy in the world."

A light went on in Luke's eyes. "That's it! Other women. She didn't care that I kissed August. I think she might have actually liked the idea. I can't get a dude pregnant. Well, there was that one time in Belfast, but that doesn't count, that was some seriously kooky magic. I could just limit myself to other men for magical energy if Sally and I were hooked up!"

Orson sighed. "Good luck with that. We might be myth-folk, and because of our uniqueness, our centuries-old historical perspective, and having been men and women in other times, we might be more inclined toward... alternate lifestyles. And gender don't always change just because sex does, from life to life. Look at Cormick. But we're still living this life, now, not those other lives we occasionally recall. We're still a bunch of rednecks in a tiny West Texas town. How many gays you think we got around here?"

Luke stood and started pacing, thinking intently. "Well, there's me. I mean, I know that part of why I'm bisexual is that I'm a satyr, and statistically speaking, we're more likely to be bi than anything else. Comes from getting turned on by other people being turned on."

"What a feedback system."

"I know, right? So there's me, and August, theoretically."

"Who will eventually leave. Who you don't even like," Orson said.

"He's OK. And he's certainly hot."

"I need another beer if we're going to have this conversation." Orson headed to the refrigerator, and Luke followed him.

"Cormick's... something. Don't know if he's gay or bi."

"But you will never get him to admit it. He might be a frickin' fairy princess, but he's still royalty. He's still gonna follow the rules if he can possibly help it," Orson pointed out, popping the lid off a beer and tossing it in the trash. Sootie came trotting in behind them, looking around expectantly as if to say, "Hey, we're in the kitchen! Are we going to do something exciting in here?"

Luke bent down and scratched the blue-ticked dog on her head. "Anything's possible. Maybe I could appeal to the council system and see if I couldn't get a proxy down here every so often."

"Using the council as a gay dating service? Unlikely in the best of circumstances."

Luke continued pacing, which in the tiny kitchen meant turning around every three steps. "No, this could work! I don't necessarily have to be involved in the action. It helps, but I can get by without, if Sally's OK with throwing some really wild parties."

"You're logicking yourself into some pretty dicey areas here, boy."

"But it's the closest I've gotten to having things work with me and Sally!"

Orson grabbed one of Luke's horns and held him still. "Good God, Luke, stop pacing."

Luke turned his head as much as he could. "You know being restrained by my horns turns me on, right?"

Orson let go of his horn with a sigh. "Yes, I know that. Tragically, I know that. It is part of the accursed wretchedness of my life that I know that. I'm just saying, maybe you and Sally aren't gonna work, you know? Have you guys even said outright that you want to be together?"

"Um... in a roundabout sort of way."

"You can't be roundabout outright. Just think on it real close before you go trying to make this work when it's such long odds. A satyr and a sensible, traditional southern woman who is... some kind of myth-folk. Has she ever said what she is?"

"Nope. I figure when she wants to tell, she will. I'm being all respectful of her boundaries and stuff, see? And yes, sir. I'll think on it."

"All right. Then I have a special request for you," Orson said.

"For my Jiminy Cricket? Name it."

"Can we go watch the game and not say another word about your sex life all day?"

Luke nodded. "Absolutely. Nothing would make me happier. Except if the Colts beat the Eagles."

"That, my friend, is something we can both finally agree on."

Chapter Seventeen

Orson came through Luke's front door without knocking. Luke was on the phone, and he waved as Orson gingerly set a heavy bag on the table.

"But I was thinking, what if it was just guys? No girls? Hello?"

Orson groaned as Luke stuck his cell phone in his pocket. "Tell me that wasn't Sally."

"I just wanted to see what she thought."

"You're a bonehead, and I have done with thee." He pulled on white gloves, drew an enormous, ancient book out of the bag, and set it on the table as if it was made of spun glass.

"What is that?" Luke asked.

"This," Orson said, "is one of the fae texts. I got it sent down from Philadelphia. I am hoping it will have something in it that we can use to track our summoner. August says he's tried every tracking measure he knows, and there is no shortage of ways to track supernatural activity. There's just nothing. It's as if someone knew all those methods already and was prepared to erase their trails."

"Sounds like either a fox or a hound to me," Luke said.

"That's worth meditating upon. Anyway, I thought if he's tried everything he knows, maybe it's time to teach a new ghost some old tricks."

Luke returned his attention to the book. He grimaced at the sheer size of it. "Don't suppose this thing's got a 'Find' function on it."

"I don't know what that is," Orson said. "The good news is that I know this text pretty well already, and the fae used a whole lotta illustration. This won't be a thing that drags on." He opened the book carefully and began to look for relevant passages on the fragile pages.

Luke grew irritable as the day turned into evening, with Orson still at his kitchen table, poring over the old fae text, eating Luke's food, and occasionally calling Cormick or August. He had a pile of notes scattered around him and a nice little collection of beer bottles, which Luke had contributed to. As Luke gathered up the bottles, he said, "Making any progress?"

"Oh yeah," Orson said, stroking his thick, walruslike mustache, as he commonly did when he was thoroughly engrossed in something. "This is great. I mean, a lot of it's going to be difficult to use since we don't have a lot of these fae artifacts, but it's useful. We can put something together. Like, there's a story about the Erlking making a fine paper out of the wind, bound by a ray of sunlight, and by flipping from back to front of the book, he could see into the past of wherever he was, and by flipping the other way, see into the future." He pointed to an elaborate sigil drawn in a sloppy hand in blue pen. "And this over here is a sigil for tracking the Wild Hunt. Which does us no good now, of course, but if we could base an imitation on this model—"

Luke rolled his eyes. "OK, Orson, that's enough fae stuff for me. I can't make paper from air or construct the Wild Hunt's compass. I'm a satyr. I'd have better luck turning water into wine. You have fun, I'm gonna take out the trash."

Since the city trash collectors didn't come all the way up the mountain to Luke's place, taking out the trash was more involved than it sounded. Luke gathered the trash from the kitchen, tied it up, and took it outside. He retrieved several other bags from a locked, heavy-duty plastic bin. Little claw marks on the lid and paw prints in the sandy dirt around it demonstrated the necessity of a bin for the trash. Sootie hopped into the truck with him, happy for any excuse for a car ride, even a short one. Luke drove down the gravel drive and the dirt road to where the pavement started and unloaded the trash into the county dumpster.

When he got back to his house, he parked in a spot with no trees above it. He climbed onto the hood of the truck and stared up at the stars. Sootie joined him, though she was uninterested in astronomy; she lay with her back against his side, just happy to be in his space. Luke lit a cigarette and felt his body relax as he gazed at the canopy of little lights above them. It was one reason for staying in the country. He lapsed into a daydream of lying out on the grass on a blanket with Sally, talking about little things, staring out into the cosmos from his own tiny pocket of the universe, this little oasis in the desert he'd made. She'd be wearing a little sundress, maybe that yellow one with the blue flowers she'd worn at her last birthday party. With cowboy boots. He imagined kissing her, running his hand up her side, feeling her make a little sound against his mouth and press against him—

His reverie was interrupted by the sound of gravel under a car's tires. He sat up and watched a new Mustang drive too fast up the driveway and come to a sliding stop by the front porch. He winced at the ruts it put in the gravel. A tall woman unfolded herself from the vehicle and walked toward the porch. The bile rose in Luke's throat when he recognized her. She carried a clutch purse in one manicured hand, a necessity since skirts that svelte did not sport pockets. Her makeup was immaculate, her hose free of runs, her jewelry and perfume expensive, and her cleavage arranged to its maximum advantage.

In short, she was not from around there.

She smiled at Luke as she walked, in high heels, through the gravel—a true professional. Sootie growled, and Luke frowned.

"Hello, Luke," she said. "Have you seen my ex-husband?"

Luke slid off the hood of the truck, stomped the cigarette out with the heel of his boot, and stood with his shoulders hunched defensively. "Orson's inside, Mae." He nodded in the direction of the house with his chin.

Mae took a few steps closer, smiling with too many teeth showing. "Oh, but let me take a look at you, you pretty thing! It's been almost eight years since I've seen you." She looked him up and down, and her eyes grew heavy lidded and suggestive. "The years have been good to you. You're looking all grown up these days."

Luke's stomach turned. Sootie growled again, and Luke hooked a thumb toward the dog. "What she said."

Mae patted his cheek with a hand that jangled from the

bracelets on her wrist. "Oh, you were always so much fun. No need to be sullen about it. I won't be long. But Luke"—and here her smile fell into a pout that was anything but pleading—"I do expect to catch up with you before I go." She turned and walked into the house without a knock.

Luke sat down in the grass with his head in his hands. "Ohhhh, Sootie," he said, "this is bad. This is really bad. Mae, here? She's going to screw things up, I just know it!" Sootie licked the backs of his hands. After a few minutes, voices inside started to rise. Luke got to his feet and brushed himself off. He couldn't let Orson face the she-bitch alone. He went in after her.

The battle was already in full swing. Orson was telling her in no uncertain terms to get out and stay out and what she could do with herself when she got there. Mae was just trying to get a word in edgewise. Luke cut in, a potentially dangerous gamble. "Mae," he said, "he clearly doesn't want to talk right now. Why don't you just go get a hotel room, and you guys can chat on neutral ground or something about whatever it is got you here in the first place."

Mae turned to face him, and Luke wished he'd kept his mouth shut. She stalked toward him, a few inches taller than him in her shoes, and put one magenta-nailed finger in his face.

"Luke Shepherdson. What's got me here, as you put it, is your predicament. You're doing big magic. You need someone to feed on, you lusty leech." She smiled, and it was anything but happy. "Historically, that's where I've come in."

Luke held up his hands. "We been down that road, and not a one of us liked where it led."

Behind her, Orson carefully closed the fae book. Mae's smile took on a wolfishness that Luke had only seen on actual wolves. "Speak for yourself." She half closed her eyes, and the air around her wavered, as if unsure of itself. Mae's magic started trickling into him, then pouring. Luke fell against the wall as the lustful magic swept into him. His body shivered involuntarily with excitement, his blood rushing through his veins with a pounding, frantic drumbeat. He had goose bumps all over, and his mouth had gone dry. If she kept summoning up her own lust-magic like she was, he was going to do something regrettable. He snarled at her and clenched his fists, leaving small half-moon indentations in his palms.

"I won't give you what you want, Mae."

She backed off a notch, raising her head to look down her nose at him. "You've gained some self-control," she said, appraising him anew. She smiled over her shoulder at Orson. "I'll be around, boys." She walked out of the house without a hurried step or a backward glance.

"Well shit," Orson said. "This just got more complicated."

Luke sat down at the table and gathered a pen and some paper to him, his breath ragged in his throat and his mind a scattered mess of panic. "OK, I'm on board with your plan now. What can I do, and what crazy fairy realm do I have to find to do it?"

Chapter Eighteen

It was a few blessed days of peace before Luke saw Mae again. Orson reassured Luke he would get her out of town as fast as possible. He didn't have a leash on her, though, so Luke was not surprised when Mae turned up at his work. Luke was bent over a board, planing it with a large electric sander, when he felt a surge of excitement and greasy, sickening, lustful energy pass through him. It was entirely unlike the playful, heartfelt yearning he picked up from Sally or the passionate abandon in Allison. No one else he had ever met could make lust feel as unwholesome and selfish as Mae. Across from him, Brent stood up and took off his safety goggles. Luke turned off the sander and stood also, knowing who would be behind him.

Mae stood at the gate to the construction yard, perfectly coiffed, chatting up the foreman. She touched his elbow in a familiar, affectionate way. He smiled and led her over to where Luke was working.

"Luke," he said, "this young thing tells me you two are friends. I don't know where you found this one, but are there more like her?" Mae laughed, pretending to be surprised and flattered.

Luke scowled. "God willing, no. Hi, Mae. What do you want?" As if sensing the chill in the air, the foreman walked a few paces away, though Luke noticed that he kept his eyes on them.

Mae lightly hit his arm. "Oh Luke, c'mon. I just came by because this is the only place I can catch you alone." She glared at Brent over Luke's shoulder, and he took the hint and backed away too.

"You mean without Orson."

"Of course I mean without Orson. You two are joined at the hip, as usual. I was always disappointed I couldn't get you two in bed at the same time."

Luke felt a little wave of nausea flutter through his body. "Orson's not into men. And I don't find him attractive."

"Trifling little things to get around. What's preference compared to pleasure? Everyone's a little bi in the dark. Now honey"—she held up a hand as Luke started to protest—"I didn't come all the way from New York to rehash old times. I came to help you."

Luke clapped his jaw shut, studied her, and said, "Help how?"

She traced her knuckles up and down his chest. "I hear through the grapevine you are having some trouble. That means big magic. Which for you means lots... and lots... of sexual energy. Since you're not getting that from my ex-husband, clearly, you must be getting it somewhere. Either that, or you're tapping reserves like crazy." Her pout widened into a smile. "And we all know what can happen when you get that low, don't we?"

Magic shoved into him, and he took a step back, rocked by the metaphysical blow. He wasn't ready for it this time. His body ached with want, his cock straining against his thick work jeans. Mae's skirt rode especially high on her long thighs, and the faint impression of her nipples showed through her thin, gauzy shirt. Or was it just Luke's perception, amplified by the lust magic she was pouring down his throat? He knew what she felt like, tasted like. He knew if he took her to his truck, she'd straddle him in the front seat, and she wouldn't be wearing any panties. He could be inside her in just a few moments, her hot, slick flesh wrapped tight around his cock. And she'd ride him harder than anyone else would, soak him with magic until he was saturated like a wet dish cloth and then wring him out and leave him a limp, strung-out addict, begging for more.

She knew he was thinking it. Her hand slid to his belly.

"Luke! Hey Luke, I gotta talk to you—"

Sally came through the front gate, wearing jeans with little holes starting in the knees and a Harley-Davidson T-shirt, her hair up in an Astros cap. She stopped when she saw Mae. Luke stepped back and breathed in deep; Mae's magic faltered, and he swept the cobwebs from his mind. Thank goodness for Sally, he thought. Sally ignored the foreman as he approached her and strode toward Luke instead.

"Hi. I gotta talk to you a sex. Sec." Her face flushed a light pink as she glanced at Mae. "If, ya know, you're not busy."

"Glad to be not busy," Luke said, taking her by the elbow and steering her away from Mae, who smirked at them.

Sally's brow wrinkled. "Who is *that?*"

"Orson's ex-wife. She enjoys tormenting me because she can use me to hurt Orson. Listen, you stay away from her if you can, she's toxic as hell."

"I can take care of myself," Sally said. "Look, I came to find out if you'd seen Glen lately. Sorry to bother you at work."

Luke paused for a second, as much to switch mental gears as to register surprise. "Glen the goblin? Huh. No, I haven't. I've left messages for him, now that you mention it, that he hasn't returned. Why didn't you just call my cell?"

"I did."

Luke pulled out his cell phone and saw several missed calls. "Dang. I must have had some machinery on, sorry. Is Glen missing or something?"

Sally shrugged. "Cormick asked me to help look for him. His house is empty, and he hasn't showed up for work this week."

"Shit. OK, keep me updated, will you?"

Sally nodded. "Yeah. And hey, Luke?" She jerked her thumb at Mae. "If she gives you trouble, just tell her you have chlamydia. Do I interpret right, her being a nymph and you being a satyr, that she troubles you with her sexiness?" Sally rolled her hips in a farce of sexuality.

"Recognized what she is, huh?"

"Kinda hard to miss it. She might as well have her license plate read NMF I69."

"Great. Hey, I'll give you a call after work, all right? But I gotta deal with her, get her out of here. Take care, Sal, all right?"

Luke walked back to Mae, and Sally followed him despite his request. Before he could introduce them, Sally lit up with a wide smile.

"Hi! I'm Sally. Luke says you're new in town, and I think it's just a shame these boys didn't think to take off work to accommodate you. Luke says he's gotta get back to work, but I'd be happy to take you around myself. My girl Allison has this great little restaurant on down the highway. My treat! You must have all kinds of stories about our boys, I'd love to hear them."

Luke died a little inside as Mae fixed him with a smile that would look more appropriate on a great white. "I'd love to," she said to Sally, and the two women walked out to the parking lot together.

Chapter Nineteen

There was no telling how many traffic laws Luke broke driving to Allison's restaurant after work. By the time he got there, the sun was setting, and only Sally's car was out front. He walked in to find Allison and Sally sitting in the far booth together, as smug and merciless as a cat with a whole nest full of canaries. Luke approached with caution.

"Hey girls," he said. "Sooooo. How did things go with Mae this afternoon?"

Allison and Sally smirked at each other. Allison looked up and said, "Bitch has gotta die."

Luke's eyebrows shot up. "Do tell."

"First she insulted my restaurant."

"And Orson's intelligence," Sally said.

"And the honor of the entire south-central US region."

"And my shoes!" Sally held up her feet, clad in steel-toed work boots.

"And she seems to think she has you wrapped around her little finger." Allison pushed out a chair with her foot. "Have a seat, satyr-boy."

"Well, she's right on one count," Luke said with a groan. "She's a nymph. She can generate more sexual energy, more lust, in any number of targets than just about anything in the world. And for me, that's a whole shitload of trouble. Sure, it's like having a supercharged battery around, but it also means that if she plays it right, I literally can't say no."

The women's faces fell. "How can you not say no?" Allison pressed. "Just tell the bitch to slag off."

"Are you not hearing me? She. Can. Control. What. I. Want. It's that simple. Away from her, I don't want to touch her at all, she makes me sick. But when she starts throwing her metaphysical weight around, there's nothing I can do to shut her out. It's like she's telepathic, just with me."

Allison and Sally exchanged significant looks. Her eyes on the table, Sally said, "If she knows you don't want to sleep with her, and she forces you to, even magically, it's rape."

"I know."

A heavy silence fell at the table. Allison said it first, plain faced. "Did she rape you?"

Luke hesitated a moment before saying, "To call what happened rape would be an insult to anyone who's ever actually been raped. But she blurred the line between consent and nonconsent, and more worrisome, she would do it again."

Allison laid a hand on Luke's shoulder. "If she hurts you, we will kick in her pearly-white teeth." Sally nodded her agreement.

Luke smiled weakly. "Thanks." The "we" in that sentence did not go unnoticed. "The truth of the matter is the only way for me to be safe is to be absent. I'm going to go talk to Orson about traveling to Tír na nÓg for one of the artifacts he's researching."

Sally's face fell. "All right.... But be careful. We'll keep an eye on Orson while you're gone."

"Thanks. Listen, Mae and Orson really loved each other for a while there. I was a big part of the reason they fell apart. She just couldn't help herself around me."

"That tempting, were you?" Sally bristled.

"Yes," Luke said, his tone very serious. "I was too tempting a target. She can be good, when her motives are pure. I mean, hardly anyone is all evil. But Orson might as well have left her for me, because he picked his friendship with me over his marriage—for lots of good reasons. Like any relationship, it's complicated. But you know what they say about a woman scorned. If she's here, she's gunning for bear. So don't underestimate her, all right?"

The women nodded. Allison got up and collected their drinks and a couple of small plates that looked like they might have had something chocolate on them. As she walked to the sink in the back, Sally put her hand on Luke's arm.

"I misjudged Allison."

Luke smiled. "I'm glad you two struck a common chord today."

Sally returned the smile. "Like she says. Nobody messes with our satyr."

He decided to take advantage of her generous mood. "You give any thought to what I said over the phone? About—"

Sally raised a hand. "I know what about. All I can promise is to think about it."

Luke nodded. "All I can ask."

Chapter Twenty

The next day, Luke drove up to Brent's house after work, an old trailer in the same area as Orson's—not so much a park as a side street that had slowly filled up with trailers. He stared at the 1980s-model single-wide over the top of his steering wheel, brow furrowed. If not for Glen's disappearance, Brent's absence from work that day would not have raised his hackles. The tinker fae was prone to bouts of both intense productivity, in which all other obligations would be forgotten in his fervor to finish some new project, and drunken stupor, a tear that could last a week if not checked. He never would have kept his job if the foreman wasn't his cousin.

He left the relative safety of the truck and went up to the trailer. The skirting was gone in the front, the undercarriage of the trailer exposed and all illusion of it being a permanent home stripped away. The stairs were narrow and rickety, and the very act of rapping on the door made them shake beneath Luke's boots. The door was locked when he tried it. He pulled out a set of keys he'd gotten from the foreman, who had been all too happy to let Luke be the one to check on Brent, and opened the door to silence and a chaotic mess.

Luke thought there had been a struggle for a minute before he remembered that this was what Brent's place normally looked like. Clothes, empty food containers, dirty dishes, adult magazines, and tools made up the top layer of debris; Luke declined to investigate any further. The place smelled like cat piss, even though Brent hadn't had a cat for years. Luke checked the bedroom and found nothing but laundry and an unmade bed. He checked the bathroom and noted that Brent's razor and hairbrush were still on the sink. In the tiny kitchen, the milk was fresh, almost a full half carton, and a pan of half-cooked bacon sat on the back burner, turning rancid in its own grease. There were bits of something on the element that smelled like burned pork. Satisfied, Luke went outside to sit on the rickety stairs, called Cormick to report, and then called the police.

⁂

Part of being in the myth-folk community was hiding what they were from the rest of society. It was surprisingly easy; it wasn't as if people went looking for satyrs and faeries anymore, and mortals who could see the myth-folk's true forms were rare. No one believed them, anyway. On the rare occasion that someone was outed, the truth was almost always discarded as ridiculous. Who would believe that the veterinarian was a kelpie?

Still, there was no sense in being careless. Part of the reason Luke had gone to Brent's house was to make sure there weren't any strange tools or gadgets lying around before he called the police. They had resources the myth-folk community didn't, and tinker fae or not, Brent could still have been the victim of a regular old murder, abduction, or other violent crime.

Luke gave his statement for the third time. He'd been interrogated often enough in his many lives to know it for what it was—they were looking for holes in his story, hoping he'd answer the same question different ways, be inconsistent. There was nothing to hide, though, so Luke was entirely truthful: Brent was absent from work with no notice, he came to check on him, the man's cousin and boss had given him the keys, Brent had been missing for over twenty-four hours, and with Glen's disappearance, it seemed more alarming than it might have otherwise.

The detective from the county station glanced up, an eyebrow raised. "So you know both of the missing men?"

Luke gave him an impatient look. "It's a small town. A lot of us know both Brent and Glen. You do too, Harold." Luke had gone to high school with Harold's youngest sister.

"Sorry, Luke, it's Detective Browning while I'm on duty, and I'm going to do my job the same whether I know your name or not." He held up Luke's cell phone, which he had asked for earlier. "And why call Cormick before you called the police?"

Luke shrugged. "I dunno, I just did. Thought he'd want to know."

"A mutual friend?"

"Yeah."

The detective jotted that down. "I know, small town, everyone knows everyone." And that made everyone suspect. "OK, Mr. Shepherdson, you can go home now. But hey, don't leave town, OK? I might think of some more questions for you."

Luke was not intimidated, but he'd do his best to follow instructions. As he walked to his truck, he saw Alan, a troll who was a traffic cop for the Fox Pass police. Long ago, the myth-folk had thought it might be of benefit to have a cop on their side. But not everyone was a sharp tack, and Alan's usefulness had been limited to getting certain tickets dismissed. Luke's father, a friend of the police chief through the Freemasons, had more influence than Alan. Now, he stood at the end of the driveway, stationed to wave off any cars that approached the scene. None did. Luke gave him a wave and climbed into his truck. Lost dreams, he thought. Nobody turns out the way they think they will, even with a dozen lifetimes behind them. Life was always a surprise, sometimes good, sometimes bad, and sometimes just disappointing.

He showed up at Sally's without calling ahead. Wilson waved to him from the barn. Luke envied him; he wanted his animals back on his farm. He went in and found Sally patching a pair of work jeans on the couch. He told her about the events of the afternoon, and her face grew grave. She put her arms around him and held him, not out of lust but out of fear for him, herself, and everyone around them. She smelled clean and sweet, like fresh-baked cookies and clean cotton, like hay and water, like comfort and love and all that was right in the world. Luke's heart seemed to collapse in his chest when he realized he was thinking that she smelled like home.

When Wilson came in, Sally let go of Luke and went to take care of a chore in the barn. Luke stayed on the couch and watched her leave. Wilson sat down in the easy chair across from the couch, two glasses of sweet tea in front of him. It took Luke a moment to realize one of them was for him.

"Something you want to talk to me about, son?" Wilson said.

Luke nodded and leaned forward on his elbows. "Yes, sir." He thought for a moment, steepled fingers against his mouth. "No sense in hemming and hawing—Wilson, I want to ask your permission to court Sally."

Wilson blinked. "That's... not quite the vocabulary I was expecting. Haven't you two already been... courting? Dating? Whatever?"

Luke shook his head. "No. We've been tiptoeing around each other for some time, but I've not been formal about pursuing her. She hasn't said as much, but I think she might be ready to come to terms with... whatever this is." He took a drink of tea and then said, with a tilt of his head, "You thought I was going to ask to marry her."

Wilson shrugged. "Apparently your amour is not as far along as I imagined."

"Sally's a good girl."

"Sally's a grown-ass woman. She's closing in on thirty, and you're long past that marker."

Luke couldn't help but smile. "We've both got some old-fashioned ideas, me and her."

Wilson snorted. "Don't be ironic. Boy, don't you think I know something about what you lot are?"

Luke's smile melted like an ice chip on the sidewalk. "Uh... sir?"

"You, Cormick, Orson, Glen, that Brent asshole—"

"Hold up now, Brent's missing."

"Then he's a missing asshole. I've seen you guys do stuff you've no business knowing how to do. I watched Sally break a dog's neck when he went after her chickens when she was seven years old, like she'd done it a hundred times. I've heard Orson mutter to himself when he gets sleepy in a language I don't even recognize. I heard that story about you and the violin."

"From who?" Luke snapped.

"From your mama, that's who. What, you think we don't trade stories about our weird kids?"

Luke wilted further.

"Now listen sharp. I know you lot are more than you seem, and I know you have reasons for not letting on. But if you want to court Sally, you want to keep one thing firmly in mind." He leaned forward and planted his calloused palm on the table between them. "If you hurt my little girl, my little girl will put you in the ICU."

Luke blinked and sat up straighter.

"I'd threaten to kick your ass on her behalf, but I know the situation better than you think. Better than you, I expect. Sally is not just my daughter; she's something dangerous, too. So I'll let Sally handle her own vengeance. You just do your best not to deserve it."

Luke stood up. "Yes, sir," he said, and he meant it.

Wilson stood and offered Luke his hand. Luke shook it. "Between you and me," Wilson said, "I hope you convince her to partner up with you. I kinda hoped it was going to be you looking after my grandbabies."

Luke let a smile crook the corner of his mouth. "I hope the same."

Chapter Twenty-One

Luke knew better than to press Sally that day or the next, when Cormick called a city meeting and informed the rest of the myth-folk community of the disappearances of Glen and Brent. He called ahead to make sure she would have time to talk with him before he showed up the next day after work.

He found her in the barn, reorganizing the feed room. He leaned against the doorframe and watched her for a minute, partly admiring her butt and partly working up the nerve to say something. Finally she turned around, a piece of hay in her hair and her hands on her hips.

"Hey, Luke. Gimme a hand here? That bag of goat minerals must weigh a hundred pounds."

"Sure. Hey, listen...." He hefted the bag up with her and moved it to a corner.

"I heard about your conversation with my daddy." She didn't meet his eyes.

"Oh. Um."

"And I got something to say about it. Several things, really. One, you been courting me in one way or another since you came back from College Station ten years ago. I assume that by taking upon the formality of asking my daddy about it at last that you either got real serious about it, or you didn't realize you were flirting so bad, or both."

Luke made a grunting sound to this and shuffled a bag of sweet feed across the floor.

"Two, I intend to treat you seriously in this respect, since you gone and made it formal."

"Thank you for that."

"And three, I'm ending this courtship here and now."

Luke stopped and stood up straight. "Excuse me? You haven't even given me a chance!"

"Yes I have," Sally said, attempting to gather up the wires of a hay bale and secure them. "You might not know it, but you've had chances, and you've failed. Luke, I'm sorry, but you can't be faithful."

"How can you possibly know that? I've had girlfriends. I'm not a cheat."

"Remember what you told me about Mae? How about that? You said yourself you didn't even really have the option of saying no."

Luke's face took on a rare darkness. "That's hardly the same thing as willing unfaithfulness, and she's a one-in-a-million case."

"More like one in four!"

Luke tilted his head in confusion. "What?"

"Nothing. It's not happening, OK?" She turned her back on him and started clearing old bags of medications and supplements from a shelf. Luke felt anger well up in him, mixing with the tingling, pins-and-needles sensation up his spine that he had come to recognize as Sally's lustful energy. He grabbed her by her shoulders, turned her around, and pinned her against the wall of the feed room with his body. Her eyes widened in surprise a few inches from his own, and he stopped just short of kissing her. A flush of excitement rippled through her, and Luke felt it in his own body too, a rush of electricity like the thrumming shock of an electric fence.

"You can't tell me you feel nothing for me," Luke said. He pressed his knee forward, between her legs.

She raised her hands to his stomach, seeming for a moment as if she was going to push him away, but then hooked her fingers into his waistband and pulled him harder against her. "Goddamn it, Luke," she said, her lips hovering above his mouth. "Don't you know it takes every bit of my self-control to keep from jumping all over you?"

"Well, why don't you?" He brushed his cheek against hers, running his lips along her jawline.

He felt her shiver against him, rolling her hips, her body

arching involuntarily, her breath coming in short gasps. She wrapped her arms around him, her fingernails pressing into him like an eagle's talons. He was sure that if he put a hand between her legs, he'd find her wet and wanting. She might not even stop him, the way her body was running away with her.

But Sally was still in control of herself, and her mind trumped her body. "Because you need more sex than you can get from one person," she said, dropping her forehead to his shoulder with a grief-stricken look. "And while the idea of you having a couple of boyfriends on the side to make up the difference is... more interesting than I like to admit, you're... you're just not trustworthy, Luke."

He grew still and drew back to look her in the eye. "How can you be so sure, when I've given you no reason to think so low of me?"

"I've seen it before, Luke! All three times before—this isn't any different!"

"What three times?"

Sally's eyes flew wide, like a child caught in a lie, and she tucked her head down. "Shit."

"Shit what?" He hooked a finger under her chin and raised her face. "You come straight with me now."

"Luke.... God, I don't know how to say this. I've just got to come out with it." She bit her lip and put her hands on his face. "Luke, we've done this dance before, you and me. In other lifetimes. You courting me, me giving in, you... doing what satyrs do. It's why I haven't told anyone what I am—I didn't want you to recognize me. I can't do it again. I can't trust you, as much as I want to. As much as I want you." Her body agreed with that last statement.

Luke stared for a long moment, his mind reeling. "You've been my lover before. And you didn't tell me this because...."

"Because we were little when I recognized you. I was ten; you were seventeen."

"God, I was wild at seventeen." He winced, thinking of what

his seventeen-year-old self would have looked like to a child.

"Yes, I know. The first time I saw you, I knew who you were. And when I couldn't tell you then... well, the secret got easier and easier to keep. Until now, when I couldn't anymore."

"When you let it slip."

Her hands dropped as she stepped away from him. "Could be I'm just tired of hiding. Go looking through your memories of your past lives, Luke. Go looking for a thunderbird."

She slipped out of his arms and walked away.

Chapter Twenty-Two

Luke slept fitfully that night, rose before dawn, and had a cup of coffee and a cigarette on the front porch before starting out in the fading dark. Sootie stayed on the porch, knowing somehow that Luke was on a solo mission. He hiked deep into his land, through the mesquite glades and the yucca patches, up and down the red-rock ravines. He knew when he'd reached the center of his land, a grassy spot that just felt right.

He sat cross-legged, watching the light change in the east, trying to stay relaxed. He had awakened his past lives before, but it was always an unsettling experience—he never knew exactly what he was going to remember. He breathed in and out with the still morning air. It was almost cool, this late in the fall, with the scent of sage blossoms in the air. His mind grew quiet, and he let his daily cares fade from his thoughts. He sought out the core of his being, the satyr who was constant not just throughout this life but in the one before, and before that, and before that—his immortal soul.

He sank back through his memories, past all the years of his life. Past the recent events with the chupacabras and their summoner, past Sally, past August and Glen and Brent. His mind flickered past his working adult life, his time in college, his teen years, wild times of machines and study and soft flesh. He went past his childhood, dramatic times of great triumphs and great pain, the glorious outdoors and the animals it contained, past the drudgery of school and the unfairness of adult tyranny. His mind touched light on the dimly recollected fog of early life, consisting mostly of the kitchen floor and his mother's bare feet, her voice a constant, lyrical background song.

Beyond that, there was more. A short life that ended in 1968 with chemicals and sex and music, a fractured childhood in the fifties in the Midwest. And back beyond that, more. A violent death in the Pacific in the forties, a rough time in the thirties, moving with his family from place to place. Dust, everywhere was dust, and locusts, and hunger, and death. Behind that was a happy childhood, a kind and wonderful father, so admirable a man that he was sorry to have forgotten that life for so long, even as difficult as it eventually became.

And beyond that.... He slowed down, pondering a curious life long forgotten. He was a farrier in New Mexico, and he met a Navajo girl of great beauty and greater pride. A thunderbird... Sally, though her name was Jane in that life. He failed her—he was drawn into an orgy by a group of satyrs and nymphs in a great magical rite with the coyote-folk of New Mexico. He could not possibly have resisted, but she would hear no word of explanation or regret from him. His heart filled with old hurt, remembering how she walked away, her anger and pain. She said he would never find her again, she would never let him in again, and he knew she meant it not just for that life, but forever.

He pushed on to the next life. She wasn't in that one, though he had a sense of searching, forever looking, and not finding what he was looking for. Another life after that, filled with violence and pain. He flipped past it as fast as he could, reminding himself to avoid Haiti at all costs.

Beyond that was a life in Europe. He was married when he met her, a wild thing in the Canadian forests. He recognized her, loved her instantly. He was not faithful to his wife, but when his business in Canada ended, he returned to her, and his children, and his European life. And in doing so, he abandoned his thunderbird lover. He longed for her for the rest of his life and called out her name as he died in a raging fever.

The farther back he went, the foggier his memories became. Moments of great pain and great pleasure stood out like splashes of red watercolor paint on gray paper. He remembered losing children, losing limbs, always so much loss in a world with primitive medicine, without laws to protect the powerless. It was easy to find purpose in a life so hell-bent on sheer survival.

And there she was, in a memory almost lost to the fog of time. An American Indian protecting her home. Beautiful, dangerous, and her eyes lit up with lust for the handsome trader with the exotic pale skin and curling horns. He could recall so little of her, only that she was a light that came into his life so briefly and went out again—she and her people. Not even their thunderbird could protect them from smallpox... but he could have warned her, he had seen it happen before in other tribes. He hadn't imagined it would spread so far. He died within a month of the epidemic, of a water moccasin bite.

When he came out of his trance, reeling from the press of centuries, the many cycles of lives, the sun was fully risen in the sky. He stood and shook off the grass and dirt of his land and went in search of his thunderbird.

Chapter Twenty-Three

Sally was sitting on the porch next to Sootie when Luke got back to his house. He stopped just outside the fringe of mesquite forest and looked at her. She was in shorts, her knobbly knees drawn up to her chest. When he looked at her, he saw the faint impression of a Navajo weaver, a Canadian lover, an American Indian girl in Mexico, and he saw through the eyes of an American farrier, a British businessman, a Greek merchant.

Of course, they were also none of those things. They were a thunderbird and a satyr. They were a pair of mortal humans in West Texas—a young woman living on her father's goat farm and a construction worker with his own small plot of land. They might have once been Jane, Dinae, and Blue Sky; Enrique, Basil, and Dmitri. But now, they were Sally and Luke. The same souls, different lives.

"I went looking," he said as he crossed the gravel drive and stopped at the bottom of the steps. "It was as you said. Three lives. Three betrayals. I want to defend the actions of my past lives, to try to explain... but it wouldn't change anything, would it?"

Sally shook her head.

"I can see why you don't want to hook up with me again. But Sal... I ain't those men, not really. I share those memories with them. I share the same soul. But I gotta believe that we are in command of our own destinies. Because if we're not... well, what the hell's the point? Why be immortal if each life doesn't have a different destiny, a new start? Without free will, what are we?"

Sally's eyes and voice were steady. "We do have free will, Luke. I can change my choices. I can choose not to let you into my heart and my bed."

Luke walked up the stairs and dropped down next to her. "That's another thing. The whole want-you-or-not? That's one choice I ain't got. Seems that's where free will stops for me."

Sally turned away from him, burying her nose in Sootie's neck. "You can't stop yourself from being in my bed, huh? How's that work?"

"You don't have to be so biting about it. Even when I don't want to, I find myself thinking about you. Remember that day August first came here, and I dropped Sootie off in the morning? That whole day, I couldn't get you out of my head. I couldn't stop imagining you and August—uh, what's wrong?"

"You were imagining me and August? Like, having sex?" Her eyes were wide, rabbitlike, her voice flung high and squeaky.

"Yes.... Uh, sorry—"

"Name details."

Luke rubbed his neck, scuffing his boot on the steps. "Well.... He had on green boxers. And there was one moment when he had you bent over the hitching post in the barn—"

"Ohhhhh, God, no no no. Luke, this can't be real!"

"You're gonna have to fill me in here, babe, because you are flipping out in ways that I did not expect."

"I'm so sorry, Luke. I... I did jump August that day."

"Holy Jesus Christ on a cracker! Seriously?"

"And I was thinking about you while I did it. I wanted you so bad, I figured here's this hot guy, a day of wild hanky-panky would take my mind off of you. But it didn't, not at all."

Luke's eyes flew wide in understanding. "And I picked up on it when you were having sex... because you were channeling it at me, a satyr."

Sally covered her face with her hands. "Shit."

"The night I was attacked by the chupacabras... what were you doing then?"

Sally chewed on her lower lip. "I was talking online to a friend of mine."

"Who?"

"Charlie."

"Oh, your gay buddy in Austin. About what?" Luke pressed.

She looked anywhere but at Luke. "About sex and you."

"That was it?"

Sally groaned. "Fine, it was an extremely graphic conversation and I was really turned on."

Luke snapped his fingers. "And at the same time, I was having an extremely erotic dream about you. Don't you see, Sal? You channel to me. It's almost like telepathy. I bet if we could trace it, every time you did something sexual and thought about me, I'd start fantasizing about you, too." He thought for a minute. "I'm not gonna think about that too hard."

"Yeah, please don't."

He put his hand over hers. Her skin was cool, and a flush of goose bumps raised on her arm. "So you see? As long as you want me, I'm gonna want you. The question is whether you can handle our history and whether you can be flexible enough to let someone else charge me up with magical energy when it's necessary."

She shook her head. "I just don't know."

He ran his thumb over her knuckles, thrilling at the small touch. "Those three lives were rough. But I can promise you this, Sal—if you want me in this life, I'm yours. You can put a halter on me, stable me in the round pen, and call me Mr. Fuzzypants if you want. Yes, there may be things that happen that are out of my control. Shit is gonna fly. Someone like Mae will turn up and throw me for a loop. But do you really think her kind of magic has any stake in what goes on in my heart? In every way that really matters, I devote myself to you."

Sally's chin had been trembling, and her face finally crumpled as she drew in a sob. "Oh God!" she said, and wrapped her arms tight around Luke's neck. He held her awkwardly from the side while her shoulders shook. She was warm, and her spaghetti-strap shirt stretched tight against her chest, and her shorts exposed more thigh than they covered. Her feet were bare, and for some reason that stood out to Luke as intensely sexy. He felt a little guilty, getting turned on while she was crying, but the guilt fled when she pulled back and kissed him.

Luke gasped as her mouth closed over his, rough and forceful in her need. She got up, not ending the kiss, and pushed her way into his lap, straddling him, pressing him against one of the poles that held up the porch. Her breath came fast and shallow, her body arching to press against as much of him as possible. Her hands found the edge of his T-shirt and slid up his bare back, nails scratching faintly down his spine. Electricity seemed to shudder out of her, and Luke yelped.

"Did I hurt you?" she said, leaving their kiss to nip and lick at his ear.

"Nope, I'm good. Just careful on the shocks." He pulled back enough to look Sally in the face. "You're sure about this? I don't want to get into this, then have you change your mind."

Sally got to her feet and offered Luke her hand. "Of course I'm not sure. I'm scared as hell. But I'm sure I can't run away from how I feel about you, either. So if you're willing to risk your immortal heart, knowing all that I do, then I'll meet you halfway."

Luke grinned and let Sally pull him to his feet. "Sounds perfect."

She led him to the front door and inside, shutting Sootie out on the porch.

Chapter Twenty-Four

Tripping over each other in their hurry, Luke and Sally made their way to the couch, the first available horizontal surface that wasn't made of wood. Sally's excitement put off great waves of magical energy that ran through Luke like shockwaves, little jolts of electrocution that left his brain happily disjointed in the rush. She lifted his shirt off of him in one smooth motion and pushed him backward onto the threadbare couch. It squeaked as he landed on it; neither of them took much notice.

Luke grinned at her as she straddled him. "You got no idea how much I've wanted to do this with you."

"Hush, satyr-boy." She silenced him with her mouth, her kisses long and deep. "I've wanted you since I knew what wanting was."

Luke ran his hands up her thighs to her shirt, lifting the cloth to feel the soft skin along her sides, up her spine, pulling the shirt higher—

Luke's cell phone began to buzz, clattering like a scolding squirrel against the table. He'd left it there when he'd gone walking earlier that morning. Luke scrunched up his nose and reached over to silence the phone. The screen read "Missed Call from August Waterford."

"Sorry, buddy," Luke said. "Not today." He reached up, twisted his fingers into the hair at the nape of Sally's neck, and pulled back to expose her throat. As he kissed his way from her chin to the hollow between her collarbones, he added, "I'm occupied." Sally gasped and slid her hips back and forth, rubbing against him so hard it almost hurt, moaning her pleasure in having him between her legs. Luke's mind reeled. She was so like she had been in his fantasies, unrestrained, fiercely demonstrative in her desire for him.

She pulled down her spaghetti-strap shirt to expose her breasts, and Luke had to hold back from hurting her, so eagerly did he suck and kiss her. He had long admired Sally's rack, and now, with her so enthusiastic for him to see and touch, he could barely hold back. He unbuttoned his jeans, and she helped him push them down. He was glad to be rid of them—denim was so restrictive. His cock throbbed beneath his boxer shorts, straining against the thin material, and Sally unbuttoned her own jean shorts. He helped her out of those, and then it was just two soft layers of cotton between them. Luke rubbed the length of his cock against her clit, and he could feel through the fabric how wet she was, how much she longed to have his cock in her pussy. She wanted him. Her wanting was charging through him like an electrical storm, almost painful in its intensity. Once wasn't going to be enough, not to satisfy her. He'd have to—

Now it was Sally's phone going off, playing the "Macarena." With a great moan of frustration, she grabbed her shorts off the floor and dug the phone out. She stopped and looked at the screen, her brow furrowing.

"It's August."

"Well don't answer it!"

"It might be important, if he's trying both of us."

"Fucking you right now is important!"

"Word," Sally said, and tossed the phone aside. Luke grabbed her around the middle and lay forward, pressing her against the other half of the couch. She hooked one leg over the back of the couch and spread wide so he could rub against her harder, moaning and bucking against him. Each thrust was a preview of what it would be like inside her. Her breasts quivered with every movement, and Luke fondled them roughly. She gasped at this, in a good way, and he bit and sucked her brown nipples. She reached her hand down his boxers and grasped his cock, chuckling darkly to herself.

"Woman, I know you're not laughing at my cock," he said. "'Cause I take that bit very seriously."

"Not out of humor, love. Out of sheer joy. Because you have

one hell of a piece of equipment here." She began to stroke him up and down. "And I can't wait to feel it in me."

"Well, what are we waiting for?"

Both phones rang, "Macarena" clashing horribly with the chattering vibration of Luke's phone on the table. Sally and Luke exchanged a dark look and grabbed their phones. They had twin text messages from August: "GET OUT NOW."

Chapter Twenty-Five

Luke called August from the cab of the pickup, shirtless and barefoot. "This better be good, because I was really goddamn busy," he growled. Beside him, Sally crossed her arms tight over her chest, staring resolutely out the window like a frustrated teenager. Sootie kept a low profile on the floorboard between them.

"I just tried to go up to your place," August said, blithely ignoring Luke's mood. "There is a bridge over a large stream that is blocked with an old sedan. I didn't get a good look, but I could swear I saw little monsters crawling around in the forest nearby."

"Sounds like chupacabras," Luke said. "And perhaps, finally, the person or people behind them."

"Exactly."

"Why didn't you charge 'em? You're big and badass, right?"

"Not if I've just crossed running water."

"Running water? That works? Seriously?"

"I'm a ghost, Luke. I can cross running water if I have to, but it grounds me out, sweeps away a ton of magical momentum. That's why in the Irving story—"

"The horseman stops at the bridge," Luke finished for him.

"Exactly. Ghosts like me are effectively useless for a time after crossing running water. One reason I was glad we waited awhile to go hunting the last time I was at your place, and your creeks were dry."

"Gotcha. I'm almost to the bridge now. I see the car, no people. Hang on." He put the phone in a cupholder on the dash as they rolled up to the bridge. It was little more than old railroad ties held together with dirt and rebar, not even any side rails, about twenty feet from bank to bank and thirty feet above a creek that ran dry in the summer and dangerously fast and deep during the fall and spring rains. As August had said, there was a 1980s-model sedan parked across the front of the bridge, and shadows a little bigger than Sootie flitted between the car and the forest, disappearing under the bridge. As they watched, larger shapes climbed monkeylike from under the bridge, and Luke groaned. "Oh no."

"What is it?"

"Bridge trolls. Fucking bridge trolls—and I bet you anything they're pegging me as a billy goat gruff."

Sally let a few beats pass before she said, "I'm sorry, what?"

"The old stories are the hardest to kick. I had it happen twice before in this life. Goddamn, they never learn, anything vaguely caprine gets cast as a goat." He rolled the window down a few inches and called, "What's the deal, hoss?"

The four trolls moved into flanking positions. Though it was a bright day, a tangible darkness hung thick beneath the bois d'arc trees where the trolls moved. They wore their magic like a cloak, old spells of camouflage and shadow, and Luke could not get a good look at any of them. One of them, he couldn't tell which, said, "All we want is you. The girl, even the dog, can go."

"You don't exactly blow me away with the generosity of your offer."

"We're not asking." The troll gestured toward the sedan.

A fifth figure climbed out of the car; Luke recognized Mae and cursed. She was more disheveled than her normally coifed self and moved with the sinuousness of a serpent. She had been channeling a lot of energy recently. She reached out a hand, and Luke felt the blood rush to his already frustrated cock, which stiffened as readily as if she had put her hand between his legs. Her magical energy thrummed into him. His stomach turned, and his skin turned clammy with a cold, fearful, fever-sick sweat.

"Your companions will be given safe passage," the troll said. His voice sounded like bubbling water and creaking trees. "You will stay. The nymph will have her revenge upon you, and when you are spent, we will use your blood to claim your land as our own. We will break the horns from your head, cleave the hooves from your ankles, and bind you with briars to the tree that shades your pathetic shack of a home. There your body will hang until it is rent to dust by the wind and the birds and the scavenging vermin. This is our bargain, our negotiation—give yourself up, and they will not join you in your suffering."

Luke might not have been able to respond, his mind so bound up in Mae's magic, but a sharp crack against his jaw broke him out of it. Sally rubbed her knuckles. "I got this, babe," she said. She cranked down her window and leaned out. "Here's our answering negotiation."

She raised her hands, and the few clouds in the sky began to darken, shading from white to gray as if smudged with charcoal. The wind picked up, bringing with it the smell of rain. She screamed her response to the trolls in a rage that Luke had not heard from her in this or any other life. "Call off this attack now, or I will rip your immortal souls from your bodies and chug them down like a diet soda. You're thousands of years old, right? Tell me now how terrified you are of the true death! You're facing off against a thunderbird, a reaper of souls. Your little rabbit hearts are beneath the raptor's shadow—you better run!" She threw her arms wide, and a bolt of lightning out of what was once a clear blue sky crashed into the sedan behind Mae. The nymph screamed and fell to the ground.

Luke put the truck into drive and slammed on the gas. Mae rolled out of the way, and they hit the sedan squarely on the side, the impact impossibly loud and jarring. The old pickup roared, but it didn't falter. The sedan slid sideways in front of them, seesawing one way, then another, and finally careening off the bridge and into the ravine. Glass and fluid showered into the creek. As soon as they were clear, Luke jammed on the gas, and the truck roared down the road, away from trolls and nymph and chupacabras alike.

Chapter Twenty-Six

Luke and Sally met August farther down the road, where they shared a shortened version of the confrontation at the bridge. August looked back toward the bridge with a curious expression almost like regret. Luke wondered if perhaps he wished he had been in on the action—or if he wished it had gone the other way. The sharp pang of doubt gnawed at him, though he had no solid reason to question August now.

They regrouped at Cormick's house, a well manicured suburban home with a lot of white stone masonry on the front façade and red brick elsewhere. No weeds were tolerated in the small, sprinkler-fed lawn. A green mustache of cubed boxwood shrubs lined the front. The interior sported a flawless coat of soft beige eggshell paint, set off by bright white crown molding and wainscoting in the dining room. There were no stains on the white carpet, no scuffs on the gleaming hardwood floor. Luke was unsure whether it was alright to actually sit on the antique furniture.

The kitchen was the only messy room that they could see, so they congregated there. They found dishes in the sink, wrappers and measuring instruments on the counters, and Cormick in a blue T-shirt with a bit of flour on it. Something delicious and sweet was in the oven. He apologized for the mess and explained that they'd caught him "in a creative mood."

Luke related their tale to Cormick and Orson, who was serendipitously already there when they arrived. Orson fished foreign beers out of the refrigerator and passed them out wordlessly. Sally hoisted herself up onto the counter and hunched glumly over hers. Luke hovered close to her, the near miss of earlier hanging between them.

Finally Cormick said, "There is a family of trolls in Fox Pass. Alan's a cop. They come to the council meetings."

"But are they bridge trolls?" Luke said. "They're a pretty specific set."

"I don't know. It never occurred to me to ask. What's the difference?"

"Sadly, I know all about them, because at least once a lifetime one of them comes trip-trapping along, determined to make a billy goat gruff out of me. Maybe it's the horns. Bridge trolls are concerned with travel, with portals and pathways. They're the guardians of those things and can get pretty ugly about them. It can be metaphysical, too—those who break the rules, cross from one kind of mental or social realm to another, the tricksters, they tend to attract the ire of the bridge trolls. They wouldn't like satyrs even if we didn't resemble goats, because we tend to switch genders from one life to another. We take unexpected partners, dare people to do things they wouldn't ordinarily do. We ask them to cross over—"

"That's it," August said with a sharp intake of breath.

"What's it?" Luke said.

"The gateway," Cormick and Orson said as one, the same revelatory light coming on in their eyes.

"Oh my God," Sally said, pressing her hands to her mouth as her eyes flew wide.

"Will someone please fill me in on what the whole room has realized?" Luke said with a snort.

Orson put a hand on Luke's shoulder. "The magical gateway, Luke—the reason we're all hanging out in West Texas, and why so many of us are born here? The big arch of stone near the river. They're trying to get rid of you because they're afraid you're going to call something over. It's the biggest bridge the trolls could find to guard, and they don't want you trip-trapping over it."

"So they called over the creature that specifically targets goats," Sally said. "The chupacabras."

"And when that failed, they did their homework on you personally and recruited Mae to cripple you magically," Orson added. "She's a hellfire bitch, but she's not normally so mustache-twirling evil. My bet is she's been influenced, maybe even magically poisoned."

Luke leaned against the counter with a deep grumbling breath and swigged his beer. "Son of a bitch. They tried to do it all legit like, too—last year somebody made me an offer on my land. Went through a real estate agent so I didn't ever know who it was. Musta been them."

"Why didn't you take it?" Sally asked.

Luke looked over at her with a meaningful smile. "There wasn't another spot like that one in Fox Pass, and I had this pretty girl I liked, wanted to stick nearby to see if she'd come round." She returned his smile.

"At last we know what we're dealing with," August said. "The council in New York will be pleased." There was a bitter note in his voice that piqued Luke's interest.

"The council can bite my hairy ass," Luke said.

"Noted. So how do we fight them?" August said.

"Tricky," Orson said, tapping his fingers against his mouth. "They're naturally camouflaged. Lose sight of them for a moment and they freeze—look just like a boulder or a dead tree or a mound of earth dotted with little white flowers. Then all of a sudden, that boulder is biting your leg off. Nasty creatures, not much for understanding or forgiveness."

"So weird," Luke said, "that they didn't take me alone, as many times as I've been up and down the mountain. It sure was lucky you were with me, Sal."

"Perhaps not lucky at all," Cormick said. "Maybe they were waiting for when you had a passenger, so they could use her escape as a negotiating chip."

"Bastards," Orson said. "Though not bad planning on their part. For all I know you're a winged mouse, Sal."

Sally shrugged. "No use keeping it secret anymore, now that Luke knows. I'm a thunderbird."

"Wow," Orson said as Cormick jumped back and said, "Jesus!"

"That explains a few things," August muttered.

"Back to the matter at hand," Sally said. "How do we fight them, and how do we know if Alan and his family are the bridge trolls we're looking for?"

"Was that a Star Wars reference?" Luke asked.

She grinned. "Course it was."

"I love you."

"Course you do."

Orson cleared his throat. "As to whether Alan and co. are bridge trolls... well, they don't look any different from other trolls. You gotta see them in action to know the difference. Or give them some kind of truth serum or something."

"Coyote had to speak the truth if asked four times," Sally mused.

"Yeah, but he became the werecoyotes, as far as we can tell. And we don't entreat with the shapeshifters," Cormick said with a shudder.

"Why is that?" August asked. "I've never even met a shapeshifter, but their magic doesn't seem all that different from ours. I mean, we almost shapeshift ourselves, choosing either our mortal or immortal selves to manifest."

"Why don't you ask your council buddies?" Orson said, clearly not yet having forgiven August for his northern heritage.

"Because they don't like their agents asking too many questions. It's easier to ask you guys."

Cormick raised an eyebrow. "And if we report to them that you asked a lot of questions?"

August snorted. "I'm not sure which is more likely—you reporting to the council, or them believing you over me."

Cormick sighed. "That's fair. The truth about the shapeshifters is, they're just dangerous, the pack animals more than others. They don't act entirely human; they're unpredictable."

"The same can be said of us," Sally observed.

"They're more animalistic," Cormick said. "Trust me on this. I've dealt with the coyotes, and they are not a fun bunch to be around. You start feeling like a lobster in a seafood tank. There is a pack right on the other side of the border, in Mexico. You feel free to go find them if you ever want to find out for yourself just how different the shapeshifters are."

August shrugged. "Just curious. Now, about the bridge trolls— my guess is, we need to bait them into showing themselves. Perhaps by having Luke do something they'd hate? Like go through the gateway to the other realms?"

Luke shifted his weight uneasily. "It's not quite so simple as going gallivanting over the edge. I've never been through a gateway like that one, not in this life or any other. The fae realms, the land of the dead, the skylands, the underworlds, a thousand and one spirit realms, they're all there waiting on the other side. To say nothing of the lands of the Hindu gods, the East Asian gods, the secret gardens guarded by the cherubim, and the many levels of Hell. I keep my cloven feet planted firmly on this side of things for a reason. The closest I been is over the rainbow bridge of Haiti, several lifetimes back, and that is one trip I would dearly love to forget."

"You have to know where you're going," Orson said. "To get to one particular land, you must have been there before."

"I've been to a lot of lands before, actually," August said, "in the service of the council."

"Yeah, but you're a ghost," Luke said. "No one cares what borders you cross. Not gonna do us any good to send you."

"I'm not suggesting myself," August said with an enigmatic smile. "I'm suggesting my horse."

Chapter Twenty-Seven

When they got out of the car at the base of the trail that led to the gateway, Luke took Sally's hand and held her back. The others took the hint and walked ahead, leaving them to their own company for a moment. Cormick and Orson headed into the woods to scout for any trolls that might be nearby, and August went straight up the trail.

Luke looped his arms around Sally's waist and pulled her up against him.

"You gotta come back," Sally said, knotting her fists in the front of his shirt.

"That's the plan," he said.

She kissed him, opening her mouth to flick her tongue against his, tasting him. Luke felt his body stir again, still frustrated from their interruption by August and the trolls. Sally obviously felt the same, because she backed against the car, pulling him along. Luke pinned her against the side of the sedan, feeling her breasts move against his chest. She was warm, and soft, and she wanted him. His cock hardened, and Sally felt it—she rolled her hips against him, making a protesting noise of frustration. He thrilled to be brought to arousal so quickly, agonizing that they couldn't jump each other right then.

"God, Luke," Sally said, "I wish we could—"

"And why can't we?"

She bit her lip. "Because I don't want our first time to be a quickie. I want it," she whispered in his ear, "to go a long damn time."

Luke agreed, but it didn't make pulling away any easier. He ducked his head and kissed along her neck. Her skin tasted salty and sweet at the same time. "When I get back," he purred in her ear, "I'm going to make a dishonest woman out of you."

She raised one leg to his hip to grind against him. "You better," she said. Her cheeks were flushed, and he knew if he slid his hand between her legs, he'd find her slick and swollen, aching to have him. It wouldn't take much—remove her shorts, take out his cock, he could fuck her right up against the car, or bent over the hood, or across the backseat.

But that wasn't how they wanted their first time to be. So he took deep, steadying breaths and stepped away from her. She took his hand, and they started up the trail together. It took until they reached the top of the hill for his cock to stand down, and it felt ready to return to attention at the slightest provocation.

Fortunately, the prospect of riding August's horse was enough to wither his soul. The horse glared at him with baleful glowing red eyes and bared its great yellow teeth, its tail whipping in agitation.

"Where the hell did the horse come from?" Luke whispered to Sally. "We drove here!"

"Under his hat?" Sally guessed.

"He is with me always," August said. "We have not been separated for so long; this will be difficult for him. And me."

"To hell with that. I want Hellion here to be nice and relaxed. Could we get him stoned first or something?" Luke squawked.

August ignored this and held the horse's head while Luke mounted. August murmured to it and stroked its cheek while Sally adjusted the stirrups to fit Luke's legs. The gateway lay to the west, a great stone wall with a natural hole worn through it by time and wind and magic. It was a good twenty feet high and twice that across—big enough for an awful lot of terrible things to pass, Luke thought.

"Be careful," Sally said for the umpteenth time. She buckled the stirrup strap and let the saddle flap fall back over it. She held the stirrup while Luke put his foot in it, then adjusted the one on the other side. The horse shifted beneath him, its great bulk feeling more like the rolling sea than a living animal. The horse was tense. Luke adjusted the soft black leather reins, resisting the urge to hold them both in one hand.

"I just wish he rode Western," Luke said. "Gonna be a trick riding English after so long. Hope he doesn't expect me to post."

"You can sit the trot if you want," August said coolly. "But don't give him an excuse to buck you off, or we will never find you."

Luke leaned down to kiss Sally. She was warm, but she shivered. He would be thinking about her the entire time he was gone. Surely they couldn't come this far, overcome the hardship of the lives they'd lived before this, and not get at least a little time to be happy together. Even as he thought it, he knew it was a dangerous train of thought.

Sally was evidently thinking the same thing, because she grabbed the front of his shirt and said, "You come back, hear?"

He straightened up and shook his horns. "My lady demands and I obey."

"I'm serious!"

"So am I."

"OK," August said, stepping back from the horse. "He's all yours. He knows where to go."

"And I know what to look for when I get there." He turned the horse's head toward the gateway and pressed his heels lightly inward. The horse stepped out briskly, covering the stony ground in great strides. When they reached the gate, Luke looked back over his shoulder. Sally stood out in bright profile, as if she had a spotlight on her, while August was nearly invisible in the darkness. As they passed through the gateway, wings of light shone around her—then she and the desert around her were gone.

Chapter Twenty-Eight

The path through the gate, through the web of roads leading to all worlds, was more dizzying and terrifying and wonderful than anything Luke had seen in all his many, many lives. Colors he had never seen before, that did not exist in his reality, blazed around him like shattered lightning. He looked into the abyss beyond the light and saw eyes gazing back at him, marking his passing, the great guardians of the chasms.

They went by worlds, entire realities, so fast he had only time to glimpse them before they were on to the next one. It was, he would think later, like running down the aisle of a great library, where the pages of the books opened up as he passed and spilled forth their guts, unfolding and refolding like maps, beautiful and terrible and immense in their breadth. The creature beneath him was no horse at all, but a shimmering dark presence the color of a raven, black as the void until the light hit it and revealed the iridescent green and purple depths within. It flew along the pathways with its feet not striking at all, navigating the cobweb of the cosmos like it was normal, like it was easy. All Luke could do was cling to its neck and try not to scream.

When at last the horse stopped, the air was still, the light pale and weak, in a stone corridor. Luke sat up, shaking, slid out of the saddle, and found his legs didn't hold him; he collapsed onto the floor and retched. The horse walked past him, huffing as if to say, "Amateur."

When Luke's head stopped spinning and his strength returned to him, he pulled himself off the ground and followed the horse into the great stone hall, his lighter trip-trapping footsteps an accent rhythm to the heavy clip-clop of the horse's hooves. Luke was fully his satyr-self here in the world of the fae, his horns and hooves as real as his olive skin and work-worn callouses. He was naked, as all satyrs inevitably prefer, and surprised himself by thinking nothing odd about it. Here, he realized, he could not manifest a human appearance; he was all satyr, and nothing else.

The enormous stone hall was cold, and still, and held more silence than he had ever heard. When the echoes of their footsteps stopped, there was no sound whatsoever. It was disconcerting, especially in a place that had once been so very alive—Tír na nÓg, the land of youth, the home of the Tuatha Dé Danann and the heroes of many lands. The arched ceiling towered many stories above him, old stonework so tight it would outlast the ages. Many columns supported it, and into them were carved the runic languages of the peoples who had visited the hall—Celtic, Welsh, and many others. One had a great spiral winding around it, intersected with the quick Ogham marks of Pictish. To Luke's great surprise, he could almost read it. He wondered what long-ago life he had led in Scotland.

"Many blessings upon you," he said aloud, running his hand over the ancient stone. His voice echoed, its hollow ringing a reminder of just how silent the hall was. "Or... something like that." He followed the script around, picking out words he understood, until it was too high to make out, though it continued all the way to the ceiling.

"Wonder how they did that," he said. He walked along the outer wall, eyeballing the many corridors that led off of the great hall. Seeing a light, he went down one corridor to a room filled with a golden glow.

A great, strangely silent fire burned in a central fire pit, the smoke curling up to a chimney-hole high in the ceiling. A circular table ringed the pit, laden with food of every kind—large slabs of meat on the bone, glistening with a honey glaze; clumps of fruit plump and brightly colored, with a hint of sugar crystals sprinkled upon them; crisp-crusted bread still steaming from the oven, with a bowl of whipped butter beside each one. Jugs of wine and mead stood beside heavy ceramic mugs. His head swam from the marvelous mix of aromas, and he could almost taste the fine food, feel the tender texture of it in his mouth.

The horse nudged him hard from behind, and he almost fell over.

"I wasn't going to taste it," he said. "I'm not stupid. The first rule of any magical land, especially Faerie, is to take no food or drink." The horse didn't look convinced. "Hey," Luke said, "weren't your eyes glowing red before? They're green now. Which, don't get me wrong, is still creepy. You look like you got the ectoplasm from *Ghostbusters* floating out of your eyes." The horse snorted derisively as it turned away from him. Luke gave the table one last sighing look; it might not be real, but it surely was tempting. After lust and pride, a satyr's favorite sin was gluttony.

He and the horse walked through many more corridors and halls. There were strange suits of armor that would fit no man or beast Luke knew. Of course, he mused, no armor he'd ever seen would fit him, either, with his tail and high joints and cloven hooves. There was a massive spear with many barbs upon its enormous iron head; it was tinged here and there with a black crust that made Luke cringe. Swords, daggers, bows, axes and flails made up the décor; there were no paintings, tapestries, sculptures, or vases for the ancient fae and their human companions. The finest art was a well made weapon.

"I can see why Orson liked it here," he muttered.

The farthest room was filled knee-deep with bones, with a raised path and a dais in the center. The bones were all wrong; they didn't seem to go together. He picked out several skulls and realized that the bones were the jumbled skeletons of humans and faeries, mixed with horses and dogs. He walked to the center, where a leather collar lay on the dais. He picked it up; no dust lay upon it. Turning to go, he heard a clink.

In any other place, one tiny sound would not have bothered him. But here, in the vast and eternal silence, that small sound set his hair on edge. He froze and watched the pile of bones.

Somewhere, another clink. Then a bone tumbled down the pile to the floor. Luke ran.

He called to the horse, who met him in the center of the stone hall, both skidding to a stop on the stones.

"We've got to go," he said, taking hold of its bridle. "Skeletons—"

The horse's nostrils flared, and it stepped away from him, its green eyes narrowed and fierce. Luke got the idea as plain as if it had flashed inside his mind—he had not gotten what they came for, a tool to use against the trolls. The horse would not take him back.

"Look," said Luke, "I got a faerie dog collar. Won't that do something? No? Crap, I'm not a goddamn faerie, I'm Greek!" He banged his fists against the base of his horns. "What do I know about faeries, what do I know about faeries.... Don't drink the drink, don't eat the food, don't break a promise, don't give a brownie clothes, don't insult them, milk curdles before them, changelings are left in place of a fae-stolen baby, someone who's crazy can be called fae struck, a fae pony will run you all over the moors and drown you, time runs differently, there's at least two courts, they tangle your hair and make a mess out of stuff, Cuchulainn loved a faerie girl, some blonde chick—" He gasped. "The spear—that's Cuchulainn's spear! Gul something! Gul Dukat? No, that's Star Trek—I dunno. Can I use that? More importantly, could Orson use that?"

Luke broke off his monologue when he heard a clatter behind him. He turned to see a thousand bones spilling out of the doorway, moving as if pulled by strings, awkward and tripping but inevitably shuffling forward. They were assembling themselves—here and there a leg found a hip joint to fit into, fingers scuttled together to form hands, spines snaked forward looking for their skulls, and ribs rattled like bundles of kindling. Luke ran to where the enormous black-crusted spear hung on the wall. He took it down and promptly dropped it to the floor—its weight was far greater than it looked. He picked it up, lugged it onto his shoulders, and turned to run.

A figure was silhouetted in the doorway, a skeleton on a thick-boned horse. Beyond her, a thousand partial skeletons churned up the dust and wavered upon her heels. August's horse was nowhere to be seen. He was trapped.

Chapter Twenty-Nine

She sat sidesaddle on a skeletal horse, and gauzy wraps draped her bones in what would have been a scandalous and enticing fashion had she been whole. Scraps and ropes of long, blonde hair clung to her scalp, held in place mostly by the deteriorating silken scarf around her brow. She crooked her finger, and the great spear Luke carried became impossibly heavy, unbearably heavy—he went down to his knees, the spear across both shoulders, both hands held in place by invisible bonds. He could not put it down.

The undead woman slid from her mount and knelt before him. He could only raise his head enough to see her shoulders. She clacked her teeth and touched one finger beneath his bearded chin.

"You are not of the people," she said, her voice surprisingly beautiful—a ghost's voice, he thought, nothing to do with how she was now. It was all in how she remembered herself. She leaned forward; he would have had a perfect view of her breasts, if she had been alive. She seemed to be sniffing him, a quick in-and-out huffing like a dog. "But you have the scent of fae love upon you. Three of them."

"Cormick and Orson," Luke said. "One is my lord. The other is my brother-in-arms, one of the Tuatha Dé Danann." His brow knit. "Three? Oh—Glen. Glen is a goblin. Goblins are fae, aren't they?"

"Strictly speaking, yes. What is he to you? He loves you."

"Just... my friend." He thought of the night he'd performed his great feat of magic, destroying the dens of the chupacabras on his land, when August had kissed him. He'd felt a great rush of lust-magic from someone else in attendance, someone who tasted like a fae. He had thought it was from Cormick. He felt almost guilty that he had never considered the possibility it had been from Glen.

"He is my friend," he said with more certainty. "I don't know if I am anything more to him."

"You have a trifecta—a lord, an equal, and a supplicant of fae blood." She rose. "You may take the spear, if you have a noble cause." The silence was pregnant with expectation as she waited.

"I take it to give to Orson, to use to defend my land, my love, and all our lives."

"The only three things worth fighting for," she said, and mounted her horse. "But I will take a toll from you."

The weight of the spear lifted, and Luke stood, relieved. She gestured him forward, and he took a few steps to stand beside her horse. She leaned down, opened her jaws, and sealed them over his mouth.

Twenty-eight hundred years seemed to open up inside of him. Hundreds of lives waited for him, some just beneath the surface, some fossilized beneath layers of memories in his mind. He heard himself screaming from a long way off, but he could no longer feel the air in his lungs or see anything of the stone hall or the undead fae woman. She dredged through his mind like a potter digs clay from a bank, leaving deep, rending trails with her fingers. She pulled great chunks of old lives away, and he tried to cling to them as she swallowed them.

A Greek woman with wild tastes and a husband who could not give her children came to run with him and the nymphs in the woods. He remembered how she wanted him, how her eyes lit up when she saw him, knowing that he would give her what she wanted. She was soft and starved for pleasure and came looking for her satyr lover more often than she should have. Their children were many, wild things who grew fierce and powerful, both the sons and the daughters. For a moment he was inside her, she was calling his name, always saying "More... more...." Then she and all his memories of her were gone.

He—no, he was a woman this time—was a priestess of some long-forgotten religion, in the temples of the forests. Men would come and pray upon the altar, and if they pleased her, she would have them upon the altar. They would rend her clothes in their eagerness to penetrate her. She loved that initial thrust when a new cock pushed inside her, not knowing if he would be rough and frenzied to spill his seed or if he would take a long time, sliding in and out, making her beg. The best, she thought, were the new ones, the ones who had never been with a woman before, and certainly never a satyr. She would laugh at them, make them flustered, until they would either pin her to the stone, push her legs aside, and take her or falter and beg her mercy. And she would give it, pleasuring herself upon them at her own pace. The women did not dare approach the near gods who lived in their woods, the feral beast-demons their men sought. At least, that was what they thought of her. She didn't care; she and her sisters were as inhuman as any wolf, and just as vicious when they were crossed.

A momentary burst of magic, and that life was gone too, sucked down the fae's throat.

A family life in early Europe, cut short by the plague. Luke clung fiercely to the memory of a blond-haired little boy, his youngest son, the sole survivor of that terrible summer, and then the boy and all the tragedy he lived through were gone. A life at sea, only a few centuries ago, as the cabin boy to a handsome and gregarious captain. He'd laughed at the pity he saw in the eyes of the other sailors—he loved the days the captain asked him to stay up late with him. He lived to be the captain's first mate, eventually, and those old sailors never did seem to understand that he enjoyed being in the captain's bed. He and the captain and the ship and everyone he knew sank into the sea, a blaze of fire above them— and then oblivion, as that life was forgotten too, consumed. A solitary life in the woods of colonial America, a true Salem witch that everyone had the good sense to leave alone—unless they wanted to pay her, with goods or with pleasure, for her services. Gone. A short life, a little girl on a large farm, a fall from a horse, a long fever, then death. All gone.

Luke fell to the ground, gasping like he'd nearly drowned, drinking in the cold, still air. He had the feeling something had been taken from him, some old part of his soul, but he no longer knew what it was. He raised his eyes to the skeletal fae—but she wasn't a skeleton, she was swelling, coloring, flesh filling in between her bones. She was beautiful and young, a blonde fae woman on a horse that also filled out, muscles and skin and fine gray fur engulfing the bones. She smiled down at Luke.

"I thank you for what you've given me. More than I thought you could have. You are old, so impossibly old—there is more in the world than I knew. You have years enough behind you, I would be surprised if you even missed what I have taken." She breathed in deep, and her eyes fluttered closed. "I have never known pleasure as you have. Satyr—that is what you are. Shall I keep you, and have you teach me all you know of bodily bliss?"

Luke rolled onto his stomach, struggling to get to all fours. "I... I have sworn an oath. I will take none to my bed without the blessings of my mate." The language of the land—oath, mate—spilled easily from him. Dimly, as if from a long way off, he thought, *I've been around Orson too long.*

"Because of all you have already given, I will allow this," she said. She looked away from him as if she could see far, over many miles. "I have quarry," she said. "I will lead the Hunt today. But look for me in the future, Satyr." She smiled, and her grin was as wide as a skull's, too wide, too many teeth. "I may hunger for you again." She gave some unseen cue to the horse, and it lunged forward. The great horde of skeletal dogs and horses and humans and faeries and more followed, and they disappeared through the stone walls.

Luke staggered to August's black horse, the dog collar from the dais in his fist and the spear upon his shoulders. This time, the horse let him mount. He braced the spear against the stirrup as he might have a flag and clung to the horse's mane, and the horse leaped through the stone walls as if they had never been there at all.

Chapter Thirty

When Luke came through the portal back into his world, his first thought was that it all looked so gray. He felt himself tilting off the side of the horse—or rather, the world slid sideways, and down he went with it. He tried to cling to the horse's neck, but his arms fell away, as if the simple act of holding on were an impossible feat of strength.

He had enough horse sense drilled into him from centuries past to kick his feet out of the stirrups. Then he tumbled out of the saddle and landed with a belly flop in the hard-packed red dirt. The spear fell beside him, and the horse trotted away. He watched, sideways, as the horse approached August, then abruptly wheeled ninety degrees and sprinted away from him, down the mountain trail. August started after it, shouting in surprise. Luke was relieved to hear the thundering hooves and shouts diminish into the distance; his head was pounding out a cantering rhythm of its own.

Other people were there, but Luke barely registered their voices. The world was so foggy, and he just wanted to sleep. Sleep sounded great. The ground wasn't even that uncomfortable. It was downright welcoming, so still and quiet and cool. He snarled as someone pulled him into a sitting position, and in rebellion against this propping up, let himself slide down into a slouch. His disturber held Luke half-upright, arms around his chest as Luke squirmed to get comfortable.

He heard Sally's voice. "Is he OK? He's so pale!"

Cormick's voice, next. "He's been in Tír na nÓg, a dead fae realm that was overtaken by specters ages ago. I expect something there lapped up as much of his magical energy as it could, like a cat drinking the juice from a can of tuna. We knew that could happen."

"And you still sent him."

"He sent his own damn self!"

"Shut up, everyone, and let's get him back on his feet." Allison's voice.

"Be my guest," grunted the man who was holding Luke half-upright. An unfamiliar voice, with only a trace of the same southern accent that rounded the long vowels of most of the Fox Pass myth-folk.

Allison huffed, a sound he had often heard her make when talking to her son. She was trying to be patient and polite with someone. "He needs magical energy. Sally, go kiss him."

"I can't! Not like this!" Luke wished he had the strength to do so much as encourage her. But his mouth wouldn't obey him when he tried to order it around.

"Fine, I will."

"Bitch, you most certainly will not."

"OK," Allison said, her voice pitching upward in a crescendo. "Look, Miss Territorial. Someone around here needs to get turned on, and it needs to involve Luke. I don't give a damn how that happens. So come up with something."

Sally's voice, strangely tentative. "Charlie, could you...."

"I am not kissing your unconscious boyfriend as an introduction," said the man holding Luke up.

"But she likes the idea," Allison said. Luke could hear the gears in her brain turning, even half-unconscious as he was. "All right, Sal, c'mere. I have a plan. Look at those guys. Smoking hot, right? I mean, for our type. Luke is tall... ish, farmer's tan and tight cords of muscle from working his well toned ass off, a bit of scruff to him. He drives a pickup. He can birth a calf. He owns tools and knows how to use them. He likes kids, both the human and the goat variety. Dude can move or fix or build anything you'd ever need. He will climb down in the dirt and get shit done."

Cormick stifled a laugh. "You have the most bizarre set of turn-ons."

"Shut up, fairy princess, if I were trying to turn you on I'd talk about how neat and clean and controlled everything was. Now, where was I? Ah yes. Your friend there—"

"My name's Charlie."

"Charlie. He's your friend, right? Your confidant. He knows you. He's kind, and funny, and frankly a good-looking fellow in his own way."

"Don't overdo it," Charlie muttered.

"Hey," Allison said, "you're too city-boy for my taste, I'm doing my best!"

"He can fix my computer," Sally said.

"What's that?" Allison asked.

"He can fix my computer. The one thing Luke couldn't do shit with. He could fix any kind of electronic, really. He taught me how to defrag my hard drive. He walked me through setting up my wireless printer. He built his own computer, a desktop of true magnificence. He taught me the basics of programming. Any time my computer spazzes out on me, he can put it right. Between the two of them, there is nothing in the world they couldn't fix."

"My God," Allison said, "they really do need to make out."

Cormick snorted. "This is just weird."

"Gawd, Cormick," Allison said, "you were a girl in past lives. Haven't you ever fancied a useful guy?"

"I always had staff for that."

"Well we don't have staff!" Sally barked. "We have ourselves, and sometimes our male relatives. But they're not always useful, or available, or healthy. And that leaves us sitting in the room with a broken thing, usually something extremely necessary like a toilet, and tools that may or may not be what we actually need, without the physical strength to do what's needed. With a useful man, at least there's two of you, and one of you has stronger hands and different tools that may or may not be what's needed!"

"Or the internet," Charlie piped up. "Best tool ever."

"Other than a welding torch, yes," Sally agreed. "Cormick, it's not just that a useful man can fix stuff. It becomes two of you against the world's endless series of bullshit problems and broken shit. It's not that I can't fix things my own girly self; it's that, with Luke and Charlie around, I *don't have to.* It's not just me taking it all on anymore. I have partners, well armed and well schooled in what to do and how. I benefit greatly from their experience, their strengths, and their willingness to work."

"Well said," Allison said. "Now Sally, fix your eyes on that pair of useful men. Luke all scruffy and his shirt torn up the side, unshaven, with his dark hair and olive-colored skin. Half lying on your friend, blue eyed and blond haired, slender and young."

Luke felt a trickle of magic seeping into him, the slow movement of water saturating the parched skin of cracked, drought-ridden earth. He forced his eyes open for a moment before even that tiny bit of strength was spent. In that moment, he got a glimpse of Charlie. He was reminded strongly of a red dun horse; perhaps it was Charlie's long nose, or the way his hair fell over his face like a horse's forelock, that shade of light brown that would have been blond as a child. Charlie was watching the girls; Luke followed his gaze, and his eyes widened.

Allison stood behind Sally, arms around her waist, chin on Sally's shoulder. Sally had a deer-in-the-headlights look, tense and uncomfortable but not pulling away. Luke found his soul stirred and was internally furious that he didn't have the strength even to sit up.

"Now Sally," Allison said, "listen close, girl, because I'm going to teach you how to charge a satyr."

Chapter Thirty-One

Sally shifted in Allison's arms; Allison only held her tighter from behind, as if willing her to listen, to heed her. "Charging a satyr isn't complicated, but simple doesn't necessarily mean easy. It's like birthing a baby—you have to know what muscles you're supposed to use, and you probably don't even know you have these magical muscles until you start using them. Direct your magic toward Luke. Funnel it toward him. Right now you radiate all over, like one of those static electricity ball thingies. You gotta be more like lightning, sending it all right to him."

"Who told you I'm a thunderbird?"

"Everyone's talking about it. Think about emotional release—how it feels, physically, when you have a huge emotional weight lifted from you, that sense of both relief and exhaustion. That slight world shift when you let go of an emotion, and the magical energy associated with. Those are the same metaphysical muscles you use to direct the flow of your erotic energy."

Luke was more aware now of the hard ground, of Charlie's knee digging into the small of his back. With enormous effort, he squirmed and shifted before falling still again, panting with the effort. He opened his eyes briefly, wanting to watch Allison instruct Sally.

"What does it feel like during?"

"Like a fist knots inside your guts, right below your rib cage, and yanks toward him. It doesn't hurt—in fact, it feels really good. But don't let go of yourself completely. He'll ground you out if you let him. He won't mean to—it's metaphysics, not choice or will with him. You gotta be careful not to drain yourself completely; once won't do you any harm, except for being totally useless the next day, but making a habit of letting go of all of your magical energy will permanently damage your capacity for your own magic. So hold onto that fist in your gut when you start to feel weak."

Luke wanted very much to be part of this conversation. He wanted to reassure Sally, to assert that Allison was right, that this, really, was why monogamy was not only difficult for a satyr but dangerous. Of course, Allison was doing a better job of explaining it than he ever had, so perhaps it was best that he was near catatonic on a blond Austinite.

"So with that in mind," Allison said, and he could hear the change in her voice, "let's charge him. You don't even need to touch him. Just get turned on thinking about him, direct your magic to him instead of throwing it in the air like confetti, and that should be enough to get him on his feet. Now.... Look at those two handsome, useful fellows. One dark, one light. One rugged and tough, the other kinda adorable in a geeky way."

"Wow. Really?" Charlie's voice was laced with irritation.

"Hush, you are," Sally said.

Allison brushed back Sally's dark hair so she could talk right in her ear. "I want you to imagine Luke waking up, grinning that shit-eating grin he gets when he is about to make trouble. He turns around, on all fours, and straddles your friend there, who is all shy and unsure about the whole thing. Luke, he doesn't care, he can taste the lust coming off that young man, and it turns him right the hell on. He lifts Charlie's face up to meet his and kisses him. Soft and full of affection at first, then deep and needful. And Charlie, he can't help himself, he kisses him back, making little noises in his throat."

Luke took a deep breath, wrapping himself up in the delicious wave of magical energy that washed over him, not only from Sally but from Allison and Charlie, too. And Cormick, he noted, sensing fae lust in the mix. Couldn't blame the guy, Allison talking like that was hot no matter what your inclinations.

Charlie's energy was unlike any magic Luke had ever tasted, and he lingered on it. He tasted the way one might imagine deep, achingly cold spring water would taste, with something like the smell of forests mixed in. Cedar wood and rich, leaf-strewn earth, rain and stone, and an animalistic aftertaste. It was hard to get a good read on him, when his magic mixed and mingled with the others'. Luke would find out soon enough. He tuned back in to what Allison was saying.

"Your friend, does he prefer to be on top or bottom?"

"Bottom," Sally said, her voice strained.

"Good. Luke kisses his neck and his ear, starts undoing his shirt. Charlie's not so sure about all this, because Luke's yours and he's never had an audience before, but he goes along with it because Luke needs this, and Sally needs Luke, and anyway he's turned on."

"I follow," Charlie said. "I'll lay off the dirty looks."

Luke forced his eyes open; it was easier now than a few minutes ago. Sally was leaning into Allison, an arm over the other woman's, which was still around her waist. He watched Allison talk to her, watched Sally begin to twitch and fidget, excited but unable to do anything about it.

"Charlie," Allison said, "give me something to work with."

"This is so not my area of expertise," Charlie said. "It's been, what—nine months since my boyfriend and I broke up? And I've only had two."

"Good enough. Luke takes off Charlie's shirt and lays him back on the ground, lies between his legs and moves against him. Luke ain't shy, he lets the boy know exactly what he wants. He takes his shirt and pants off, takes Charlie's off. Luke's a satyr, full of earth magic, old magic, older than Christianity. He knows how to touch Charlie to pleasure him, how hard to bite, to scratch, to rub and grind. There's nothing like a partner who is experienced and confident. Luke takes his time with him, tasting him, teasing him, making him ache like a bruise to be fucked. Are you aching yet, Sally?"

"Gawd, yes I am."

"Can I help?"

Sally hesitated a long moment, then said, "OK."

Luke's breath was coming easier now, not the shallow panting of before. He looked at the girls, and his heart thudded hard against his breastbone, magical starvation be damned. Allison slid her hand down the front of Sally's cargo pants and whispered in her ear. When Sally suddenly gasped and bucked in her arms, Allison smiled, and her voice rose again to where Luke could make out what she was saying.

"Luke's not rough, or selfish—he takes the time to slide his fingers, one at a time, inside Charlie, to rub him with oil, to make sure he's ready. And Charlie, oh, all he wants is that man's cock up his ass, but he doesn't want to say it. His body writhes under Luke, who is stroking him now, enjoying watching his partner losing control for want of him. Finally he gives Charlie what he wants, and enters him."

Sally cried out, a good cry, barely restrained. It was like an electric jolt, and Luke was brought into full consciousness quite suddenly. He took a surreptitious look around, not wanting to interrupt the delicious scene before him. Sally gasped, ecstatic, and arched against Allison, making the most interesting little noises. Luke imagined that Allison had slid her fingers inside Sally, mirroring her description of the boys. He noticed Cormick wasn't giving a snide commentary now, just quietly listening off to the side, eyes wide. Charlie had his face buried behind Luke's ear, evidently too self-conscious to look at anyone anymore, but Luke felt Charlie's breath, hot and shallow, on his neck, and his fingers twisted in Luke's shirt. He was as tense as a drum. Luke turned his head to whisper to him, "I like how you smell."

The only indication of his surprise was a momentary hesitation, then a soft, "Thank you." But he did unclench just a little bit.

"Ohhh!" Sally said, a whine of protest.

"We'll get there, girl, just hang on. Think about where your magical core is, the tight little ball of magical energy that forms in your abdomen. Think of rolling it all up together, like a ball of dough. And when you come, I want you to use that rush of relief to throw it all to Luke."

"Like a hadouken," Sally breathed.

"Sure. Whatever that is."

"It's from *Street Fighter!*"

"Of course it is. Look now—Luke's got Charlie pinned to the ground and is thrusting into him with deep, fast strokes. He rolls his hips, shifts his angle, looking to find exactly how Charlie likes to be fucked. Because that's what an old satyr can do—he can find your weaknesses, your triggers. He's... creative. And once he's found the way that makes Charlie throw his head back and open his legs, beg for more, Luke gives it to him, does him exactly the way he's always wanted to be fucked."

It was hard to say who was the most aroused in the little clearing in the woods—Sally, Luke, or the apparently deathly shy young man holding him. Charlie stayed absolutely still, as if moving would make it more difficult to control himself, his body totally tense. Waves of lustful energy fell off of him like swirls of leaves in a fall storm. Luke slid against him, sat up now that he had the strength to do so, let the girls see how well their plan was working. Sally met Luke's eyes and bit her lip hard, her expression one of surprise and want and encouragement.

Luke turned his head back to murmur in Charlie's ear. "Can I kiss you?"

Charlie was still and silent, then nodded, the movement barely perceptible. Luke reached a hand behind Charlie's neck and pulled him in for a kiss. He tasted tangy and sweet, his mouth stronger than Sally's.

"Aw hell yeah!" Luke heard Sally say.

A moment later she was making less comprehensible sounds, and Allison was saying, "When they come, their bodies rock together with the incredible pleasure of their ecstasy, and—"

"Shut up, Allison, I get it!" Sally managed to bark in between her cries. As she rocked her hips hard against Allison's hand, Luke's body was suddenly seized with pleasure. A rush of tingling heat filled him, almost hurting with its intensity. He shuddered and moaned against Charlie, whose own lustful magic, while nowhere near Sally's level, contributed not insignificantly to the burning shock of magical energy barreling through Luke's system.

When the majority of the aftershocks had passed through him, Luke sat up under his own power, though still dizzy, and grinned sloppily. "Hi. I'm Luke."

"So I gathered. I'm Charlie."

Luke stood up and held out a hand to pull Charlie to his feet. "Nice to meet you, Charlie. Welcome to Fox Pass."

Chapter Thirty-Two

Allison let Sally slide down to the ground at last. She watched the girl pant on all fours for a minute before declaring loudly, "I am so goddamn good. That was one of the coolest things ever."

"Very impressive," Luke said, drumming his fingers against his leg and rocking slightly. He felt like he could go bouncing off the trees around the clearing, a shiny steel ball in a pinball machine, a complete turnaround from his near-coma of earlier. He walked over to Sally. When he knelt beside her to ask how she was, she tackled him and kissed him, hard and sloppy.

"You," she said, "are trouble."

"This is all adorable and whatnot," Cormick chimed in, "but we've got to get out of here. The trolls will have some way of knowing Luke is back, remember? They showed up after you went through the portal the first time, Luke, pissed off something fierce."

"I gave them what-for last time, I'll do it again," Sally said, cracking her knuckles.

"Oh, and you have the, ahem, juice left to do that after charging your satyr boyfriend?" Cormick said, not unkindly.

Sally's face fell. "Crap. I don't know."

"Then let's get going. Best not to tempt fate by getting cocky. No pun intended."

In true suburban style, Cormick was driving a massive SUV borrowed from his aunt, a Boy Scouts den mother. Allison called shotgun, and Orson sat in the middle row with a very put-out August, who had been unable to catch his rogue mount. Luke sat, silent and fidgeting, between Charlie and Sally in the third row of seating, the events of the evening catching up to him. He didn't know why Charlie was there, what his intentions or his relationship with Sally really were. The more he thought about it, the weirder he felt about having kissed the man earlier. Well, he thought, that's the way of intimate encounters. They so frequently sounded like good ideas at the time.

The ride down the mountain from the portal was tense, with all parties staring out the windows at the surrounding trees, normally so lovely but now a menacing sight, almost claustrophobic. What looked to be a boulder on the side of the road might be an ambush. Anything might come out of those trees, a troll or a troll's ally. When they were off the mountain and the trees thinned to sage and mesquite brush, Luke breathed a little easier.

Orson turned in his seat to look at Luke. "Tír na nÓg didn't treat you so badly, then."

"Oh, it did," Luke growled. "Sally, Allison, and Charlie got me back on my feet. I was nearly catatonic when I came back through."

"What happened in there?"

Luke described the hall, watching Orson's face crumple with the old hurt. Orson perked up when he heard about the woman who had sucked something away from Luke, though Luke couldn't put his finger on what, exactly, she had taken.

"A part of my soul, perhaps," he said, "though I hope it's not as dire as that."

"She could have sucked away part of your life—your memories, and the emotions associated with them," Orson said. "Remember the old stories about how the fae would kidnap people, keep them awhile, and when those people came back, they'd find a hundred years or more had passed? And they'd age suddenly and die? There's more than one way that happened, not the least of which was time passing differently there, but one way is that the human lived those hundred-plus years and every so often the faerie host would drain those memories away from them, and place a youthful glamour upon them, so they didn't know they'd been there all that time. When they escaped, or were set free, or failed to follow a geas like Cuchulainn did, the glamour would break and they'd find out how old they really were. I bet that's what happened to you, too. You certainly have memories enough to take. Do you remember your mother?"

"Yes. And high school and college, and Mae and working, and moving to Fox Pass...."

"Might not even be this life. Let's try some others." Orson listed off moments he'd shared with Luke in their past lives, and for a time, Luke remembered them. Then, "Do you remember Salem?"

"Is that a place or a person?"

"Salem, Massachusetts. Before the witch trials. You sold agricultural charms to the peasants, before that one hysterical bitch set fire to your house, and you moved up to Canada."

Luke's eyes grew wide, and he shook his head. "Doesn't sound familiar."

Orson's lips grew thin underneath his bushy mustache. "You, uh.... You were a woman. Very busty. Kinda whorish."

"You say that as if it were a bad thing," Luke quipped.

"It wasn't."

"Oh." Luke's smirk vanished. "I understand you now. I would remember that. And I don't."

Orson sighed, the resigned noise of a man long accustomed to loss. "Pity. Sounds like she consumed some of your memories. We can puzzle out more about which ones later, if you want. You and I, we don't have many secrets from each other."

"Funny, I would have said we don't have *any* secrets."

"No one shares everything. Thank God for that."

Chapter Thirty-Three

Orson considered the spear in his lap. "Cuchulainn's spear.... It's strange to see it after so many years, and in such a different setting. Like seeing your kindergarten teacher in the supermarket—a collision of worlds." He looked back up at Luke. "So you paid for the spear with some of your past life memories—that's good, actually. Frankly I'm surprised she'd barter with you, those fae wraiths are a dangerous lot. Normally she would have just drunk you dry, or at least hung you up for later."

"She said I had a trio or something of fae affection—a superior, a peer, and a subordinate. Or supplicant. Started with an s-u." He pointed past Orson to Cormick in the driver's seat. "Our illustrious leader... you... and Glen."

Orson's brow knit. "Glen? I didn't know you guys were that close."

Luke dropped his head into his hands. "We weren't. But apparently he thought highly enough of me to leave a magical mark upon me. Makes me feel like crap, actually, that I didn't pay him more attention."

"You talk as if he's already dead."

"Well, we don't know what's happened to him, do we?"

"Wouldn't his magic disappear if he were dead?" August chimed in.

"Not necessarily." Everyone looked at Charlie, whose dour expression turned deadly serious. "Myth-folk magic can be preserved after death if certain precautions are taken. He could be dead, and the magic he worked in life still lingering, if he were magically contained."

August narrowed his eyes at Charlie. "How would you know

about that?" he asked. "What are you?"

Charlie's hesitation was just long enough to be noticeable. "A Jersey Devil."

"Jesus!" August bellowed, jumping back as far as his seat belt allowed.

"And you're, what, an Easter Bunny? C'mon, none of us are exactly made of sunshine."

"Naw. Just lightning," Sally quipped, making explosion gestures with her hands.

"This isn't funny!" August said. "Those things are dangerous!"

"Like dude already pointed out," Luke said, leaning forward, "so is everyone in this car, everyone in this community. Even Allison is dangerous, when in her element."

There was a moment in which everyone considered this. Then Cormick said, "In her restaurant?"

"No, jackass, when she's in the water! Cripes."

"I'm plenty dangerous!" Allison protested.

"You're not," Orson said, "not the way the rest of us are. Not unless we're all swimming."

"You guys, Allison still has hundreds of years of experience, she can swing with the rest of us," Sally said, a line appearing between her eyes.

"Thank you!" Allison said.

"Swing what? A frying pan?" Orson griped.

"Spoken like a man who's never been hit with one!"

"Shut up!" Cormick yelled over the din. "Gawd. You people. Focus! We are all of us scary nightmarish beings. Now August, you go first, tell us why Jersey Devils are scary, and then Charlie, you can tell us all why he's wrong. If you all start trying to talk at once again, I will pull this car over, pick up a rock, and we'll have to pass the rock to determine who can speak. Do you want to play Pass the Rock of Speaking?" A moment of silence passed. "Do you?"

"No," everyone in the car muttered with a communal pout.

"Good. Now August, talk."

August eyeballed Charlie warily. "I've never met one that was civilized. They're a lot like the chupacabras, more animal than human. There are people around now who actually believe in them, so they are influenced by those beliefs. They are vicious, demonic predators. And, none of the ones I have ever met could cloak themselves in a human guise, the way we can. They are their myth-selves, and nothing else. C'mon, if you met someone who introduced himself as a chupacabra, would you trust him?"

"That's enough, August. Interesting. Charlie, go," Cormick said.

"When I was a child my mother contacted a magic-user. I'm sorry, I don't know exactly what she was. She cloaked me in a myth-folk type of magic. Under its influence I became... almost human."

Orson studied him through narrowed eyes. "You're wearing someone else's magic."

"Yes."

"Fuck me, that's sick." He rubbed his eyes with his hand. "It's like wearing someone else's skin. A skin-changer, essentially. I might actually be sick. Cormick—"

"Swallow your imagination, Tuatha. Charlie, where did the magic come from? Or more specifically, from whom?"

"I don't know. I was a child. And I was a Devil; I wouldn't have cared."

In the silence that followed, Luke looked at Sally. "He's your friend."

"Yes," she said, "and I can vouch for his character. He's not evil, Cormick. If anything his origin gives him cause to carefully monitor and consider the morality of his actions."

"You're the head of the Fox Pass council," Orson said. "Cormick, you are the one who decides if he can stay or not."

Cormick sighed. "He can stay, of course. We are none of us culpable for the actions of our parents, only for what we choose upon maturity. He's clearly been making good choices or he wouldn't have won Sally's good opinion. And I already told Sally her friend could be here under her protection."

"You didn't ask what he was?" August snapped.

"Of course I did. Sally vouched for him then and said it was his secret to tell. Coming from a thunderbird who kept her own counsel on the truth of her nature for so long, I felt it appropriate. And I still feel it appropriate," he said over the protests that began. "Hush. The boy is welcome."

"I'm hardly a boy," Charlie said.

August snorted. "Yeah. You're twenty-four, right? This is your first life? You're a boy. No one else in this car is less than three hundred."

Charlie eyed August. "A headless horseman? You're one to talk, Irving's story was nineteenth century."

"And the headless wild huntsman of European folklore is much older." He leaned over the back of the seat a bit, menacingly. "And much more dangerous than a colonial folktale."

"Guys, chill," Sally said. "Can we just agree that you all have scary big cocks and get on with solving the mystery of the chupacabra-summoning bridge trolls?"

Allison laughed out loud and didn't seem to care that no one else in the car was laughing.

Chapter Thirty-Four

Luke's brow furrowed as Cormick turned onto the highway that would lead to Sally's house—or rather, Sally's parents' house. "We going to your place?" he asked her.

"Yeah," Sally said, "it's kinda become our base of operations."

"Since when?" Luke felt like he'd missed something important, some little detail that would pop the whole scene into focus. "How long was I gone? Felt like a few hours to me."

The car was silent for a moment, as if the others were all catching on at once. Sally filled in the void. "Ten days."

"Ten days?" Luke screeched. He felt Charlie draw away from him, and Orson dropped his eyes. "Ten? Son of a bitch, oh God.... Oh God, I'm so fired."

"Maybe not," Sally said, putting a hand on his leg.

"Yeah? And what am I supposed to tell my boss about where I been for a week and a half? Something besides 'in fairyland, looking for weapons to use against bridge trolls.'" After a few moments of silence, he let his head fall forward and rest with a thud on the back of the seat in front of him. "So. Fired."

"We'll deal with it in the morning," Orson said. "In the meantime, you should know what's been going on. Sally's folks got wind that something was up with our community—to which we ask no questions, so Sally will tell us no lies—and they took their RV on walkabout in New Mexico so we could use their place. We got all kinds of wards up, so it's as secure as we can make it without seriously changing the landscape."

"Jesus, where'd you get a warder?" Luke said.

August raised his hand.

"Well shit, that might have come in handy earlier. Nice of you to speak up."

August curled his lip. "I owe you nothing, including justification."

"Fine. The trolls been at you guys, then?"

"Yes," Cormick said. "Five more myth-folk have gone missing, this time folk from the city council itself. So the whole town is on lockdown. We'll bed down for the night and regroup in the morning."

Luke was still reeling from the implications of losing his job when they arrived at Sally's parents' house. The Palm Harbor double-wide was usually bright and cheerful, but after the vivid unreality of the worlds beyond the portal, it looked startlingly shabby and dim to Luke's eyes. He imagined his own home, by comparison, would look like a hovel. He hoped the sensation of everything being gray and sad and still would fade with time, like an ecstatic hangover.

He took a silent smoke break with Orson on the front steps while the others filed inside. He heard Sally readying the coffeepot for the morning, Cormick saying he was going to take a shower, Allison raiding the fridge. August came out a few minutes later with the keys to Sally's car. He left without a word, but Luke could guess where he was going—to look for the horse that had so curiously run from him. Orson didn't say anything to Luke about his newly unemployed status or his lost lives. When he was done with his cigarette, he clapped Luke's shoulder before leaving him to his thoughts. And that, Luke thought, was the difference between men and women. A woman would've wanted to talk about it all, which was the last thing Luke wanted to do.

Cormick took the master bedroom, and Allison and Orson folded out the sleeper couch in the living room. Charlie curled up in the recliner under a crocheted afghan. Sally took Luke's hand and led him back to her bedroom.

Sally's room had not endured much in the way of redecorating since she had been a child. It was a small room, with pink rosebuds dotting both the curtains and the wallpaper. Her narrow bed was white and matched the small chest of drawers and nightstand. The heavy bookshelf was the major addition in her maturity, crammed into the wall space between the bed and the window. It was laden with paperbacks two deep, tracing the trail of her favorites throughout her life. Horse stories by Marguerite Henry and dog stories by Jack London gave way to high school serials and romance novels, and a smattering of classics left from English Lit. The top shelf held a few textbooks, computer books, home repair how-to guides, cookbooks, and mystery novels. Luke noted, with interest, a wedding-planning book.

He couldn't let her off too easily, though. He made a show of looking around the room and said, "No boy band posters?"

She smacked his arm. "Shut up, you know my folks left this room as some kind of surreal shrine to me when I left home. I haven't had the heart to change it up much, since I'll be leaving soon enough anyway."

"Oh yeah? Where you going? Somewhere nice?"

She smirked, leaning against the chest of drawers. "Well, I was thinking about Austin, but lately I been hoping I might have a roommate. To share the rent and all. And since my job is portable, it kinda depends on where he goes."

"Oh yeah?" Luke said, sliding his arms around her waist. "This roommate... is he a sexy roommate?"

"He ain't bad." She grinned. "He's gotta find himself a job first, of course. But stuff's gotta get built everywhere, so looks like we can go anywhere we want."

The reminder of his new status as unemployed wilted Luke's mood a little. "True, I suppose we are free to go wherever, now.... But I have my land."

"Sell it."

"I can't sell it! I've sunk magic into that land, it's linked to me now."

"So sell it to Orson! For whatever he can pay for it."

"Can't lose that kind of money."

"Luke," Sally said, her brow furrowing, "it's money. It's possessions. It don't mean squat. Let it go, like a kite over the sea. Then we can get out of here, we can start somewhere new, somewhere there's opportunity and growth and excitement and energy! There's nothing for us here but a big gate." She hooked her fingers into his belt loops. "Besides. I have money."

His eyebrow rose. "Do you really."

"I do. I been doing a lot of freelance work, web graphics and stuff. Charlie taught me the software. It's really not hard, not like most computer stuff, it's just another art tool. I've got a few thousand dollars tucked away now, not a big pile, but it's sure enough to get us started."

Luke was quiet for a moment. He wavered between excitement at the idea of running off with Sally and a pang of hurt pride that it would have to be her who got them off right. Predictably, he went with the latter. "I oughta be the one providing," he said, lowering his eyes. "I'm crap with finances."

"Well turns out I'm really good at them. I been doing Daddy's books for years. Matter of fact, I been doing *your* daddy's books for years."

Luke gawked. "You're doing the books for Dad's bar?"

She grinned. "Li'l girl came back from college with a minor in accounting. Ta-da! Besides, you can make it up to me; I start us off, and you can take care of me and all our babies for the rest of our lives. Sound like a fair deal?"

Luke's eyebrows shot up. "Babies?"

Chapter Thirty-Five

For a moment, Sally looked alarmed. "Do you... ah... want kids?" she asked Luke.

Luke looked down at Sally's stomach. A series of images flashed though his mind in quick succession, like a film montage—Sally holding a baby, following an exploring toddler at the park, sitting with a young child doing homework, reading a dark-haired little girl to sleep. He tried to imagine Sally pregnant. Pregnant with his baby, her tummy round and smooth. He brought his hands around to the front of her waist and ran his thumbs over her currently mostly flat stomach.

"Yeah," he said, "I do want kids. You and I, we'd make some pretty ones."

"Let's see.... Your mom's Greek, right?"

"Yup. And Dad's of vaguely Germanic descent. All-American mutt."

"So's my mom, though she calls herself Cherokee if pressed." Luke snorted. "So she's got black hair."

"I said if pressed! And Dad, of course, is Navajo and Italian."

Luke nodded. "Yeah, sounds like we have the makings of true Americans. But I like mutts." He froze in the middle of nuzzling her ear. "Did someone—"

"Yes, I took care of Sootie. She's sound asleep in Dad's office."

"OK, good, thank you." He moved against her, pressing his body along the length of hers. His cock stiffened, and from the way she tilted her hips and moved her knee to the outside of his, she was well aware of it. "The idea of you being pregnant from me.... It's a major turn-on. I hope it doesn't weird you out."

"Seems like the most natural turn-on in the world," she said, grinning.

"You know, we do have a bedroom all to ourselves...."

"Not exactly. The bed Cormick is in is right on the other side of this very thin wall. And Luke, look around—when I'm in this room, I feel like a little girl. I cannot fuck you good and proper in this room."

Luke glanced around and sighed. He could see her point. "Damn. It's just as well, I've been up over twenty-four hours, and I've been utterly drained and recharged in an incredibly short time, on top of finding out I lost my job and kissing some guy I've never met. I am positively loopy."

Sally giggled. "That was really hot, by the way."

"Excuse me if I feel odd about it."

"Don't feel odd. It's good for Charlie to get some attention. His last boyfriend was a bastard, and he thinks you're hot."

"You can fill me in on his history later."

"Or you can ask him about it."

Luke snorted. "We're guys. We don't typically give a lot of backstory."

"Fine," Sally said, rolling her eyes. "Later. Right now, though, given that I can't jump your bones, let's get some sleep."

She made him leave the room while she changed into a set of soft gray and pink pajamas. Luke stripped down to boxers and slipped into the bed beside her. It squeaked tremendously with every motion, settling any doubt in Luke's mind that they could possibly have sex without alerting everyone in the house. He wondered if her parents had left it that way on purpose.

Sally smelled good, like lavender and chamomile. Luke put his arm over her and slipped his hand under her shirt, feeling the soft skin of her belly. He imagined once more a baby growing in her, a new life moving under his hand, their child. He felt a great swell of emotion, remembering in a rush all the times in past lives he'd shared the creation of a child with a woman. Sometimes it was wrong, or a mistake, but most of the time, it had been on purpose. The best times were with his wives, when it was their second, or fifth, or ninth pregnancy. So many children created and lost. He wondered what their lives had been like after he'd died. He had looked some of them up, but not all of them, and of course most had no records to look for.

He'd been on the other side of it too, as a woman. He was grateful for the times it had been easy and tried to forget the times it had been hard. The best life he'd had as a mother, he decided, had been in Italy, when he'd had seven children, and every one had outlived him. He pressed his hand protectively over Sally's stomach. Prenatal care was good these days, he thought. Childbirth wasn't the great danger that it used to be, to mother or child. Sally would be OK. Their children would be OK. It would be a great life. The best ever.

Sally stirred slightly. "You thinkin' about babies?"

"Yeah."

"Me too."

Luke kissed the back of Sally's neck. "You gonna marry me, Sally?"

"Well yeah, if we're gonna have babies."

"Oh good."

Chapter Thirty-Six

Luke woke with the dawn, as he had for the past several hundred years. Sally lay beside him, significantly more rumpled than she had been the night before. She was, Luke had just discovered, an active sleeper.

She breathed deep, almost huffing, the lines of worry on her face slackened. Her dark hair lay in a careless tangle around her face; her spaghetti-strap pajamas were pulled askew by her midnight squirming. Luke bit his lip, looking her over, so touchable and pretty. He could see the outline of her breasts against the thin pajama fabric, and the cleft of her cleavage, the curve of her hip where her shirt had pulled up in the night. He ran a hand down her side; she muttered in her sleep, like a grumbling squirrel, and was still again.

She looked so peaceful and sweet while she was asleep, and Luke wanted to kiss her on her soft, plump cheek. As he leaned over her, she stirred, and smacked him in the nose as she threw her arm up. Wincing, he disentangled their limbs and went to the kitchen to make coffee. Kissing would have to wait until she was more engaged.

To his surprise, someone else was already up. There was hot coffee in the carafe and a hiss of steam rising from the percolator. Luke poured a cup and walked out onto the front porch, where Charlie sat hunched over his clutched mug.

"You're up early," Luke said by way of greeting.

"That recliner is not made for extended napping."

"Gotcha."

Charlie took a drink, slurping like a child. "August came back late last night. Or early this morning, however you want it. He didn't catch his horse."

"That's the weirdest freaking thing," Luke said. "I never seen anything like that. There ain't many myth-folk got a second half to them like that." The idea of having something run off with a bit of his soul was unsettling. He took out a crushed pack of Camels, fished out the least bent one, lit it, and drew in a lungful of smoke.

"I've seen it before," Charlie said. "I... well, I've studied, we'll leave it at that for now. I think the closest equivalent outside our own sphere of magic is the witch's familiar. It's like a separate entity, but neither can exist fully without the other. To have a schism like that must be distressing. Did anything happen to it while you were on the other side of the gate?"

Luke chewed over the question for a minute. The horse had been out of sight several times during their otherworldly trip, but nothing he knew of had distressed it. "Only thing I can think of is, his eyes changed color from red to green."

"Huh. They were red in our world before you went into the gate?"

"Yup."

"They were green when I saw it. I guess the significance of that depends on what made his eyes glow in the first place, which is a question I don't know that even August would know the answer to. My first guess would be some kind of ectoplasm, given what they are."

"The only other time I've heard that word," Luke said, "was in *Ghostbusters*."

Charlie waved his hand dismissively. "It's an otherworldly discharge, like the physical manifestation of psykinetic energy before it's dissipated."

"Now you're just trying to use big words. You got a thesaurus in your pocket, or are you just happy to see me?"

Charlie gracefully ignored Luke and continued his analysis. "If it changed color when it entered the portal... I wonder what changed. Does the portal act as a filter of any kind?"

Luke shrugged. "It's got to, I suppose. Otherwise any old thing could come waltzing in or out, ya know? Most times, if you're not a native to a world, you gotta be called to come through, or be a specialist in spirit walking. Which August and his horse, being ghosts, would be."

"So maybe instead of adding something in... the portal took something out."

Luke was silent, digesting this piece of information. He rolled the cigarette, mostly gone, between his thumb and fingers. "Huh. Like passing milk through a cheesecloth."

"I don't know why you would do such a thing, but I suspect you get the idea."

Luke patted Charlie's head. "You're young. Soon enough you'll be using phrases like ROTFL and young folk will look at you the way you're looking at me."

"Still doesn't seem real, the whole living forever thing."

"Well, it ain't really living forever, is it? You're not the same person every time. Really, you're not. And the memories aren't there all the time; you gotta go looking for them, or you might even forget they're there, like a box of pictures under the bed. Good thing, too, because we'd all go mad otherwise. Then one day you gotta go dragging them all out looking for something in particular, and come across stuff long forgotten that punches you in the gut or makes you laugh out loud." He sighed. "It's a wonderful, terrible burden and privilege."

"Better than the alternative." Charlie's face took on a thoughtful expression. It suited him, Luke thought. "Do you believe in heaven?"

Luke shrugged and put out his cigarette on the bottom of his boot. "Don't know. Ain't never been." He stuck the butt of the cigarette into the coffee can full of butts. There seemed to be one of those coffee cans, rusted and half full of butts and sand, on every front porch he'd ever known. He stood up. "C'mon. Let's go pester a ghost."

Chapter Thirty-Seven

"Hey. Hey August. August, wake up. What color are your horse's eyes normally?"

August growled low in his throat as he slowly opened menacing blue eyes. Luke decided he looked scarier when he was rudely awakened than he did throwing his flaming skull around. He was in Sally's parents' bed; beside him, Cormick was still mostly asleep. When August stirred, Cormick pulled the blankets up over his head.

"What the hell?" August snarled.

"Your horse's eyes changed color from red to green when I went through the gate. We were thinking it might be related to why he ran off."

The anger turned to confusion. "His eyes are usually green."

"No, they were red when you got here."

August pulled himself ever so slightly upright, letting the blanket fall down his chest. OK, Luke had to admit to himself, the ghost was nice looking mostly naked. Behind him, he felt Charlie's magic paying close attention. Focus, Luke thought, this was no time for lust magic. August muttered something, and Luke shook his head. "What was that?"

"I'm color-blind. I didn't know they were red. I've no idea why they would be."

Charlie pressed in between Luke and the side table. "We're thinking the portal may have acted as a filter and removed some magical element that was at work."

August nodded slowly, mulling this over. "I gotta get a cup of coffee," he said, "before I think this hard."

"That's fair," Luke said, taking a step back. August swung his legs over the side of the bed and got to his feet. He was wearing black pajama bottoms of a silky fabric that slid over his legs, and his feet were bare. Luke was in the midst of admiring this sight— strictly from an aesthetic point of view, he thought; he still considered August a jerk—when with shocking speed, August darted out his hand, grabbed Luke by one of his horns, and slammed Luke's head against the solid oak headboard.

Cormick and Charlie shrieked as lights danced in front of Luke's eyes; the pain was incredible, and he would have a headache for the rest of the day. But he did not, as August so clearly intended, crumple, incapacitated, to the ground. He kicked backward, blindly, and connected with soft tissue and bone. Luke spun like a reining horse and launched himself at the place he imagined August would be. He was only a little off. He grabbed, grappled, and took August enough off balance that they both fell to the floor.

Luke didn't have a chance against August in a fair fight, not here, away from his land. August was faster and stronger, at least thirty pounds heavier, and formally trained, and when pressed, he had a fiery skull weapon he would most assuredly use. So Luke didn't fight fair. He locked his legs around August and clung tightly to him; he swung his horns ferociously, clawed and bit. In short, he fought dirty, like the desperate backwoods scrap that he was. Suddenly a thick cloth was over his face. He let go of August, pawed frantically at the cloth—then it was off of him, and he scooted backward on his butt.

He figured out what had happened pretty quickly. Charlie had thrown the comforter from Sally's parents' bed over the fighting men, and now both Charlie and Orson were sitting on a comforter-wrapped August. Luke got to his feet, the adrenaline making his limbs tremble like aspen leaves.

"Fear not, you look good in floral," Charlie called to August over his enraged howls.

"What the hell?" Cormick cried.

"Pretty boy here had some bad juju worked on him," Luke said. He explained their theory to Cormick, who paled. Luke's head was beginning to throb painfully; he dropped his head into his hands and made a miserable noise of caprine unhappiness.

"What can we do about it?" Cormick asked.

"Well, we could throw him through the portal," Orson suggested.

"If you think we can handle fighting the trolls *and* August," Cormick said, his usual scowl returning.

"I could try something," Charlie suggested. All eyes turned to Charlie. He held up his hands. "I haven't tried this, exactly, but it might be our best option." Protesting noises came from beneath the blanket.

"Keep talking," Cormick said.

"This requires some explanation. When I was a young child, I was given the ability to consume the magic of other myth-folk. I haven't done it in twenty years, but... it's not exactly the kind of thing you forget. It's kind of like using a katana to go after a splinter, though."

There was a horrified silence. Luke expressed the group's collective thoughts: "Dude."

"Yeah, I know. There was a good reason at the time."

"You're going to have to explain that one further," Cormick said, "but I don't know that we have another option at this point. Myth-folk are disappearing fast, and August is a massive liability if he's on the other side. Let's do it."

August shrieked and resumed kicking and struggling. It took Cormick, Luke, and Orson to hold him down, and the noise woke the girls. Allison and Sally took up guard positions at the door and window once they had been filled in, Sally armed with her father's shotgun and Allison with a machete that had seen recent work as a weedwacker.

Charlie crouched on the floor in front of August, whose eyes now glowed red as his horse's had done. His black hair, normally slicked back or artfully tossed, now hung in tangled locks around his pale face. He snarled incoherently at his captors; he looked every bit his myth, the mindless ghost, possessed.

"This is going to be disconcerting," Charlie said. "I have to drop the façade of my human form to do it. It's not really like what you folk do; I am not two beings at once. I am really and truly one thing only, and it is the cloak of another person's magic that disguises what I am, that allows me to feel and think and act human. Magic is part of you in a way that it is not part of me. For me to take some of it from you... well, it goes against our very natures."

"In short," he said as he moved toward August, "this is going to hurt."

Chapter Thirty-Eight

August did not react well to being informed that metaphysically ripping out the corrupt influence on his magic would hurt. Orson whipped behind him and put him in an armlock, and Sally warned August from the door that the shotgun was, in fact, loaded and in capable hands. Luke, whose head was still spinning, could do little more than threaten loudly in colorful language. Cormick went for his cell phone in the kitchen, to call in what few reinforcements they had left.

Luke felt a pang of pity for August as Charlie stalked toward him. He looked more than afraid; his face was clouded with the rage and disbelief of betrayal.

"I'll get it over with as fast as I can," Charlie said. "Like a Band-Aid."

"Charlie," Sally said, not lowering her gun, "are you sure this is a good idea?"

"Hell no, I've never tried it like this. I don't know that anyone has ever tried this."

"No, I mean.... Dropping your magic entirely, letting yourself be nothing but your myth. You've worked so hard to be good, to come to grips with your duality." Her eyes filled with concern, though the effect was diminished since they were looking over the top of a shotgun. "I just don't want to see you get hurt, sweetie."

Charlie smiled at her, but it didn't reach his eyes. "Trust me," he said. He turned back to August and all but stepped out of his own skin.

The transformation was not at all like how it was with normal myth-folk, who flickered back and forth between their selves like a chameleon changing colors. No, this was like a skin-walker, Luke thought. The magic that made Charlie look human peeled away from him like the skin of a butchered animal. The beast within was terrible, his emaciated body as big as a man, with wings that made him seem much larger. He walked on all fours, using the claws on his wings like a bat as he moved across the thin beige carpet. His face and neck were long like a horse's, but with an enormous maw of jagged teeth. Nothing of the quiet young man Luke had kissed the night before seemed to remain.

August screamed as the creature rushed upon him. The devil roared and sank his teeth into August's chest, over his heart. Luke gave a shout and rushed forward but was knocked off his feet by one of the great leathery wings. Luke flicked his eyes to Orson, just visible above August and the devil. He was still holding August fast, looking grim but steady.

The devil was no longer biting but sucking, his throat working in steady gulps. August was still screaming, but something else, something far away and almost beyond the bounds of sound, screamed too. Orson fought to keep control of August, who struggled frantically now with the deep, racking sobs of one who felt death pressing in on him.

The devil let go of August and fell away, mouth dripping red. Then the creature was Charlie again, as if it had slipped back into Charlie's skin, and it was Charlie who was wiping blood from his mouth and drawing deep, ragged breaths. His knees buckled, and he fell backward onto the bed, leaving a bright red slash of a stain on the floral comforter. August hung limp and silent in Orson's grip.

Sally was the first to speak. "Charlie? You OK?"

Charlie shook his head. "Nope."

"Going to be OK?"

"Eventually."

"August?" Luke pressed.

August picked up his head and slowly swung round to look at Luke. "When I get out of here," he said, "I'm going to kill you all."

"Gonna have to clear that with the council, lawman," Orson said, and dropped him onto the floor.

"The council," August breathed as he sat up, arms shaking with the effort. "I... don't remember...."

"You have amnesia?" Sally said, incredulous.

"No, God no, I almost wish I did. I... I just don't remember the meeting with the council that sent me down here. It's like it's been erased."

"Or a false memory that's been corrected," Luke said.

To his surprise, August said softly, "Could be." He accepted a hand towel from Cormick, who had rejoined the party, and pressed it to his bleeding chest. "God," he said, wincing, "that was horrible. Just about torturous—" He stopped, and a strange, faraway look came over him. His eyes flew wide, and he struggled to stand, pressing against Sally's parents' antique wardrobe. "Cormick. I think I may know where the missing myth-folk are. Come with me."

"Ohhhh no," Orson said, laying a heavy hand on August's shoulder, "you're not going anywhere with anyone alone for a while."

"Fine," he said, sounding suddenly in a great hurry, "then you and some other of my assaulters come with me. I have to see if this blurry memory that's surfacing is real."

"You get a phone call," Orson said, and handed him a cell phone.

"My stars and garters, does no one have any respect? He's injured!" Allison said. "I'm going to get the first aid kit."

Sally was sitting by Charlie, an arm over his shoulders, talking low and nodding. Luke approached them carefully and sat down on the bed as well.

"That was some trick," he said.

"Don't expect to ever see it again," Charlie said.

"Hope not to. I can see why you have a hard time playing well with others. That is about the most violent act of magical surgery I ever seen, and I'm older than Christianity."

"Psh," Sally said, "I'm prehistoric."

"It's not a contest," Luke said, smirking over Charlie's head.

"Says the loser. Charlie, baby, you sure you're gonna be all right?"

"Yeah," Charlie said, straightening. His features suddenly hardened. "Excuse me," he muttered. He hurried to the master bathroom, almost running into Allison, who emerged with the first aid kit. A second later Luke heard retching.

"OK, thanks," August was saying. He closed Orson's phone, handed it back to him, and breathed out a long, low sigh. "I owe you all an apology, and a thank you. It seems the council never sent me down here... and I do know where the missing myth-folk are. It could have gone tremendously worse if you all hadn't recognized what was going on, for me as well as you." He shifted the bloody towel on his chest. "Though your methods leave something to be desired."

Sally's bright smile was full of a terrifying malice. Over the sound of her friend being sick in the bathroom she said, "You can thank Charlie when he's done throwing up your evil."

Chapter Thirty-Nine

August was still talking about rushing out to find the missing myth-folk when the adrenaline wore off and he seemed to begin to feel the deep gashes in his chest. In only a few minutes time, he gave up the idea and sank to the carpet, light-headed.

"We should take him to a hospital," Charlie said. He was out of the bathroom and now lay curled up on the bed with his head in Sally's lap.

"With wounds that look like a giant lamprey took a bite out of him?" Cormick jerked his head at Allison. "Patch him up, I'm going to make some calls. Orson, can you take the perimeter? If whatever magicked August felt the magic go, they might come looking for him."

"Sounds likely." Orson took the shotgun from Sally and went on patrol, while Cormick went phone-treeing in the kitchen at great volume and velocity.

"OK, the biggest egos in the room are out of the way," Allison said, kneeling in front of August. "Lemme take a look, phantom boy." She peeled the wet cotton towel away from his chest and winced for him. "We'd better take this outside, where I can see better. Luke, give me a hand? Sally—"

"I'm staying in here with Charlie," she said. Luke could tell by her tone that this was not up for debate.

"Fair enough. C'mon, guys. Luke, maybe you can ground him out—this is not going to be fun."

"This morning is full of things that aren't fun," August said, a boyish whine in his voice that was very unlike him.

"We'll see if we can't make it at least tolerable," Luke said, helping August stand. He pulled August's arm over his shoulders and let the larger man rest his weight on him. Slight concussion or no, he was currently in better shape than August. It seemed like a long walk down the hallway, past the gallery of photos of smiling people and a timeline of Sally pictures.

They got out the front door and across the lawn to a large bois d'arc tree. There was a chill in the air that Luke hadn't felt when he first went out that morning; a cold front was blowing in from the northwest, a biting wind tinged with sand. Luke sat against the tree, and August sat against Luke. Allison sat beside them, arranging her supplies. She pulled the towel, now heavily soaked with blood, away from August's chest and hissed.

"The bleeding has pretty much stopped. The cuts aren't long, but they're deep," she said. "I'm going to have to stitch them. Don't worry, I'm up to it. But, well, it hurts. Luke?"

"I'm on it," Luke said. He looped his arms around August and leaned forward to nuzzle his neck, reaching out with his magic, like the butterflies in his stomach flying out. "August, relax. I'm all about earth magic, remember? Part of earth magic is grounding. I can ground out pain the same way you can ground out electricity. But you do have to let me in."

August, who had gone stiff at Luke's initial touch, loosed his shoulders and settled against Luke's chest. Luke repressed a flutter of arousal; August had a wonderful back, smooth pale skin with rippling cords of muscle, broad shoulders, and a slender waist. Just aesthetics, Luke reminded himself. He didn't have to like the guy to appreciate beauty.

"Any port in a storm," August said.

"You're welcome. Picture the pain going out of you, through me, into the earth. Being against a tree ought to help."

"Okay," August said, but he didn't sound reassured.

After getting a gallon of water from the house, Allison put on a pair of plastic gloves and cleaned the wounds, pouring water slowly across August's chest. After that, she cleaned the wounds with hydrogen peroxide. Luke focused on the ground beneath him, the tree behind him, on the roots running thick and wide and shallow, the grass sending little tendrils through the topsoil, and his own magic tunneling down deep, deep through the red clay to the bedrock far below. His headache was little better, but it seemed far away and unimportant. He felt the beginning rumblings of August's pain, a burn in his own chest, and pushed it down, down, into the earth, out through the roots.

Allison was done cleaning. She dried the wounds thoroughly and daubed an antibiotic ointment on them. She threaded a needle, dipped it in hydrogen peroxide, and began to sew shut the gashes that Charlie's teeth had left in August's chest. August didn't cry out, but he breathed fast and shallow, his back muscles tightening.

"Don't hyperventilate," Luke said. "Breath in deep and let it out in little puffs. Like a woman in labor. And concentrate on giving the pain to me, sending it away."

August nodded almost imperceptibly. Luke closed his eyes as a wave of pain came through to him, hot and fierce as only a deep injury can be. He sent it down and away, down and away, pushing it down into the cool dirt. August pressed against him, leaned his head back on Luke's shoulder. Luke tightened his grip, gratified by the show of faith. August's neck was exposed, the clean line of his throat. Luke had the impulse to bite him, suck his neck, lick his ear—

He came back to himself in a rush and centered himself on his task. He *didn't like* August. He was determined not to like him, not one little bit, and he would not indulge his satyr appetites with someone he didn't personally care for. It didn't matter that August's hair was cool and silky on his neck, or that he smelled good, or that the faint, almost inaudible whimpers of pain from August's throat sounded very much like the noises the man might make in bed, in the midst of pleasure. The two were so close.

"Done," Allison said. She smeared a little more ointment over the top of the sutures, to keep them from catching, and put a square of gauze over the whole thing. "Hold that there, I'll tape it down."

Luke was glad for the interruption to his thoughts, even though it brought his headache back into focus and made him lose the grounding connection that had let him wick away most of August's pain. He was entirely too close to enjoying himself. August looked back over his shoulder at Luke with something like new appreciation in his eyes.

"I feel so lucky, Luke," Allison said. "This is twice in one twenty-four-hour period I've watched you work your magic with another hot guy." She winked at him; she knew how uncomfortable he was and enjoyed pushing his buttons.

"Oh go to hell," he said, smirking.

"Happily, I'll never have to! Hahaha, I'm immortal!" she singsonged, and snipped the last piece of tape.

"Were you a nurse in a past life or something?" August asked.

"Nope. Shepherdess. You gotta know these things with livestock." She applied the tape and motioned to his chest. "You, uh, might want to have that looked at by a real doctor sometime soon. Unless you're a fan of the 'chicks dig scars' mentality."

"You're awfully chipper for a girl who just sewed up a guy's chest," August said.

"Humor: it's the greatest defense mechanism ever. Besides. It was a nice chest." She clapped August appreciatively on the shoulder. "Now go get some clothes on before we all start thinking too hard about you and Cormick sharing a bed in a state of partial undress."

"It wasn't like that," August protested, but he allowed himself to be pulled to his feet and helped back inside.

As August dressed in the bathroom, Luke pouted at Allison. "He's hot? Nice chest? C'mon, girl! Where's the love?"

Allison took hold of Luke's horn and shook it. "You have a thunderbird now," she said. "I have needs; I won't have you anymore to take care of business! So you can't go getting jealous on me." She tilted her head, studying Luke intently with renewed interest. "What gives on that? You never been jealous before." She narrowed her eyes at him. "There is an element here I am missing. I can smell it. But you lot go on and keep your secrets," she said with a wave of her hand. "I'm gonna go see if Cormick is done being dramatic at the world so we can go."

Chapter Forty

Luke, August, and Orson stared out the car windows at the self-storage facility just outside the two-block strip that claimed to be downtown Fox Pass. A quarter mile away, people went about their business at the post office, the courthouse, the pharmacy, and the library. In the back seat, Luke lit a cigarette, gave it to Orson wordlessly out of long-formed habit, and lit another for himself. August rolled down the window on the passenger side.

There was one way in or out of the facility, a gate in the seven-foot iron fence surrounding the two rows of storage units. An office in a portable building squatted up front, and there was a keypad with an entry code by the gate.

"We take the car in," Luke said. "Don't get too far from it."

"It won't bust through that fence," August said.

"But it'll bust through a troll," Orson said, "and at least slow down bullets. You guys feeling all right?"

"Between Luke's grounding and the pain meds Sally found for me, I'm functional," August said. "I actually feel pretty damn good, now that I've got that poison out of me."

"She gave me half a pill," Luke said. "My head's all right, and I feel clear. Grounding will do that for a guy. Gotta love earth magic."

"Then we're going in."

Orson drove up to the gate, and August told him the code to enter. The gate gave a great screech as its unoiled gears grated, but it swung away, and they drove through.

"We need to clear the office first," August said.

They parked in front of the office, knowing that anyone inside would have been alerted to their presence already. No measure of surprise was left to them. August went first, holding a sleek Glock like he'd used it before. He swung open the door and stood aside, and when no attack came, he slid in and cleared the corners before motioning for the others. Orson stayed near the front with the shotgun, watching their back, while August and Luke, who had Sally's father's hunting rifle, cleared the rest of the building silently. When they were assured no one was present, they met Orson back at the front.

"Nice to be working with a pair of professionals," August said to them.

"Most good ol' boys around here would pass for professional," Luke said, "but thanks. It helps to have been in combat so many lives before."

"Just glad we got the girls to stay home," Orson grumbled.

"You shouldn't give them such a hard time," Luke said. "They'd hold their own."

"Yeah," Orson said, "but we'd be looking out for them, and that might be the fatal flaw in a combat situation. Ain't a matter of their competence, it's just the way men and women work. The men are always going to want to keep the women alive. Especially those two, with you involved."

Luke nodded. "OK, I see your point. August, where do we go from here?"

They got back in the car and circled the lot, checking for security officers or guards; they found none. Satisfied that they were not going to be taken unaware, August led them to unit 43. He took a pair of heavy-duty bolt cutters from the car, cut the lock, and slid the door up and open.

A gorgon lay on the concrete floor. She raised her head and hissed when she saw August, but her demonic face twisted in confusion upon spying the other two. The room smelled of ammonia and filth; a bucket with a dirty towel draped over it stood in one corner, and two empty water bottles littered the floor. Her hands were bound, and her feet were shackled to the concrete.

"Meredith," Luke breathed, going down on his knees beside her. He pulled out his pocketknife and slit through the ropes on her wrists. August handed the bolt cutters to Orson, who went to work on the shackles.

In her human form, Meredith was in her fifties, all bone and paper-thin skin stretched over sharp angles. Only her hair, thick black curls now even more striking with shocks of gray throughout, could be called beautiful. In her myth form, she was a powerful member of the council, ancient and vicious. In her human life, she ran the cosmetics department of the pharmacy and organized fund-raising for the pitifully small high school marching band, which only recently could boast that all the usual instruments were represented.

She didn't speak, but she pulled herself into Luke's arms, her shoulders quaking with silent sobs. Luke held her a moment, stroking her hair, murmuring reassurance. It didn't matter what he said; his voice was what mattered, an ally come to take her away from the darkness and rot. He walked her to the car, and she collapsed in the backseat and did not move.

Luke met August's eyes as he shut the door and stood. "Did you collect her?" he asked. His voice was cool, even, but there was a promise of rage.

August shook his head. "Not her. But there were others I did. Luke, I didn't even know it had happened until that... possession was sucked out of me. Even now, it's like watching a movie of someone else's life, remembering what happened." His brow knit. "You can't possibly hold me responsible for what I did while possessed."

"Never known trolls to possess anyone."

"I've never known trolls to kidnap and torture multiple myth-folk in an effort to take possession of a portal, either. I'd say this is a truly unique situation."

"Fair enough," Luke said. "Next unit."

They collected Carl Mendez, a high school chemistry teacher who was also a Mexican demon myth (his students would not be surprised), and Fern Yates, who worked at the Motel 6 and sat on the council as an embodiment of the Wolf, enormous and bloody in her myth-folk form but much reduced in her current state. They went into the car with Meredith.

Luke's breath caught as August raised the next door. "Brent!" he cried, and rushed in. His friend and coworker skittered into the corner, his nerves as shot as his eyes. He waved his hands frantically, as if trying desperately to ward off anyone coming close to him.

"Not him! Not him!" Brent yelped.

"Him?" Luke looked over his shoulder at August. "Ah. Brent, he switched sides. He's a good guy now."

"Good guy? Good guys don't—don't bust into your house while you're fixing your motherfucking breakfast and slam your hand down on the stove element before saying a goddamn word!" He said this all in one slurred breath.

Luke focused on Brent's hands. One of them bore a nasty wound, clearly infected despite sloppy bandaging. There were circular red marks on his skin, filling with pus in spots. Luke wished they weren't on concrete, wished he could ground himself, reach out with his magic for something stabilizing. He cursed modern civilization for the umpteenth time.

"We're leaving," Luke said. "C'mon, get in the car. It's gonna be tight."

"Thank you," Brent said as Luke and Orson started working on his bonds. "I'm so sorry. God, I was so scared that you'd never find me, that you'd leave me here, after that happened—"

"Don't be absurd," Luke said. "You getting left behind—it'd never happen."

"You're a better man than I am, Luke. I'm so sorry."

"You keep saying that." The bonds came loose, and Orson cracked through the first shackle.

"Well I am. I had no idea how far they were going to go with the chupacabras. It doesn't make any sense, them wanting to kill you. Hurt you, yeah, or frighten, but killing and kidnapping and possessing? I had no idea."

Luke leveled his gaze at Brent, a man he'd known all his life, and a shadow of doubt crept into his heart. If he confessed he didn't know what Brent was babbling about, Brent might explain...

or if he'd done wrong, he might clam up, and they might never know the truth. The question was whether he believed Brent, who had worked at his side for the past several years, was capable of doing him harm. How much did he trust the tinker fae?

Not enough, he decided. He stood up, pulling Brent with him. "We'll discuss it later, man. Don't waste your strength."

"I could say the same thing to you."

A hundred feet away, a man stepped out of the shadows and leveled a gun at the four of them. Alan wore his police officer's uniform, and his troll magic made him appear bigger than he was. Luke was helpless; his rifle was in the trunk of the car, and Orson's shotgun lay several feet away in the shadows. August alone returned the gesture with his Glock.

Alan's trollish face curled into a snarl. "It's time for your part in this to end."

Chapter Forty-One

Across the aisle of the storage facility, Alan cocked his handgun. It was police issue, and Alan made no secret of his marksmanship with it, but it was the monstrous, hungry eyes narrowed at him over the barrel that really made Luke fearful. Alan would not hesitate to shoot him, and Luke knew what it was to be shot.

Perhaps if he hadn't so recently gone looking through his past lives, he would not have been so affected, but then, violence leaves its mark, no matter how far removed. Memories, terrible memories from almost seventy years ago, came back to him in a rush. The scalding force of the bullets, flying back to land on his face in mud that was wet not from rain but from blood. He screamed for help, for his long-absent family while his fellow soldiers stepped over him to take his post before he was even really dead. The smell—he would never truly be free of that smell, of blood and rot and filth, all mixed into the great whirlpool that sucked him down into oblivion. His legs gave way beneath Brent's weight, and he landed on his knees on the concrete. He hardly felt it. He thought of Sally.

"We were so close this time," he tried to say, but his throat closed up and speech threatened to choke him like a noose.

"You better put down that gun, boy," Orson said.

All eyes moved to Orson. He stood, casting aside the bolt cutters. He was a tall man, but he stooped, and slumped, and rarely spoke in mixed company. Luke forgot sometimes just how big Orson was. His face reddened, splotchy with anger, his fists clenched and unclenched, but his blue eyes were steady and fierce behind his round wire glasses. He took a few steps toward Alan, giving up any hope of cover from the storage unit. Luke wanted to scream at him to run, to get down, to fear death, but then, death didn't seem to be a concern for this bull of a man.

"You must know there's no scenario where you come out on top after this. You and your family have left evidence all over this place; you fire that gun, your cop buddies will be here in minutes. You don't fire, I kill you." He held out his hand, his casual demeanor putting Luke in mind of a father telling a small child to surrender a forbidden treasure. "There's only one move left to you."

"Keep coming," Alan said, taking a step back. "You'll die first."

"Nope. Kill Brent. Kill Luke. Kill August. But you won't be killing me, not with that. Ask yourself why I'm not carrying a gun. My shotgun was right over there, and I didn't go for it. Then consider... just what was it Luke went to Tír na nÓg to get?"

Alan's eyes went wide and blank. His thoughts were written all over his face; he didn't know what he was up against anymore. Whether he knew anything about the fae world of Tír na nÓg or not, his imagination could fill in the gaps. What was unknown was always more frightening than what was known. He took a few more steps back and lowered the gun. Luke's chest unclenched; he could breathe again. He realized he'd broken out in a cold sweat as it trickled down his temples and wet the T-shirt down his spine.

Alan continued backing away, toward the gate. "No police," he said through a mouthful of bared troll teeth. "We're myth-folk; we handle our own."

"No police," Orson said. "Not yet, anyway. Though the situation smacks of irony. Hey Alan."

Alan had been about to turn the corner, presumably to get to his car and make his escape. He tilted his head, indicating he was listening.

Orson smiled, full of promise. "I'm coming for you. You and all your family."

"We'll be ready for you."

"No," Orson said. "You won't be."

Alan was gone. Luke shifted Brent's weight. "C'mon, tinker fae," he said, "we have an extra life, as it turns out."

"Motherfucker!" Brent said, his voice high and tight.

"Indeed. Get in the car; let's scram."

"Hold on," August said, lowering his gun but not holstering it. "There's one more."

Luke lowered Brent into the passenger seat with a groan. "Crap. We're already going to be overloaded here."

August retrieved the bolt cutters and headed down the lane. "We won't need a seat. The trunk will do." He looked over his shoulder, a grieving pain on his face. "I'm sorry. I didn't know what was happening until it was too late."

August cut the lock and raised the door. Glen lay on the floor, recently dead. Luke knelt by his small, knobbly-kneed friend and touched his ginger hair. Glen's goblin-self was not evident at all; his soul was gone. A deep ache opened up in Luke's heart.

"Oh Glen," he said, "I'm so sorry. I didn't know. That seems to be the defense of the day, but really, I didn't know. You hid it real well." He rocked back, holding his knees. "Dammit, I'm fixing to cry. I was such a dumbass, never paying him no mind. So he was kind of dim. So what? He was good, and loyal, and a scrapper, and he worked hard. I didn't give him the credit he deserved." Luke's chin threatened to crumple, and he held his breath, trusting to stillness to keep him from breaking over into tears. When it was safe to breathe, he rubbed his face and stood.

Orson clapped him on the shoulder. "It wasn't just you that dismissed Glen. He was always at the bottom of the pack."

"Yeah, but he didn't love you. That fae bitch said he did. As soon as she said it, I knew it was true. Funny how some lightbulb moments are like that. I'd never have known otherwise."

Orson let his hand fall. "Get in the car. August and I will handle this."

Luke shook his head. "No, he was my friend, I'll—"

"This ain't an Ol' Yeller moment. You don't have to prove your manliness or your strength or your devotion by handling a dead body. He doesn't know any difference now. So let us do this for you, and let's get back to the house. There will be plenty of time for manual labor later."

Luke gave in and got into the car, sitting in the middle of the front seat beside Brent. It was only the old sedans that could handle so many passengers. He stared out the front window, thinking about Sally and everyone back at Sally's parents' house. As Orson got into the driver's seat and August squeezed into the back seat with three other people, Luke's brow knit, a horrible thought occurring to him.

"Hey August? You did the warding at Sally's, right?"

"Yes I did."

"Are you sure you didn't leave loopholes for the trolls, seeing as how you were under their influence?"

August clearly hadn't thought of that. "I'm... I'm not sure. Warding magic is so very particular. I might have."

Orson and Luke exchanged a dark look. Orson started the car, and floored it.

Chapter Forty-Two

The drive to Sally's parents' home was tense and quiet. The released prisoners were dehydrated and weak, more fit for a hospital than a showdown with a group of deranged trolls. Brent suggested that a detour to the hospital might be the right course, but Luke pointed out that questions would inevitably rise about how they got in such a state, and when left unanswered, would certainly delay their return to Sally and company and might even result in a search of the car. Including the trunk, which contained a dead goblin in a cracked blue tarp. All discussion was tabled.

Orson slowed as he approached the yellow double-wide, painfully cheery in the clear fall light. "How do we tell if the wards are still up?" he asked August.

"They're up. But that doesn't tell us anything, since I was possessed when I was doing the magic. I might not have warded out the trolls at all. They certainly knew the magic broke, since Alan found us at the storage place. Strange that he was the only one."

"The rest might have come here. Though I don't see any unfamiliar cars," Luke said. "We could give it a wide berth and drive around back first. Pity there's no cover between the house and the barn."

The words were barely out of his mouth before the front door opened a crack and shotgun pellets peppered the side of the sedan. They were fortunate it was bird shot and not a heavier pellet. They were fortunate also that Sally's mother's sedan was a steel-bodied suburban tank from the eighties and not a modern fiberglass model. The windows shattered, and everyone but Orson dropped as low as they could. Orson floored the gas pedal and made for the barn. There was blood and glass all over them, and they were thrown about in their seats as the sedan thundered over rough-trod, rocky pasture. Orson hit the metal pole gate that closed off the barn at full speed and skidded to the other end of the barn, the gate clinging like a great, twisted hand to the front end of the sedan.

"Get out," Luke barked, kicking the council members nearest him. Their wounds from glass and bird shot could wait. "Get out, there's a storm shelter in the first stall. No, left! Other left!" He herded them to the storm shelter, jerked on it, and found it locked. His fist hammered the door. "Hey! It's Luke!"

Behind him, Orson and August took up positions on either side of the broad doorway, occasionally firing when they saw something to fire at. The door to the storm shelter opened, and Luke stared down at Cormick and Allison. "Where's Sally?" he said.

Cormick came up the stairs to allow the others to descend. "She and Charlie are still in the house. They took on the trolls at the front door; Allison and I went out the back. We've phoned for help, but I don't know when anyone will get here. We've only been down there a few minutes." He looked down at the people in the shelter. "I'll deal with being shocked and appalled at the condition of my fellow myth-folk, and relieved at their recovery, shortly. Glen? The other two who are missing?"

Luke shook his head. "Get in the shelter and stay there. The three of us will see if we can stall for time until reinforcements get here. Who'd you call?"

"Paul, Kristin, Jerri, and your mom."

"Boy, that will be fun to explain. OK, hole up now." He shut the door behind Cormick, wiped blood from his forehead, retrieved his rifle from the car, and joined Orson at the entrance to the barn. He arrived just in time to see Sally and Charlie emerge from the house, bound at the wrists, with two figures behind them, herding them at gunpoint.

"We want the satyr," one of them called.

"It's nice to want things. I want your head on a pike," Orson replied.

"Here's how it's going to play out. You put down your weapons and surrender. We take the satyr, everyone else lives. Or, we kill the man. You get another chance to surrender. Then we kill the woman.

You get another chance. Then we set fire to the barn and you can all burn alive while we shoot whoever runs out."

Luke looked pleadingly at Orson. "No," Orson said. "We can't trust anything they say."

"We can trust that they'll kill us."

"They don't know you have a weapon. You'd put it away before Alan found us. Give it to Cormick."

Luke passed the rifle down into the storm shelter, shut the door in Cormick's face as he started to argue, and walked out into the broad aisle of the barn with his hands up. Orson and August walked into the open too, looking disgusted about slowly, deliberately laying their guns on the ground. Sally gave a cry of alarm, which surely would have turned into angry yelling if she had not been so frightened.

Mae walked out from behind Sally and Charlie. She was wearing a black silk robe far too short and conscious of its appeal to belong to anyone but her. She was barefoot, and her black curls flew around her face in wild locks, far from her usual coiffed mane. She wore no makeup; dark circles ringed her eyes, and her lips were as pale as her drawn cheeks. She looked, Luke thought, like a woman possessed.

As she entered the barn, she pulled on the robe's belt, and it slid open. She was naked beneath it, and she drew the sides open to show her breasts. There was no pretense, no opening gambit this time. She raised her arms, and the lust-magic of the nymph hit Luke like a physical blow, breaking upon him and knocking him off his feet. His body writhed on the red dirt floor, completely out of his control, suddenly mad with want. Blood rushed through him as his heart pounded a frenzied rhythm; he choked, couldn't speak or breathe, couldn't even focus his eyes. Bodily pleasure wrenched him backward, making him arch his back and cry out, incoherent and babbling.

Mae stood over him. She took his hand and drew it between her legs. He entered her with his fingers, found her clit with his thumb, and she tossed back her head with gasping delight as he rubbed and worked her. Somewhere in the distance, Sally screamed. He barely registered it. He fumbled with the button on his jeans; he freed his cock, stiff and aching with want, and began to stroke himself. There was not room in his mind for who was around him, or whether he wanted what was happening. She poured her magic into him and consumed his will.

And that of his companions. Orson appeared at his side and took her in his arms, biting her neck and grasping her breasts roughly. He fell to his knees and took one, then the other nipple in his mouth, sucking and moaning. August was behind her, his pants open, rocking his hips as he rubbed against her bottom through the fabric of the robe. He murmured in her ear, nipping and licking, and pulled the robe off of her entirely. Her eyes rolled back in her head; she was entirely lost. They all were.

Chapter Forty-Three

Somewhere beyond the nymph-induced bliss that rode roughshod over Luke's mind, there was a tiny, screaming remnant of his psyche that understood what was happening. That distant bit of consciousness looked out of his eyes but could not speak, or move, or stop. The rest of him, like August and Orson, was wholly engulfed by Mae's magic. He had never seen her cut loose to this extent; on an intellectual level it was an impressive show of power, but one he wouldn't appreciate until later.

He heard the scuff of boots behind him, and a rough hand grabbed one of his horns. The troll jerked Luke's head back, exposing his throat, and Luke could do nothing but stare up at the snarling, stonelike face. It was granite gray with blue and white lines of marbling and the pockmarked texture of old tombstones. The troll held a knife—one of Sally's mother's good kitchen knives, a thin, sharp blade for fileting fish. He lowered it to Luke's throat.

"You damned satyr," the troll snarled, his tongue thick in his mouth. "It was never supposed to be like this. We just wanted our toll—at this portal and all the others. It's our right once more to claim the bridges as we choose—not that the rest of the myth-folk understand that."

Luke's body moved on its own; he rubbed against the troll's legs, his skin aching for any contact. Inside he wanted to scream, enraged and horrified at how Mae's magic—which he had seen used in beautiful and wondrous ways in the past—twisted him, and Orson, and August, and most likely Mae herself. Even with a knife at his throat, he could not stop stroking his cock. It wasn't enough; he wanted to fuck, and be fucked, repeatedly, roughly, it didn't matter who, or how. Mae was drinking in his sexual energy, siphoning him. If it went on, there was no telling what he might do, and she would drink him dry.

She'd done it before.

Not that he had to worry about that, not with a sliced throat in his near future. What little was left of Luke's mind howled, fought frantically for any scrap of control, but there was none to be had. Dying was not the worst part. There would be another life for him, as there always had been, and this one would be just another memory to sift through, a life to hang up and strip for parts. It wasn't even the painfully close miss with Sally. No, the worst part was the helplessness, watching it come with no way to stop it and knowing that Sally was watching. She was going to watch him and their friends die while he pleasured himself in thrall to a nymph, before she was killed herself. That moment would be a thorn in his immortal side long after his body's bones turned to dust, and he did not want to live with it forever after.

The troll went to cut him once, twice, and stopped. He shifted his grip and spoke again, as if using his opportunity for monologue to delay the act of violence. "It was supposed to be just you! But now—now everyone here has to die, and the others who found out, and anyone else who looks into it. All because you, this one old goat, wouldn't fucking die!"

The troll moved once more as if to slice Luke's throat, and stopped. Luke watched a war wage in the troll's eyes and understood in a startling moment of clarity—he had been trying not to kill anyone, and now that he perceived he had no choice, he wasn't able to make himself do it. He raised the knife high, his eyes locked with Luke's. Luke wondered, as seconds stretched on with the knife poised in the air, teetering as if on a thin edge, if a reluctant murderer was really any better than an enthusiastic one; the troll's guilt would not make any difference to his victims.

Everyone spooked as a gunshot fired at close range—then another, and another. Luke and the troll looked up past Mae, August, and Orson to where the other troll had a gun on Sally and Charlie. That troll was now on the ground writhing in pain, and

Charlie wrestled him for his gun. Now that the threat was removed from her friend, Sally raised her bound wrists, fingers held as wide as she could. A net of electricity coalesced around her, crackling with blue-white fire. A fierce snarl split her face; it was a very avian look, full of hate and uncompromising intent.

"Hadouken, motherfucker!" she screamed, and a lightning bolt arched through the air to hit the troll standing behind Luke. Charlie rushed past her, the gun now in his hand, and closed on Mae. He raised the sawed-off shotgun to shoulder level. Luke couldn't help but notice he was holding it totally wrong; it wasn't even cocked. If the gun had a safety, it was probably on, and if he managed to fire it, the kickback would knock his teeth in.

"On your knees!" Charlie barked at Mae, as if attempting to sound intimidating, but the break in his voice betrayed his terror. "Let them go!"

Mae only smiled and raised her hand. "I think not," she said. "You're a pretty one. Come join us. You haven't known pleasure till you've surrendered to a nymph." Luke felt the magic uncoiling from her like a serpent, reaching for him, tendrils of powers looking to penetrate him and master him.

Charlie's face contorted in confusion, then lapsed into annoyance. He darted in, swung the shotgun around, and clocked her in the temple. She fell to the ground, too shocked to say a word.

Charlie raised the butt of the shotgun. "Your wiles don't work on me, bitch, I'm gay!" he said before slamming her on the head with the gun again. This time, she was out.

And her victims were free. For the first time in many lifetimes, Luke was in a rush to close up his pants. So too were August and Orson, though Orson did so as he knelt to pick up Mae, cradling her limp body to him. August stumbled backward and found a corner to slump into, his pretty blue eyes wide with horror. Luke had just enough time to observe that it took a lot to rattle a headless horseman when Sally barreled into him and knocked him flat on his back in the dirt.

"You dumbass!" she shrieked while she kissed him repeatedly.

"Putting your guns down for us—we all could've been killed—"

"Ow," Luke said. He managed to sit up and gave her a firm and resounding kiss as punctuation. A large part of him would have been interested in a literal roll in the hay at that moment, if not for spectators, but Mae's magic had left him with a lingering nausea like seasickness or morning sickness. Strange, he thought, the memories that stayed, the sensations that never faded. With Sally's help, he rose up on shaking limbs, and together, they towered over the troll that had almost destroyed him.

"No more kitchen knives, huh?" Luke said. "Pity. I got a whole houseful. Let's you and me have us a little talk."

Chapter Forty-Four

Luke followed Sally up the front steps and into the house. His body shook from the adrenaline of the battle with the troll, with Mae, with himself. His head was back to hurting; had it been only that morning that August had given him a mild concussion? It seemed like days ago. The grounding magic from earlier wasn't going to hold off the pain and fatigue forever. He was hungry—no, he decided, he was ravenous. He hadn't eaten since before he'd gone through the portal on August's horse. August couldn't be a whole lot better off.

They'd left the others in the barn and come inside to gather supplies: water and easily digested food for the recently rescued, pain meds for the recently injured, and the spear for Orson. Luke considered making good on his threat to the troll, but torture didn't suit him. When it came down to it, no matter what experiences he could draw upon or how gray his morality became, Luke wanted to be a good person. And good people didn't torture other people, even when they were murdering bastards, and especially when the bulk of the danger had passed.

Luke was in the middle of these musings when Sally turned around and put a hand on his chest as they entered the kitchen. She was especially pretty right now, he thought—in her pajama shirt, old boots, and jeans with the knees blown out, with no make-up, only the most cursory of attempts to tame her hair, and the exhilaration of danger lighting up her eyes and pinking her cheeks. She was rumpled, to say the least, and it gave him ideas about rumpling her further.

"I just wanted to look at you," she said, letting out a slow breath between her teeth, "and be reminded that you're real. That you're you. That I didn't lose you." She stepped up to him and looped her arms around his waist, fingers trailing up his spine.

"I've wanted you so bad, I'm gonna hunt trolls down for generations to come if we don't get to have a peaceful spell."

"Girl," he said, drawing her against him, "I got no intention of letting you have any peace." He kissed her, and she kissed him back, matching his passion. He picked her up and put her on the kitchen island; she wrapped her legs around him and held him close. She wasn't wearing a bra, and he could feel the press of her breasts through the soft cloth. He moaned at the electric buzz of her lust-magic, her energy soaking into him whether he went looking for it or not, a warm, insistent hum of excitement.

"I want you," she said. "This isn't the time or place, but I can't get over wanting you. I see you and I just want to tear your shirt off and look at you and touch you." She grazed her fingers over his face, as if memorizing every plane. "You with your dark good looks, I swear you could've come out of a movie."

"Never seen a movie star who needed so much dental work, or had a farmer's tan," he joked, giving her the tilted grin that he knew got to her the best.

"Well they oughta come that way," she insisted. "Or maybe you just make it look good."

"Even the horns?" He buried his nose in her neck, breathing in her scent, unmasked by perfume or soap. Just her. It was wonderful.

"Especially the horns." He could feel her grinning. "Maybe it's weird, but I really like the horns."

"You know it turns me right the hell on for someone to grab them and hold me by the horns."

"Oh yeah?" She ran her hands down his horns, from the base where they grew from his forehead, just behind his hairline, to the tips, one slightly shorter than the other where it had broken, long ago. He shivered, twitching like he was unsettled. She drew out the satyr magic in him and egged it on.

"Does the fur go up to your waist?" she asked, running her hands down his back to his waist.

"No," he said, pushing her hand to his hamstring, just below his ass, "it ends about there. No hairy butts, sorry."

"Do you have a tail?"

"I do."

"Eeee, I want to see your tail!"

"You first," he said, dropping his hands to cup her ass and pull her hard against him. She made a small noise of frustration and want; he knew she could feel that he was hard, that pleasure was available for the taking, just a few layers of denim away. She ground against him, squeezing him with her thighs. He ran his hand up her side, cupped her breast, thumbed her hardening nipple, and kissed her deeply, their tongues flitting and circling each other, each wanting to drown in the sheer presence of the other—

There came a bang and shout from the door. "Goddammit Luke, not now!"

Luke and Sally jumped as one, spinning to see Orson charge through the front door and cross the living room at a gallop, Sally's father's hunting rifle in one hand. He threw open the door to the front hall closet, where a collection of brooms and mops were propped up with their business ends in a plastic bin that had long ago parted company with its lid. He yanked out the black barbed spear from Tír na nÓg, sending the cleaning implements into a confused jumble on the floor. He strode back to the door and threw the rifle to Luke. "C'mon, Romeo. Fight now, fuck later."

"What?" Luke said. "Who are we fighting?"

"Alan, the cop troll," Orson said, "and a whole flock of chupacabras."

Chapter Forty-Five

Alan didn't look like a cop anymore. He'd left his police cruiser in
the grass; his uniform was shredded into a tattered rag that clung
to his body, stony as the others, dark and sharp like dull obsidian.
He showed a jagged mouth full of teeth to Luke as the satyr
stepped out of Sally's house and crossed the front porch, rifle at
ease but ready. The body of the troll who had been shot still lay in
the yard.

"I felt my brother go," Alan said, barely restrained. He went
down on all fours, a spectral nightmare stalking through Sally's
mother's pink rosebushes. Petals dropped around him as he
brushed against them, clearly counting on the cover to keep Luke
from getting a good shot. "And now I find you here.... You and
your whore."

"Give the girl a ranged weapon," Orson said.

"She is a ranged weapon," Luke answered.

"My precision sucks," Sally admitted, unruffled by the insult.
"Get him closer."

Luke returned his attention to the troll. "Can't say I'm too sorry
about your brother. He had a gun on my friends. You might say he
had it coming. What now?"

"I leave with his body."

"Fair enough."

"And yours."

"Now that I take exception to."

"Surrender now, and I won't hurt your friends."

"Funny," Luke said, bringing the rifle to his shoulder and
stepping back into a firing stance, "but this ain't the first time you
lot have made that particular sorry offer. So far it hasn't worked
out so well for you."

"The goblin is dead," the troll snarled. "He swore loyalty to you, and spit in my face. Love for you has already cost one person his life."

"And the other council members?"

"They were not able to see reason, when they discovered our plans. Unfair, unfeeling for the plight of our kind."

"Yeah, can't say I'm feeling much sympathy myself. So we weren't the only ones looking into what was going on, and they wouldn't be bribed or threatened into silence," Luke said. "Good to know. Tell you what, I'll make you a similar deal: you call off your chupacabras, take your dead with you, don't pursue this tolling-the-portals business anymore, and I, in return, won't hunt your asses down and put your heads up on spikes. Because that's my current plan."

"Fool," Alan spat. "Let it be death for you all!"

He pulled something out of his pocket and blew into it. A shrill warble in a minor key sounded from it. A swarm of chupacabras left the surrounding brush and swept forward, over and under the fence, across the lawn and the gravel drive, to attack en masse.

They were horrid beasts, now that Luke saw them in the light. Their too-thin bodies were corded with muscle that knotted and rippled under loose folds of naked, mottled flesh. Spikes jutted from their backs at odd angles, less like reptilian spines than mutated, cutaneous growths, like antlers gone wrong. Their faces were hideous, contorted, all mouth and black, bugging eyes, their toothy maws open and screaming, two enormous forward fangs jutting out. Their hands—for they were hands, opposable thumbs and all—ended in long claws for burrowing, and their feet were the same, churning up the earth as they charged.

Great, Luke thought, I'm going to be sucked dry by a demonic armadillo. At least when the fairy bitch drank me, I got something out of it.

A glimmer of an idea sparked in Luke's mind. He sighted down the barrel of the rifle and backed up to the front door. "Let one through," he said to Sally and Orson, who fanned out to the sides of the porch. He and Orson began to fire, and Sally's lightning split the air into a million jagged bits of white fire.

They agreed without speaking on which one to let through. A

small beast headed straight up the porch steps, and all three of them let it. As it reached him, Luke spun to the side, dropped to his knees, and yanked its legs out from under it. He dropped his weight on top of it to hold it down. Instantly his chest was a world of hurt. Spines or antlers, the hard bits on the chupacabra's back were not fun to land on.

It swung its head around, surprisingly dexterous, and sank its fangs into Luke's upper arm, but Luke had handled enough livestock in this life and in others to know how to deal with a pissed animal. He got his knee on its neck and loosed his arm from its bite. Beating back his terror of the thing that squabbled and screamed beneath him, he reached into his pocket—he was still wearing the same pair of pants from last night, when he'd returned from Tír na nÓg—and pulled out the dog collar he'd taken from the dais.

Funny, he thought as he secured it around the chupacabra's neck, how a dog collar from several hundred years ago was still recognizable. It was made out of braided leather instead of nylon and was secured by a set of knots instead of a metal buckle, but a collar it was, complete with a little loop onto which to fasten a leash. The chupacabra grew still beneath him, watching him with its great, flat black eyes.

"Yeah, you're collared all right," he growled down at it. "I'm gonna send you back down the throats of the trolls, and hell's gonna follow with you."

Luke stood up and held the chupacabra aloft, now hanging limp as a rag. The rest of the chupacabras saw and backed away, hesitation and doubt quelling their enthusiasm for blood. "I don't know what this does," Luke yelled, "but it came from Faerie so it's sure to be hell to deal with! You want to attack me, call off your demons and attack me yourself, you dumbass sumbitch!"

Alan was surprisingly fast. Luke backpedaled, yelping in surprise, as Alan crossed the yard in two bounds and slammed into him. They fell to the porch, grappling each other. The chupacabra fell to the side, momentarily forgotten. The troll rolled so Luke was on top—it would be difficult for Orson and Sally to attack, especially while the few remaining chupacabras were still looking for a piece of them—and gripped Luke's throat in one enormous stone hand. The hand began to close. Luke struggled, threw himself backward, wrenched from side to side, to no effect. He couldn't get air, couldn't fill the burning emptiness in his lungs. He beat at the troll beneath him, but it may as well have been bird wings on a mountain. The world began to get very dark, very fast.

There was a thick-sounding thunk, metal cutting into wood. It was jarring how fast the commotion stopped. Fighting and screaming and violence everywhere, then everything went still and silent. The hand around Luke's throat wavered, and he drew in one enormous, wonderful breath while his attacker hesitated. His vision cleared; a wooden pole stood straight up, right in front of his eyes. He looked down. The pole went through the middle of Alan's chest, but there was no blood. Alan's hand fell away. He stared unseeing at the ceiling of the porch, still breathing, still blinking. Luke scrambled backwards and almost fell down the steps.

"What the hell—"

"Cuchulainn's spear," Orson said.

Luke registered at last that Orson wasn't holding the big black spear. Alan screamed and arched upward, moving his body up the pole. Both Sally and Luke screamed with him; Luke scrambled up and stepped in front of Sally, and she clutched at his back. Only Orson had the presence of mind and fortitude to pull Alan up and off the great spear, letting it exit out through his back, the only way its ferocious barbs would allow. The spear stayed upright, lodged in the old decking of the porch. Orson dropped Alan, who howled and clutched at his chest—but there was no wound. They all abruptly stopped screaming; their horror and misery had turned to confusion. Alan looked pleadingly at them.

He didn't look like a troll anymore. The stone façade of spirit that lived beneath his human self was gone.

"I don't remember," he said, pawing at Sally's leg. "My lives— I don't remember.... Give me my lives back! Hundreds of years...."

He felt for his horns, his teeth, his arms and face. He looked frantically among them, and then his face twisted up and he launched himself at Orson. *"Give them back to me!"*

Luke stood, a horrified expression on his face. "Did that spear... just make him completely human? Mortal?"

"Looks that way," Orson said. He and Luke exchanged a look. Fear was contagious.

Sally caught it next. "Holy shit," she said, her voice breaking, "we can die." She looked down at Alan, at the last life of a very old troll whose myth-folk self had been slain. "We can die for real, forever. Oh, God, we killed him."

Alan made no move to protect himself. He curled up on his side with his face in his hands and wept.

Chapter Forty-Six

Luke, Orson, and Sally surrounded the sobbing former troll in silence, stunned by the unprecedented death of a myth-folk's immortal soul. Luke was the first to move, to press on with what had to be done, though he did so with the feeling he had just acquired several new nightmares. There were still the chupacabras to deal with. They were currently hiding in the shrubs, waiting to see how things developed before committing themselves, but they would not hold back for the sake of reverence for the fallen.

A set of pan pipes hung from Alan's belt. On seeing them, Luke struck upon an idea—this was what Alan had used to call the chupacabras. He took the pipes from Alan's belt; Alan didn't stop him. His sobs had quieted to near catatonia. The pipes were wood, made of reed or bamboo, and Luke suspected they had been repurposed from some other object, like a wind chime. They were braced with popsicle sticks and red acrylic yarn—hardly the stuff of legend. He glanced at the collared chupacabra; it sat up, gazing at him in a terrible parody of a dog.

"Hey," he said abruptly, turning to Sally, "where's Sootie? I thought you said she was here."

"Yeah, as soon as August attacked you this morning she ran into my bedroom, and is presumably still there, hiding under my covers."

"Gawd, useless little piece of—all right." He fixed the chupacabra with a narrow-eyed glare. "You're part of the Wild Hunt now. You and your brethren. And the Wild Hunt is going to go looking for bridge trolls."

"You can do that?" Sally said. "Order the Wild Hunt around?"

"I think using the collar, which connects this chupacabra to the Hunt, in conjunction with the pipe, which controls the chupacabras en masse, will have that effect. Who knows; magical items are hard to predict when combined. But it's worth a shot, ain't it?"

Sally and Orson exchanged doubtful expressions, to which Luke made a rude noise before returning his attention to the pipes. He closed his eyes and reached back for a memory of life long ago and far away. Salty air, sandy earth, grape leaves and olive trees, wine and cheese, laughter and beautiful music, and his first lover from his very first life teaching the young satyr to play the pan pipes. He recalled the angle against his lips, the shape of his mouth, the strength of his breath, coaxing reedy notes of music from the slender instrument. He remembered leaning against his lover, lounging under the olive trees while he practiced the pipes, the lustful hands of the older man roaming his body, the hungry excitement as he drew in his first taste of sexual magic during that first shaky melody.

A song—he needed a song to summon them to hunt. Another memory flickered across his mind, of the last time he'd played an instrument purely from memories of a past life. He was six years old, dragged along to a meeting between his mother and his older brother's music teacher. He tried to be still, tried to listen or otherwise occupy his thoughts, but little by little he slid out of his seat and onto the floor, bored out of his mind. His mother admonished him to get up, this was no place to lie on the floor. So he did, and walked around the office, looking at things and getting minute-by-minute reminders not to touch anything. He picked up a child-size violin; his mother barked at him, and the music teacher stayed her. It was all right, he said, that instrument was for a small child, Luke could mess with it if he wanted, and if he promised to be very, very careful. Luke agreed and was delighted to find he could hold it between his chin and shoulder, just the way he should.

It did not register at the time that he should not have known what to do with it. He plucked the fine metal strings, pressing them against the bridge with his small fingers, twisting the fine-tuning knobs on the tailpiece until it was just right. It took a few minutes more for him to figure out (remember?) how the fingering for certain notes went, how to hold the bow and draw it across the strings just so. But all at once he got the angles right, the old skill from long ago snapped into place, and a song leaped into his mind as if he had heard it every day of his life. It was a song far older than old, ancient, a fast patter of notes like the rhythm of many dancers, or many hooves. Luke flew through the song, joy flooding his heart as old memories—not imaginings, memories—came to him, of dancing and playing around a bonfire. It was a hunting song, to stir the heart before setting out after a stag or another large, fast, dangerous prey. It was the first time the song had been heard aloud for eighteen hundred years, and six-year-old Luke played the ancient song in a music teacher's office in Fox Pass, Texas.

With a screech the song was interrupted—the teacher snatched the violin out of Luke's hands. The man was bone white, shaking and sweating. He spoke rapidly to Luke's mother, who was also pale. Luke went to her, and she hesitated before putting out a hand to him, drawing him close to her. It was the first time he'd ever seen his mother frightened of anything. She was afraid of him.

They left the office in a cloud of shouting that Luke didn't understand. What was the teacher accusing him of? Why were they angry, and afraid? He had liked playing the little wooden instrument, the man had said it was all right! He cried in the car, tears of frustration, humiliation, fear, and a shadow of rage. Luke's mother took him home and held him on the couch, and stroked his hair while they listened to a gospel CD.

Finally, she bade him sit up and raised shaking fingers to the tiny knobs on his head. "I thought I was imagining things," she said. "I thought I was going crazy."

"I'm growing horns I think," Luke said happily, hoping this would cheer her up. "Aren't they cool? Just like the goats!" Their dairy goats were special pets to Luke. "But Mark couldn't see them when I tried to show him, or Daddy too. I didn't think anyone else could see them, and so they must be magic."

"They are," his mother said. "I don't know why I can see them and no one else can. But Luke, you must keep this secret. You are special, and the world does not understand people who are special. They will hurt you, and judge you, and they will not listen."

"Like Matt's music teacher?"

"Yes, like that."

"Why didn't he like my song? It was a great song."

"Yes," she said, "but he wasn't ready to hear it. How did you know how to play the violin? Was someone talking to you, telling you how to do it?"

"No... I just remembered. I did it before. A long time ago, though. I think it was before we moved here."

She nodded. They had moved to their new house the year before. "I don't think we had a violin at our old house, either."

"No, it was before that. I mean a long, loooooong time ago. Like, before we talked like we talk now. And you weren't my mommy, I had a different mommy and daddy, and we lived somewhere else. It was a little house, and it was near the ocean. I played a lot of violin back then, but we didn't call it a violin, we called it... a lyra, I think."

"You've never talked about it before."

"Well, I didn't remember it before. Picking up the violin, that's what made me remember. I don't know why I forgot, it seems a big thing to forget. But I remember lots of things, and sometimes I forget them again. Not like how Grandpa forgets, it's different, I think."

Luke's mother studied him very seriously and nodded solemnly. She was an excellent mother, in Luke's opinion, not only because she made good food and was glad to stop cleaning to have picnics but because she took him seriously. Other adults never wanted to listen to the wild stories he spun up about his adventures, played out in the creeks and fields near his home, but his mother would always listen, and ask questions, and be interested. She, at least, he could talk to. She listened now with the same air of importance and belief. But this time at the end she didn't smile and encourage him to think on it more, or draw a picture of it, or run out and get the other kids to come along with him (which just as often landed him playing with the goats as with the human children.) This time, she took his face in her hands.

"You must never tell other people when you remember something like that, honestly remember, not imagine it. I don't understand it, Luke, but you tapped into something today that frightened that teacher and will frighten other people. They will always fear what they do not understand. There will be other people you can talk to in your life, but you must look for those people carefully. Hide this like a valuable secret, like a treasure chest of gold that they will snatch away from you if they can. Do not trust." Her face softened, and he thought then that she looked very old and sad. "But always tell me, all right my darling? Secrets don't count when it is your mother. I am on your side now and always, no matter what your side is."

He hugged her, and was afraid. They both were.

And now, thirty-something years later, he played that song again.

Chapter Forty-Seven

Luke played the ancient song, the first time he'd played it since that day so long ago. It hung in the chill air like the baying of a hound. It was not the happy song he once thought. It was enthusiastic, exciting, but for no wholesome reason. It was a call to arms, an invitation to rabid violence. It was the kind of song felt bone deep, an inevitable, terrible melody recognized by all who heard it because it hibernated in the deep reservoirs of human ancestral memory, burned into the minds and souls of those who had it ringing in their ears as they died. It was an old song about old blood. Luke understood now how right his mother and the teacher had been to be frightened when a six-year-old in Texas drew that song out of thin air and a cheap child's violin.

He came down off the porch and into the yard, still playing. The chupacabras drew out of the hedges, out of the rosebushes, and stalked around him, black eyes gleaming. The collared one followed at his heels, trembling like a greyhound before a race, and began to dance with terrible leaps and scrapes and howls as it shadowboxed an unseen foe. One by one the other chupacabras joined in, their knobbed, fleshy bodies writhing in a circle around him. The satyr danced too, his cloven hooves twisting the grass and gravel. His body knew the dance, a Wild Hunt dance, a maenad kind of dance.

Shadows closed in around them, growing from dark corners and crevices. First they swept across the lawn, pale patches of dark, drifting nearer and farther like a comet's irregular orbit, but they couldn't escape. They drew in, spinning faster and faster, growing dark and turgid, mixing among the chupacabras like black smoke. The Wild Hunt reached toward them through the thin veil between worlds. Bridge trolls, Luke thought, willing the thought through the pipes, through the song, to the chupacabras, to the gathering Wild Hunt. *Our quarry is the bridge trolls drawing on the portals,* he thought. *All the portals, all around the world—no more tolls, no more sacrifices. The portals would be free, bathed in the blood of any troll that tried to draw upon unwary travelers.*

The song ended, and the sudden silence was jarring, like the ringing in his ears after a gunshot. The chupacabras scattered in all directions; released from the circle, they were surprisingly fast, as if the song had been a chain that held them to Luke. For a moment he could see one or two of them rushing pell-mell across the land, and the shadows went with them. Then they were all of them gone, leaving him in the center of Sally's lawn, the earth and gravel churned around him in a terrible sort of fae ring.

And his mother was there. She got out of her car and stood staring at him, her long gray hair blowing around her face in the cold wind. She wore a familiar expression. She stopped at the edge of the ring and stuck her hands in the pocket of her jacket, looking small and old and afraid.

"Are you all right?" she asked.

Luke got to his feet, limbs shaking, and nodded. "Yeah. I just sicced the chupacabras and the Wild Hunt on the bridge trolls."

"I'm guessing that makes more sense if you're you."

"Not as much as you'd think." He picked his way across the upturned ground.

She wrapped him in a hug. "I'm just glad you didn't get hurt." She pulled away, and he left a streak of blood on the shoulder of her jacket. He'd forgotten about where the chupacabra had bitten him. She grimaced. "Much. Glad you didn't get hurt much."

"Eh, I'd already forgotten about it."

"Silly billy." She turned him toward the house. "Let's get you fixed up, then you can fail to tell me all about it."

He touched his forehead gently to hers, a gesture she had long ago accepted from him as affectionate, in a caprine way. She held on to his elbow as they went to the porch to rejoin Orson and Sally, two more beings she both feared and loved. Luke wondered who was supporting whom.

Orson was helping a glassy-eyed Alan down the porch steps.

"Hi, Mrs. Shepherdson," he said, as if he were still one of Luke's many teenage friends who had felt quite at home in the Shepherdson house (and refrigerator). Sally motioned them into the house, holding her mother's first aid kit, a repurposed laundry detergent bucket from the bulk supply store. Luke sat down on the floral couch, and his mother and girlfriend set to fixing him up.

"Mom, you remember Sally...?" Luke said.

"Hi, Agatha," Sally said. "Cormick said he'd called you."

Agatha Shepherdson made a rude sound. "Do I remember Sally indeed. Sally honey, how are things going?" It was a loaded question, its tone heavy with meaning.

"Oh, swimmingly," Sally said with a broad grin. "He's come round."

Luke looked back and forth between his beaming girlfriend and his approving mother. "That is not cool," he said. "You can't plot behind my back. You should not even be talking where I can't see."

"If we didn't, nothing would ever get done," his mother answered, fishing cleanser, antiseptic, and bandages out of the bucket. "Have you talked about a wedding?"

"Not yet. Lotsa stuff going on. We'll get there."

Luke said nothing but couldn't help letting a hint of a smile pull at his mouth. Life seemed to take shape while he wasn't paying attention. Sally sat next to him, close to him, on the couch and held his hand while his mother bandaged his chupacabra wound. Sootie, the long-in-hiding blue heeler, emerged from the bedroom. Apparently the friendly voices and lack of gunfire had convinced her it was safe. She hopped up on the couch and snuggled next to Sally, casting forlorn eyes up at Luke.

"No, I don't forgive you either," said Luke.

"Don't give Sootie grief," Sally said, hugging the dog. "She's had a hard day." Sootie rolled onto her back in Sally's lap.

"Haven't we all."

Luke thought about the dead bridge troll Cormick or Allison had shot, his body still in the yard. He thought about Alan, having lost his immortal self to Cuchulainn's spear. The remaining troll, theoretically still alive in the barn with the myth-folk he'd imprisoned, and Brent, and Glen. He thought about Mae, who in the trolls' possession had become a crumpled, perverted version of what she really was, and Orson, who'd had to see her like that, be enthralled by her magic in that state. August, who'd also endured the nymph's magic, who'd been possessed by the troll's magic, who had done all kinds of things under their influence, lost his horse, and had the black magic sucked out of him by Charlie. And Charlie, who had endured much for Sally, and would probably endure more before it was all over... where did Charlie fit into it? He'd been brave so far, especially for one in his first life.

Luke squeezed Sally's hand. He was glad Sally had not endured worse. "Stay by me till all this is done?" he said.

She squeezed back. "Always."

Chapter Forty-Eight

All things considered, the puncture wound in Luke's arm was the least of their problems, but Sally and Agatha insisted on dressing it. When they came out of the house, Alan was gone, collected by the reinforcements Cormick had called for before Luke and the others left for the storage facility. The dead troll in the middle of the yard was gone, as was Sally's mother's sedan—riddled with bullets, windows shot out, the front half crushed from its encounter with the gate, bloodstained from several different people, and containing the body of Glen the goblin. Luke wondered which of the myth-folk locals had used what sort of magic to rid the place of the car so quickly and quietly. The three council members from the troll prison had left for San Antonio for long-term treatment with a myth-folk doctor.

In the barn, Mae was pressed into one corner, glaring at the world from inside a tarp, and August was in another, curled up in a little ball under a turnout blanket meant for a horse. In the center, guarded over by Allison with a sawed-off shotgun, was the troll who had tried and failed to slit Luke's throat.

Luke walked over to him and stood uncomfortably close. "Alan's dead," he said. "At least, the important part of him."

"I know. I saw."

"I'm gonna be sick about it later, when it sinks in. I've never seen such a thing, didn't know it was possible." He knelt down so he could look the troll in the eye. "This had to end. Tolling the portals now is only going to bring more blood, more death for your kind. You brought this fight. Not just to me, but to the whole myth-folk community, and I've sent it back after you. I know you lot think you're the good guys in this, and you can cast yourselves as the heroes all you want, but it don't change this one fact: bridge trolls are a hunted race now. So you tell every bridge troll you know, you spread the word, to leave the great portals of the world alone. If I really wanted you dead, I wouldn't tell you, I'd let you lot walk into it unawares. And if you come after this community, if you come for vengeance...." He pointed to Orson, still holding the spear, and Sally, who looked like she would like to put another bolt of lightning through the troll. "You got those guys to deal with. And me, though personally I'll take guns over what little damage I can do with my horns."

Luke stood and thought the troll looked very small, for all that he was a huge man. "You got anything to say?"

The troll shook his head. "I wish it had turned out differently."

"Me too. But you would have had to not try to kill us first."

Orson stepped up beside Luke. "Take the enchantment off of Mae."

The troll looked over his shoulder. "She is of no use to me anymore. Done."

Orson handed the spear to Luke and walked to Mae. She kicked out at him, pushing farther back into the corner, as if she could wedge herself into a crevice there like a spider. She fought him, slapped at him, but he was insistent, gentle and strong. He drew her to him, and she finally collapsed against his chest, abandoning the tarp. Her beautiful face showed the lines of her age, bordering on forty; neither nymph magic nor makeup disguised her now. Her body was lovely, well kept, but it sagged, the inevitable weight of time stealing her youthful appeal. At the roots of her hair, a touch of gray had begun to show. Orson and Mae talked, but all Luke could hear were her great, gulping sobs. Though he bore her no love, her raw vulnerability struck Luke like a punch in the sternum. No wonder Orson, who could not help but still love her a little, had to reach out to her. Luke was amazed that Mae, one of the most stalwart and powerful myth-folk he knew, could be brought low by a troll's possession magic. They had gotten that magic from somewhere. He resolved to find out where.

In the other corner, Cormick was talking to August. He knelt in front of the headless horseman, pushing his hair off his forehead, talking to him softly. August suddenly jerked back, a snarl twisting his handsome face.

"How would you know anything about it? You didn't even see what happened, you were safe in the storm shelter! It was humiliating, terrible—a violation—a desecration. I can't stand to think, to be in my own skin!"

Luke started toward them, but Cormick held up a hand. He stood and squared his shoulders. "August," he said in a commanding voice that left no one in doubt of his royal heritage, "you are a knight of the council, and you are commanded to control yourself. You were ensnared by an enchantment, in which terrible things happened. But you are not relieved of your duties, both what the council has entrusted to you and what I expect of you. You will not lapse into self-pity. You will not attempt to deal with this internally. You will accept treatment, you will recover, and you will go forth in greater compassion and understanding for what has happened here today." His voice softened. "You are not lessened in my estimation. You are still mine. Kneel."

August did a strange thing then. His muscles relaxed, as if a great burden had been taken from his shoulders. He sank to one knee in front of Cormick, and Cormick touched the back of August's head affectionately. "Thank you, my liege," he said.

Cormick looked up, past the wall of the barn, and Luke heard the sound of a heavy animal walking. August stayed still and kneeling beneath Cormick's hand while his long-absent horse walked up behind him and lipped at his shoulder.

"You may rise," Cormick said, and stepped away from him.

August stood and turned around. The horse pressed its long face against his chest, and August buried his face in its mane. He didn't sob, like Mae did, but Luke suspected from the tremor in his shoulders that in the absence of company, he would have. Luke looked away and let August keep what little remained of his secrets.

Chapter Forty-Nine

Luke noticed Sally's absence during dinner, which was sandwiches and microwaved soup eaten in near silence in the living room; the weight of exhaustion and violence hung over the group like a drug haze. He washed out his soup bowl and went looking for her. Sootie trotted along behind him, happy to be wherever he was, peripherally involved in whatever he was doing.

He found Sally in the barn, leaning against the thick-beamed door frame and staring at the empty space full of footprints and recent trauma. He came up behind her and put his arms around her waist; she leaned against him, and her tensed muscles relaxed at his touch. The dog found a pile of hay and curled up to doze, one ear alert in case her people wandered.

"What's on your mind, love?" Luke murmured. "Anything in particular, or is it just... everything?"

"Had to get away for a minute," she said. "I was lucky today, and that bothers me. I came out relatively unscathed. I'm old— possibly the oldest one here. It doesn't always make me wise, but it does make me stalwart. I could've handled some of these awful things happening to me... but not watching it happen to others. Some of the younger ones, August and Charlie in particular... I just don't know how they're holding up."

"They're tougher than you think. Kids usually are."

"Do you think August will be all right?"

Luke brought up a mental image of August, of leaning against him by the oak tree, siphoning pain away from him and sending it into the earth. He remembered the cold, lost chill of the headless horseman's magic. "I don't know. He has certainly taken a beating. Depends on whether he can process what happened with Mae. Touching and being touched without consent... it can strip away your sense of control in the world, that's for sure."

"Control," Sally said. "That's a big one for him."

Luke felt a pang of annoyance that almost immediately disappeared. Satyrs were not jealous by nature, even when they tried to be. "I forgot you guys slept together."

Sally shook her head. "It was just once. Frankly I think it confused the hell out of him. I hope whatever connection it is he has with Cormick will help him. Maybe you can ground him again before he leaves."

"You wouldn't mind?" Luke asked, a little surprised. "I wouldn't have figured he would be on the list."

He could feel Sally's smile, even with her facing away from him. A trickle of lustful energy ran from her, confirming his suspicion that she was now picturing him and August getting it on. "Grounding is hardly a full penetration magic. Need I ask what list you're talking about?"

"I dunno. Need you?" he asked, nuzzling her. "Seemed like maybe strict monogamy, especially where there was a magical need, didn't seem so vital to you anymore."

Sally was silent a minute, swaying ever so slightly. "Maybe not. There are at least two I've warmed up to. In theory. Don't really know how I'd react if I walked in on you and them."

"Don't need to find out," Luke said. "Won't nothing ever happen without your blessing. But one way or another, I am not sleeping with August, the guy gets my hackles up."

"Awww, is that all?" Sally said, and he felt her smile again. It seemed to Luke that she smiled with her whole body. "What about Charlie?"

"What about Charlie?" Luke asked, turning the question around on her. "You know him way better. If anything, I'd think today might end up being good for him—confirm that he's part of the myth community, concrete his faith in his own magic, in his courage. I gotta admit, him cracking Mae on the skull was pretty funny, in hindsight."

"I will always and forever love him for that," Sally said. "You know what that troll said to us as he brought us out? He said whichever of us made a move first, he'd shoot the other one. Isn't that sick? I could risk myself, but I couldn't risk him. Thank goodness for Allison and my dad's rifle. I think Charlie will be all right, once he gets over having sucked the bad magic out of August. But... do you think he could be on the list?"

"Oh, what list is that?" Luke teased her. "And yes, I think so. He's got balls and brains and he's kinda cute."

"Good. Very good. He had a boyfriend for a while, but frankly that guy was a real jackass; I think Charlie has had the shit kicked out of him a couple of times, metaphysically. You and I would be good for him. I'm not sure about Allison yet. How do you think she's doing?"

"Allison will be fine. The worst she's got to contend with is killing a troll who had a gun on her friends. That's a flesh wound as far as mental anguish goes."

"Orson and Cormick are definitely not on the list."

"No no no and no. And of course there's Mae.... Another messed up one I'm not ever gonna sleep with, not the least of which is because she's a crazy bitch, and likely getting crazier. Being forced to use her nymph powers without her own consent? That's gonna fuck up a girl."

"She was already fucked up," Sally growled.

"That's unfair, you didn't know her before."

"You did, and you can defend her? You told Allison and me what she did. And you just called her a crazy bitch."

Luke thought a minute. "I knew her way before. I knew her when she and Orson were really in love, really happy. I watched it all go wrong, like a train wreck in slow motion." He breathed a heavy sigh of resignation. "I watched her break a little when Orson chose his friendship with me over his marriage to her. There's more to her."

"Which means Orson's got to be hurting too."

"Oh yeah. Whatever she is now, she was once his wife. We are all of us the sum of our stories."

Sally turned and pressed her face against Luke's chest. "All our dear friends are hurting, and there's nothing we, the old codgers, can do about it! It's so unfair."

Luke set his goateed chin on top of her head—she was short enough he could do that—and held her close. "Well, there is something, really. But I'd have to be fully, uh, charged to do it."

"Oh?"

"There is an element of healing to sex. I can confer some of my magical energy to others, if they'll receive it. If I have enough oomph to spare, it doesn't even have to be sexual, though I do have to touch them. Magic is more about intent than physical ritual, after all." He drew back so he could look at her face. "But I am drained like crazy. I grounded August, I got sucked on—metaphorically—by a nymph, and I summoned the Wild Hunt. Magically speaking, I'm surprised I'm not comatose. I think maybe it's shock keeping me awake."

"So you need sex." She said it flatly, without the angry tone she might have had at another time.

"Frankly, yes." He took a deep breath. "You and Allison had a moment, and you seemed to like imagining me with Charlie. I could approach one of them."

"And why not me?"

He bit his lip. "I didn't know how you'd react to our first time being magically necessary."

"Luke," she said, reaching up to touch his hair, "it's not anyone else who's going to be there for you this time. It's going to be me." She went up on tiptoe to kiss him, and he returned the kiss with gratitude and passion.

Chapter Fifty

A cedar trunk in the hayloft held old cotton quilts, their patterns long faded, their batting poking out of frayed seams and edging. The antique and heirloom quilts were safe in the house; these were the quilts of picnics in the pasture, forts in the tack room, and makeshift pallets in the alley outside a sick animal's stall. It was one of these old quilts that Sally flung over the loose hay when she took Luke up to the loft in the barn.

Sally touched him slowly and deliberately, tracing her fingers over him as if she were drawing him, bringing every inch of him to life. He pulled her T-shirt off of her, his breath catching a little at the lavender lace bra she wore. She straddled him and pulled him up to a sitting position so she could divest him of his own dark blue T-shirt. He felt his skin turn to gooseflesh in the newly chill air; the hair on his neck and arms stood on end. There was electricity in the air—and some of it was the fluttering fingers of Sally's lustful sexual energy, feeling him out, finding its way into him. The wind found its way through cracks in the walls, and it smelled like rain.

"Storm's coming," he said, tracing the backs of his nails up her arms.

"Oh," she said, "there is."

He pressed his lips against her sternum, kissing his way up her chest. "Your storm?"

"Hell yeah." There was a light in her eye that was unfamiliar to him, avian and predatory. In that moment she could only have ever been a bird of prey, and his caprine heart shivered.

He ran his hands down her spine, to her lower back, to her ass, and pulled her firmly against him. In a quick, practiced motion, he undid her bra and slid it off her shoulders. He caressed her breasts, cupped them in his hands, felt of them with his mouth and tongue.

He took her brown nipple in his mouth and sucked, swirling his tongue. She gasped and squirmed, grinding against him, her legs flexing around him to get closer, to press harder. Luke felt her magic flowing into him, little trickles of power seeping into his flesh. He needed more. He stretched up to whisper in her ear.

"Do you want me, Sally?"

"Do I want you," she said. She reached between them and began undoing his belt and pants. "I have wanted you for years. Ached for you. I've fumed and raged and damn near foamed at the mouth in frustration that I couldn't have you—not the way I wanted. I've had you in my dreams, in my past lives, and more nights than not, when I pleasured myself, it was your cock I imagined was between my legs. I want you more than I've ever wanted anyone. I tried to substitute, and found the rest of the world a pale shade." She bit her lip, her dark eyes wide and vulnerable. "I did pretty well, for a while, hiding it, pretending I didn't want you. I convinced myself I didn't need you. Then this whole chupacabra and troll thing happened, and all of a sudden, you needed me. And that just sunk me. If I don't get to fuck you now, I might just go mad."

Luke drew in a hissing breath, looking up at Sally with wide eyes. "Girl, you could've just come over, you know."

"Not knowing what I'd wake up to? Where we were going? I'm too old for that, Luke. One thing being so ancient's done to me, I can't hardly act for fear of repeating the past. And I sure can't act all rash and impetuous, out of my own need. They're just not my engines." She unzipped his jeans. "But now that you know me, for who I am, and who we were—now that you are on the same page with me—things are a lot different."

He cupped her cheek, stared earnestly into her eyes. "They sure as hell are, and won't nothing ever be quite the same from here on out."

He kicked off his boots, and she helped him out of his pants. It was harder to get hers off, as they were tighter, and she finally grunted in frustration and just stood up to take the blasted things off. He glimpsed ever so briefly that her panties matched her bra.

He imagined she had gotten up that morning and dressed with the idea that she might get to fuck him that night.

She straddled him again and stroked her clit against his cock. She was soft, and hot, and wet, and he was almost painfully hard, his skin tight and bulging. He slid his hand under her ass, between her legs, and rubbed her with his fingers. She made little pleading noises, her muscles flexing against him. She moved as if to guide him into her; Luke held out a little longer, sliding one finger, then two into her, making sure she was ready. Thunder rumbled somewhere not too far away.

"Luke," she said, "goddamn it, please, don't make me wait any more!"

She was definitely ready, he decided. He wrapped his arms around her and rolled them both over. She raised her hips, and he pressed against her, into her, slowly, letting the soft folds of her flesh part around his cock. She was tight, and hot, and his body thrummed with pleasure as he entered her. She cried out, good noises, the gathering storm covering her enthusiastic cries with wind and thunder. Her hips bucked as she rose to meet him, spreading her legs wider to take him in deeper. Lightning crashed nearby, and the wind picked up. He drew out, then pushed back in, and she gasped in pleasure, over and over. The whole world seemed to narrow to the pulsing energy flooding into him, lighting him up from the inside out, and the thrumming pleasure of his cock inside her, pumping in and out and of her pussy.

He drew out, almost suddenly, and said to her with a pannish grin, "Roll over." She did, and he drew her ass back toward him. She eagerly raised her pussy. He stroked his fingertips lazily up the back of her legs. "Do you want it, Sally?"

"Of course I do, you old goat!"

He pressed the tip of his cock just inside the opening of her pussy. "How much do you want me?"

"Lots! Crazy lots! For years! Please, pretty satyr-boy? Please?" She looked over her shoulder at him, just her dark eyes and long lashes visible. It was the look that did it; he couldn't tease her anymore. He thrust into her, panting with exertion; she cried out, wanting more, and he gave her as much as he could, withdrawing to nearly his entire length with each stroke. The magical energy in Sally vibrated through him, pouring into him as she charged him, as she had been taught. It made his whole body pulse with ecstatic pleasure. Through the haze of euphoria, he reached beneath her and found her clit; he rubbed her in tight circles, experimenting until he found the way that made her nearly scream with pleasure, and she came loudly, her body bucking beneath him as he fucked her for all he was worth. Outside, the storm broke, and rain beat down on the tin roof of the barn.

She lay beneath him, and he was still for a minute, letting her breathe, before he started moving again, pulling out and then slowly, almost agonizingly slowly, sliding back in. The buzz of her lustful energy wasn't quite so overwhelming, and the storm held steady. As she stirred beneath him, he purred in her ear, "We'd better put a condom on."

She made an unhappy noise and squirmed. "Do we have to?"

He rolled his hips and nibbled her shoulder. "Only if you don't want a baby in nine months. I hear tell this activity can lead to babies."

She smiled over her shoulder at him. "Babies aren't so bad." She rolled over and pulled him down between her legs again.

He protested at being drawn out and shuddered at the pleasure of entering her again. "Personally, I think we'd make damn pretty kids, all dark hair and old souls and snarky attitudes." He began to speed up, turned on by the idea of Sally pregnant. Sally with a little round tummy, gradually growing bigger.

For a moment all he heard was her breath, in and out, her rapid heartbeat. Then—"I want you to be the father of my babies."

Luke made a low keening noise, his body shuddering from head to toe. A magical surge of energy thrust into him like a sword through his chest, and he rode it by increasing the speed and power of his strokes as he fucked Sally. He felt dizzy, almost cross-eyed at the intensity of the magic she poured into him. The howling wind and rain of the storm outside didn't even register anymore. He almost couldn't speak as he raised his lips to her ear. "Sally, I love you. I want you to be my family."

She breathed out like she'd been holding on to a breath for years. "Then keep going."

So he did, nothing between them at all. He fucked her now with greater intent, their bodies fusing. She sat up, pushed him over, rolled on top of him. She grabbed his horns and held him down on the quilt in the hay, and began riding him up and down, pleasuring herself upon his cock, which was stiff as a spear. She swirled her hips, changed her rhythm, and watched while Luke's eyes went in and out of focus as she charged him with all the sexual energy she could muster.

This time when she came, Luke came with her, both of them crying out as their bodies shuddered around their thrusting cores. She rode him as he spent himself in her, grinding her clit against him. And faintly in the back of his mind, was the idea that even now—or at least very shortly—she might be pregnant. By him. Carrying his child, theirs together. The idea flooded him with joy.

Chapter Fifty-One

Back inside Sally's parents' double-wide, the mood had only worsened with the storm Sally had summoned up. Luke found that Orson had Mae in the spare room, trying to keep her calm and collected until they could take her somewhere safe; Cormick and August were back in Sally's parents' room, talking quietly; Allison and Agatha were in the kitchen, cleaning up after dinner; and Charlie dozed under a crocheted afghan on Sally's bed, curled up into a little ball of traumatized Jersey Devil.

"Let's start with Cormick and August," Luke murmured in Sally's ear.

"I'm following your lead," she said. "I didn't see you do much healing stuff in prior lives. This aspect of your magical penis is new to me."

Luke smirked. "I told you, this part of my magic doesn't need full-on sex, though it's sure nice when it happens that way. It's a lot like grounding, only once the negative energy has drained out, I put a warm and fuzzy kind of magic in its place."

"You've got the fuzzy taken care of anyway." She smacked him on the butt.

Luke opened the door to Sally's parents' bedroom. Cormick and August sat on the bed, newly made up without the bloodstains from that morning. Luke wondered who had managed to magic all the blood out of the sheets, the blankets, the carpet, the drywall. He winced a little, seeing the headboard August had thrown him into, and realized his head no longer hurt. Whether it had been a concussion or not, apparently the sheer amount of magic that had run through him that day had taken care of his injury, too. How handy was that, he thought as he sat next to August.

"How are you holding up?" he asked. Sally climbed up next to Cormick and leaned against his back.

"How do you think?" August said. His voice was bitter and sharp. "In the course of a day, I've learned that I was possessed and used. I was physically, magically, and sexually assaulted. I find myself unprepared to deal with the emotional fallout." He nodded toward Cormick. "He's trying to help."

Luke raised his eyes to Cormick. "You guys have a thing then, huh?"

Cormick sighed, more tired than irritated. "I've said it a hundred times, I'm not gay. I'm truly not into men. If you must know—not that it's any of your business—August needed someone to hold his leash, so to speak. He has been under a great deal of stress, not just today, and he needed someone to be firm with him, tell him what to do, and make him feel secure. And frankly, I kind of liked someone blatantly needing me like that. It really isn't sexual at all."

"I would call it dysfunctional if it wasn't so clearly functional," Sally said.

"Whatever works," Luke said. "August, I grounded you this morning. I can do something like that again. It won't get rid of the hurt, but it may speed the healing process, so to speak. Clears your head, makes you feel centered, at peace, refreshed. You still better get a therapist when you get back to New England, but you'll have more clarity and calm as you go through it."

"New York's not part of New England," August corrected.

"It'll last that long?" Sally asked.

"It's like an extra battery. It'll last till he uses it all."

"That sounds fantastic," August said. "After grounding this morning, I felt better than I'd felt in a long time. Of course, I'd also just had a bunch of magical poison sucked out of me, so that probably had something to do with it."

"It had a lot to do with it," Luke affirmed. "How's your chest, by the way?"

August touched his chest and winced. "It's stitches, so it smarts, but it's not so bad. Allison did a good job dressing it, and she just changed the bandages a little bit ago. She says I'll have a wicked cool scar."

"Oooh, sexy," Luke said as they both smirked. "Now listen. There's a bunch of different ways to do this, but the most direct way is for me to breathe into your lungs. You ever shotgunned a cigarette? It's like that."

August raised his eyebrows. "So, uh, we have to make out." He didn't sound like it was an entirely unwelcome idea.

"It can be clean and clinical, full of platonic affection, hot and heavy, whatever is appropriate to the situation. It's a healing magic. Though it's sure easier if one or both of us is turned on. I'm a satyr, I can't help it, it's just how the magic works."

August flicked his gaze to Sally and Cormick. "I don't mind if you stay. And I don't mind if you go."

"I'll stay, keep an eye on you," Cormick said.

"And I'm staying to keep an eye on him," Sally said. "That there's my mate."

Luke grinned at the title. "We could say fiancé."

"You haven't asked all formal-like. I want a ring, even if it costs a quarter and comes in a little plastic bubble from a gumball machine outside the grocery store."

Luke made a rude noise. "You give me no credit, woman." He turned from her and faced August. The young man—for he was young, both in age and as a myth-folk, compared to Luke—dropped his gaze to the floral comforter, letting his black hair fall around his face. He looked much diminished from the haughty creature he'd seemed when Luke first met him. Luke could hardly sense the ghost within him, the headless horseman quiet and distant. He cupped August's cheek in his hand, admiring the man's fine features and pale skin, so aristocratic, so different from Luke's scruffy mutt looks. He kissed August; the man's lips were cold and thin, almost lifeless. August opened his mouth, and Luke felt his breath coming and going. Luke drew up the magic within him, feeling it coalesce in his chest behind his sternum, like a steam-powered boiler about to blow its seams. He breathed it out, pushing it into August's mouth, slow and steady, insistent. August breathed in, unsure at first, then gasping to take in more. He pulled away from Luke, his eyes wide with shock. He wanted to say something, but Luke kissed him again, looked for his opportunity, and breathed in another mouthful of magic. August moaned against him, sucking on his mouth, taking in all the magic he could.

Luke's magic welled up in him, coming easier now. His cock stiffened inside his jeans, almost painful. August was handsome enough, but he wasn't Luke's type. It was the magic that excited him; simply using it stirred his body. He answered August's moans with little sounds of his own, pressing forward as if to push the magic into him with greater insistence. August yielded easily, lying back on the bed and taking Luke with him. Luke's head swam with pleasure and want, in spite of himself, as he breathed magic down August's throat. They found a good rhythm; breathe, breathe, breathe, then a strong exhale from Luke as August inhaled his magic. He could feel their hands wandering, could sense his control of his body and his magic faltering.

He broke away, gasping, and backed up awkwardly on hands and knees on an impressively fluffy comforter. His gut cramped, and he sprawled across the foot of the bed, back arching as he tried to get his muscles to stop spasming.

August and Sally peered down at him. "Are you all right?" they both asked.

"Yes," he said. "It'll pass. Maybe I should have stretched first."

"And in the barn wasn't a warm-up?" Sally grinned.

"Girl, between you and this household, I'll have gone through a magical pentathlon by the time the evening's done."

"Like you won't enjoy it."

"So you guys are, you know, really a thing now, huh?" August asked.

"Yeah," Sally said, brushing her hair out of her eyes. "I've waited three lifetimes to have him for life, so I'm holding on to him this time, come hell or sex magic."

August leaned forward and kissed her cheek. "I'm happy for you."

"Thanks. Um. Sorry I was such a bitch before."

August shrugged. "Thank you for that. Frankly, you really were. But I understand now it wasn't personal."

Sally smiled. "I hope you get to feeling better."

August pushed his hair back out of his eyes, which were now bright and active, interested in the world again. "I already do. I feel a rush and a calm at the same time, like I just took a whole lot of Xanax."

Luke managed to sit up, looking between the two of them. "Didn't you guys sleep together?" he said.

"Yeah," Sally said, biting her lip. "Only I didn't make it clear at the time it was, uh, a one-time thing. I wasn't very nice to him later."

August shrugged. "I heard what I wanted to hear. Water under the bridge."

Cormick, nearly forgotten until that moment, clapped Sally and Luke on the shoulders. "Thank you both," he said, "but now that he's stabilized, I think I'm going to take August back to my place and order him around for a bit before bed. Thank you."

"Take care of him," Luke said.

Luke and Sally watched Cormick lead August out of the bedroom. Sally put her hand on Luke's. "Orson and Mae?"

Luke nodded grimly. "Orson and Mae."

Chapter Fifty-Two

Luke rapped his knuckles on the door of the spare bedroom and entered when he heard Orson's voice give a muffled "Come in." He'd never been in this room of Sally's house. Orson and Mae sat on a white metal daybed with enough decorative pillows to double as a couch. An old Singer sewing machine and a bookcase with an impressive array of cotton print fabrics and half-finished projects was on one side of the room; a pegboard with enough unfathomable tools to fill a dungeon hung on the adjoining wall. The closet door had a sign written in calligraphy: "Craft Closet: Open at Your Own Risk." The room was awash in blush pink, lavender, and sunshine yellow. This was, clearly, Sally's mother's domain.

Luke's mental vision of Mae was of a woman of fine taste and an invincible poker face. He'd seen her budget once, when he and Orson had been roommates after college, and it included things like "dry cleaning," "gym," "salon," and "Nordstrom." He hadn't seen "feed store" or "beer" anywhere on there and wondered why "therapist" wasn't present. Then again, that might have been on Orson's budget.

The Mae before him now reflected none of that. None of Sally's clothes fit her, given that Sally was both more rounded and six inches shorter than Mae. They'd had to go with an ancient pink nightgown with a faded gray tabby kitten and too-short sweatpants with the drawstring cinched tight. She sat with her legs pulled up to her chest, the sweatpants halfway up her unshaven shins. Her nail and toenail polish was chipped and grown out, her hair pulled back into a frizzy ponytail. She wore no make-up, and no defense. Her pain and fury were written there for the world to see.

Orson wasn't a whole lot better. Mae leaned against him, his arm around her shoulders. All his centuries seemed to show in the

lines and worry of his face. Most telling was that they didn't shoo
Luke off; they let him come in, stand before them, study them. He
extended his right hand to Mae, and she took it in her left, just
holding on to him, on to anything solid and warm.

Finally she said, "I'm sorry."

"Of course you are. But it was hardly you who done it all."

"No, I mean.... Well yes, I'm sorry this whole thing happened.
Thing is, they couldn't have used me if I hadn't been so damn
public about... not getting along."

"That's one way to put it."

"I made us all vulnerable."

"No use fretting on it now. You know you were already
forgiven, right?"

Mae sniffed and wiped her eyes with her wrist. "Goddamnit.
Why've you got to be so easy about it? Why can't you have the
decency to treat me the way I would've treated you?"

"How can I resist, when you're so charming?" Luke said, his
voice dry, bordering on snarky. He sat down on the edge of the
bed. "Listen, I have something to offer. You and I, we're all about
control. I give it up happily. I encourage others to give it up. You,
you take control, wrest it away from others. There is a part of me
that is vengeful, that wants to ask how it felt to have your control
taken away."

She looked away, her brow furrowed, frowning. She wasn't
crying yet. She would, soon. But not yet.

He soldiered on. "But I won't, because I know very well that it
sucks ass, and I wouldn't wish it on anyone. Especially not someone
who once shared love with my closest, oldest friend." He cast a
glance at Orson, who nodded in appreciation. To Mae he continued,
"If you'll let me, I can give you a little of your control back to you.
You remember the night Randy went through the Harrowing?"

She nodded. "He didn't know it was a blood moon, and came
back staggering and babbling about deer skeletons and black
foxes." She chewed her lip, thinking. "You did something out on
the porch with him, and he came in and slept for two days. And

then he turned into this philosophic git who wanted to talk about everything in maddening depth for the next semester."

Luke nodded. "Uh, yeah, I guess he did. It's a kind of earth magic similar to grounding. It won't fix any of the problems, but it'll give you a good, solid touchstone to come back to. A big chunk of satyr magic to push around."

Mae was silent for a minute, wrestling with something internally. Finally Luke said, "Do you want me to give you this?"

Mae nodded.

Luke pursed his lips, wondering how he could possibly manage this with someone who made a regular appearance in his nightmares, now that he was committed. He couldn't kiss her on the mouth. He just couldn't. Finally he said, "Sally, help me." He drew Sally's arm over his shoulders; she put her other arm over Mae's. Luke leaned in and kissed Mae on the forehead, her hands in his. He pressed his cheek to hers and drew up as much magic as he could. It was awkward and forced, and the magic clung to him like bits of styrofoam, not wanting to go to her. But slowly, little pieces of magic, like faint gasps of wind, left him and sank into her. He felt her body quiver and knew if he opened his eyes to look at her, he would see tears sliding down her cheeks. When she sat up and the tears stopped, and she let go of his hands, Luke stood—and almost fell over.

"Whoa," Mae said, her eyes filled with concern. It was a foreign expression on her features. "Are you OK? It didn't feel like I took that much."

"You didn't," Luke said. "It was just really hard to give it to you." He pointed at Orson. "You're next."

Orson held up his hands. "I'm all right."

Luke got his balance back and put his hands on Orson's shoulders. "Bullshit. You put up a good show, but you need to be centered and grounded and given a port in the storm as much as anyone here." He touched his forehead to Orson's, feeling the base of his horns touch Orson's shaved hairline. It was easier to do with Orson than with Mae. He drew up all his emotions for Orson, their many years together, his absolute trust and confidence in the man. He thought of when he'd been afraid for Orson, in battle and in life. He thought of when Orson had been there for him, sometimes when no one else was. He thought of Orson's walrus mustache, his old but tidy trailer, everything he associated with Orson. His magic liked Orson, even if there was no sexuality between them. The fae was his rock. He gave back to Orson all he had been given.

Luke was beginning to feel weak when he straightened this time. He was surprised to see Orson reach for a tissue and wipe his nose. No tears, not him, but he had gotten close.

"Thank you," Orson said softly. "Go take care of someone else. We're all right now." He put his arms around Mae, and she leaned against him. Just as they had been when Luke came in, but with a great look of relief mirrored between them. Luke nodded good night to them and guided Sally out the door ahead of him. He'd done all he could. The rest was up to them.

Sally hugged him once they were out in the hallway. "My big-hearted billy," she said, burying her face in his chest.

"If I'm a billy, does that make you a hen?"

"Fuck no." She looked up at him. "Do you have enough left to do anything for Charlie?"

"I hope so. If you'll help me." He let her lead the way toward her bedroom.

Chapter Fifty-Three

Charlie was sitting up in Sally's bed when they came in, a battered paperback copy of The Hobbit propped on his knees. He looked over the top of his glasses at them, a childlike librarian. "Am I getting kicked out?"

Sally smiled as she sat down on the bed next to him and laid her cheek against his shoulder. "No honey, of course not. Luke and I thought we might could help you. You know, get centered, get past the worst of the trauma. Satyrs work with earth magic, they're good at that kind of thing."

Charlie put the book on the bedside table. "I appreciate the gesture, but I'm actually doing fine."

Sally brushed his hair off his forehead. It fell right back. "You don't have to put on a brave face, love, we know how traumatic this has all been. It really does help. He did it for August, and Orson, and Mae."

"The hell-bitch?"

Luke sat down on the other side of him. "Yes, her. It doesn't have to be real sexual. Easier that way," Luke said, then quickly added, "but it's by no means a requirement."

"I really do appreciate the offer," Charlie said, pushing down the blankets and sitting up, "but I actually, truly am doing all right." His blue eyes were bright, and Luke could see the thoughts bubbling up inside of him, wanting to burst out, like a shaken bottle of soda. "It's like... I've been so passive for so long, staying out of the center of things, staying safe, so afraid the other myth-folk would turn against me if they really knew what I was, if they understood my magic. And they didn't!"

"Course not," Luke said. "All myth-folk can be dangerous, capable of evil and violence. Your myth ain't any more terrible than anyone else's, though I can see why you'd get some flak for it."

"It's not just that," Charlie said. "It's that the magic that allows me to pass for human isn't mine. I forget if I told you already—or if Sally told you—"

"Tell me again," Luke crooned. Sally curled up against Charlie's other side.

"When I was little, my mother took me to see a human woman who could work magic. I guess you'd call her a witch, though she sure wasn't any Wiccan. She wanted to change me into a human, or at least let me look human. The witch took another myth-folk's magic and put it over mine, like a slipcover on an ugly sofa." His brow furrowed. "Of course, I only figured out later that she would have had to kill the myth-folk to obtain that kind of magic. It's kind of sick, you know, like wearing someone's skin."

Luke shook his head. "You were a child. You can't hold yourself responsible for that."

Charlie waved him off. "I've been through all that with Sally, she's helped me come to grips with it. But other myth-folk frequently got creeped out by me. I come here, and yeah, it's in the midst of a major crisis, but...." His eyes softened as he smiled. "You guys trusted me. You let me help. You let me try. And you didn't give me a bunch of shit."

Sally threw her arms around Charlie's neck. "Ohhh, didn't I tell you so, sweetie? Those guys in Austin are jackasses. People out here are good people."

"Yes, I can see that now." Charlie smiled at Luke over Sally's shoulder. "So thanks for the offer, but I'm more likely to be able to offer you warm fuzzies than vice versa."

Sally pulled back suddenly. "Oh," she said, "I wanted to talk to you about that." She looked over at Luke and bit her lower lip. "Luke, you said something once about... maybe it would be OK for you to draw on other people sometimes. As long as I got to be there, I'd be totally cool with you and Charlie."

Luke raised his eyebrows. "You sure about that?"

Charlie furrowed his brow. "What are we debating? Are we talking about sex?"

Sally started to answer, and Luke held up a hand. "Let me lead a minute," Luke said. He trailed the backs of his fingernails up the young man's arms, watching the goosebumps rise. "Part of being a satyr is that I can tell when someone's attracted to me, unless they're actively suppressing it, like Sally did for so long." Sally stuck out her tongue at him. "And you, son...." He gave him a grin. "You think I'm purdy."

Charlie rolled his eyes. "Great. Now I can't even fantasize in peace."

"Don't have to be a fantasy," Luke said. "I think you're pretty spiffy too. You can do computers, which is badass, you're smart, you're willing to step up and help people even when you don't know how they'll take it. You just show up and work. That takes a big heart." He leaned in a little closer, near Charlie's ear. "And you suit my taste just fine."

"What taste is that?" Charlie smirked. "Saucy, loyal, dry wit, and prone to fits of violence?"

Luke sighed. "Fine, you have me pegged."

"Oh, I'd like to peg you in more ways than that," Charlie said, showing a heretofore undemonstrated forwardness. "But I'd have to have Sally's approval—no, her enthusiasm."

"Gawd!" Sally said. "Will you please just kiss?"

Luke cupped Charlie's cheek in one calloused hand and kissed him. It was so different from that first magic-drunk kiss. He felt the prickling, energetic thrust of Sally's magic, seeping into him, saturating him, and Charlie's magic, fluid and fresh. He smelled like the forest after a rain, and Luke breathed him in, making small sounds against his mouth. Charlie opened his mouth and gasped as Luke gave some of that magic back to him, right to the center of him. Luke's hands strayed over the young man's chest, pulled him close, enjoyed the warmth of his skin and the brush of his hair. He was so unlike Sally, with her soft curves; Charlie was angular and thin, with a faint peach-colored five o'clock shadow. His heart beat fast and fierce, and his kiss was needful, hungry.

"Son of a bitch," Charlie hiccuped when Luke pulled back. "OK, so there are benefits to many lifetimes worth of experience."

"I'd love to demonstrate further," Luke purred.

"You bastard. I haven't gotten laid in like, two years."

"Well," Luke said, making himself a little more comfortable, "I'm not prepared to bed you right this moment, in the middle of Sally's very girly bedroom. But perhaps we can work up to that." He nodded to Sally. "With her alongside, of course. From that epic grin I'd say her enthusiasm is not lacking."

Charlie nestled a little closer against Luke, almost as if he wanted to occupy the same space. "Given how often she's described this particular fantasy, I can't imagine it otherwise."

Luke raised his eyebrows at Sally. "Seriously?"

She elbowed Charlie. "Dude, be cool."

Luke ran his hand down Charlie's side to his waist and found the edge of his shirt. He slid his hand under the soft cotton and felt up Charlie's chest, letting the shirt ride up against his arm. Charlie shivered, wriggling with excitement that he had no idea how to express. Luke sat up and unceremoniously stripped off his own T-shirt. Nothing like bare skin, he thought, to up the ante. He lay down and guided Charlie to lie down next to him. The young man's skin was hot against his, arousal evident in every aspect of his being.

"This is going to be a tight fit, with three of us on a twin bed," Sally said.

"I'm staying here with the satyr," Charlie purred.

"How about the floor?" Luke suggested. "It's a thick carpet, Sally's comforter is crazy bouncy, and I suspect after today we are all going to sleep like the dead."

"Sounds good to me," Sally said. With some doing and maneuvering, the three made themselves something of a nest, with Luke in the middle and all their boots kicked off by the door.

Their kisses were deep and searching, exploring each other with hands and mouths. Luke's body throbbed with want, aching to hold down the handsome young man beside him and ride him, or to fuck the hell out of the girl on his other side. The satyr in him wanted penetration, possession, his cock deep inside another's body, pleasure rocking them both senseless. He was quietly smug about his self-control, catering to the needs of his partners, letting them set the pace. Charlie had to be reassured several times that it was OK, that Luke didn't care he hadn't brushed his teeth or shaved, and that sex truly wasn't necessary or even on the table at this early stage. At one point Sally sat up and reminded Charlie that "The Ex" was not in the room. After that he settled down and fretted no more.

At about ten o'clock, Luke heard his mother's car start up on the front lawn. He'd forgotten she was in the kitchen, and felt a pang of embarrassment. It didn't last long, as Allison rapped on the door once and opened it.

"Well you don't you guys look snug," she said, hands on her hips. Charlie was right, Luke realized; he did have a type.

Sally half sat up, sleepy and satisfied from a terrible, long day that culminated in sex and realized fantasies. "You can join us if you want," she said.

"Really?" said all three others in the room.

"Sure," Sally said. "Allison's cool, as it turns out. I can see why you like her, Luke." She lay back down and snuggled against Luke's back—he had been deeply involved in leaving a mark on Charlie's neck until a moment ago.

"The sentiment of a woman secure in her relationship," Allison said. "I approve. And I will sure as heck join in the sleeping pile of puppies. After I shower and brush my teeth." She patted the bag on her shoulder.

Sally pointed. "Hey, when did you get an overnight bag?"

"Are you kidding?" Allison said as she stepped out the door. "I've been hanging around Luke long enough to keep a go bag within reach at all times. Makes life a lot more comfortable." She closed the door on the sleepy trio. When she returned a half hour later in bright turquoise pajamas, they were all beginning to drift off.

"Why do I feel," she said as she lay down next to Sally and wrestled a corner of blanket from her, "that I have missed something important?"

"Don't worry about it," Sally said. "Luke's got it all figured out."

From the other side of the pallet, Luke guffawed like a fog horn. That was the last noise he made. The day, and the sheer quantity of magic he'd channeled, had finally caught up to him. He thought he could think of no greater contentment than being curled up with these three people, safe and secure and happy. Then Sootie came in and lay on his cold feet, and the world was perfect. He fell into a bone-deep, dreamless sleep.

Chapter Fifty-Four

The next morning, Luke was up with the dawn, and the rest of his entourage followed suit not too long after. He handed them each a cup of coffee as they staggered from the bedroom, each declaring him far too cheerful and energetic.

They took turns in the shower. It crossed Luke's mind to suggest to Sally that they shower together, but a look at the incredibly tiny bathroom dashed that idea. He wistfully stowed the thought away for another time, perhaps at a nice hotel on their honeymoon, and contented himself with quietly being aware that she was naked a few rooms away. And then with the idea that Charlie was naked. Luke's own shower might have been more exciting, given how stirred up he was by then, but the hot water ran out early, and he rushed through rinsing the shampoo out of his hair. He used a pink plastic disposable razor with daisies on it to shave, leaving a neat goatee, sharp sideburns, and just a couple of nicks. His hair disobeyed his instructions to comb out, preferring instead to follow the whims of his cowlicks. Finally he just got the tangles out and let it go, hoping for artfully messy. He borrowed a set of clothes from Charlie, who had packed more than enough: a pair of jeans with intact knees and hems and a T-shirt proclaiming support for a band Luke had never heard of. He didn't feel like himself until he put on his boots.

Sally took Charlie with her to collect eggs from the hens' nest boxes, a process he found absolutely thrilling. He was disappointed there was nothing to milk.

"The Saanens are milk goats," Sally explained, "but the does are all pregnant, so we've dried them off."

"What does the goat being wet have to do with milking?"

Sally shook her head. "It means we got them to stop making milk."

Charlie looked taken aback. "You can do that? Is it special food? Something in the water?"

Sally held up her hands. "Dear heart, your urbanism is showing."

Luke cooked the eggs, along with a hearty portion of bacon, and presented it to the others with a flourish. "Ta-da! Fresh from the chicken's butt!"

The girls rolled their eyes and tucked in, but Charlie looked a little pale. "The eggs come out of their butts?"

"They only have one rear orifice," Luke said. "Eat up!"

"C'mon, Jersey Devil," Sally kidded him, "join us in consuming the mangled unborn!"

It clearly took Charlie a minute to regain his sense of isolation from the reality of eating bird embryos, but the aroma of fresh-scrambled eggs with sharp cheddar cheese, freshly ground pepper, and bacon soon convinced him not to care.

Clean bodies, fresh clothes, and warm food soon had all four myth-folk feeling more human. While they were finishing the remains of breakfast, Charlie reached behind him and picked up the panpipes from the kitchen bar. "So this is what the trolls were using to call and command the chupacabras?"

Luke nodded. "That's the one bit that doesn't fit. Sure, they could make a pipe like that. You could get all the parts for it at Walmart. But how did they imbue it with magic? That's not troll magic. It had to be someone else, someone who knew a lot about chupacabras."

"Or someone who specialized in the creation of magical objects," Charlie said. "It might not be just chupacabras it can command."

The table grew silent, and Luke exchanged worried looks with the others as he thought of August and Mae.

"In that case," Allison said, "why not use it on all of us?"

"Well, good tools don't make the carpenter," Luke said. "Maybe they tried. Maybe they tried it on a whole assload of people and only managed to snag August and Mae. And chupacabras. August because with him present, no one would call the council, and Mae to rob me of my greatest strength—you girls. If she disrupted my relationships, or drained my magic, I couldn't possibly have stood up to them magically." He took the pipe from Charlie and gazed into the pipes, turning it over, as if hoping it was signed somewhere.

Sally looked suddenly grave. "Can I see that?" Luke handed her the pipes, and her expression deepened. "This... looks like it was made out of popsicle sticks, acrylic yarn, and a wind chime."

Allison guffawed. "Jeez, who would make a powerful magical object out of dollar store crap?"

"Brent," Sally said definitively.

Luke and Allison stared at her, and Charlie piped up, "Who's Brent?"

Luke shook his head. "Sally, I know you don't like Brent and you think he's a creep. But he's worked with me for four years. We're friends. And he was one of the ones kidnapped by the trolls, remem... ber...." He trailed off, trying to recall what Brent was blubbering about when they rescued him. Some kind of apology? He couldn't summon it up through the tumultuous recollection of violence and fear that was yesterday.

Sally set the pipe on the table. "I saw him at Walmart. I hate that place, but it was two a.m. and I was buying Pepto Bismol for a sick goat."

"Like ya do," Charlie muttered.

"I turned a corner heading to the checkout and ran into Brent, almost literally. It was real awkward, you know, because he was such a twit toward me before. But he was carrying an armload of stuff, including a wind chime and red yarn. I smiled at him and said, 'Craft night?' 'Cause, you know, it's two a.m. Of course you need to pick up that stuff right then. I only remember because it struck me as such a random bunch of stuff at a funny hour. In classic Brent style, he told me to fuck off. Such a classy dude. And he could definitely do this kind of magic."

Luke dropped his face into his hands. "Oh wow. When was this?"

"Months ago. Well before the first attack."

"Shit. Shit shit shit shit."

"Where's Brent now?" Allison asked.

"He went with the other damaged myth-folk to Austin. That's five hours away....Who took them?"

"Kristin," Allison said. "She can handle herself. She's one of mine, a sea serpent."

"She can handle herself when she's expecting an attack," Luke said, pulling out his cell phone. "But any one of us is vulnerable to a gunshot to the back of the head when we're not expecting it." Luke looked around the table. "Did anyone account for all the guns yesterday?"

"Crap, no," Allison said. "We were either fucked up or taking care of the fucked up."

"I'm gonna call Kristin. You have her number, Allison?" Allison gave Luke the number, and he called. It went straight to voice mail. Luke stood up, the pine chair squeaking on the linoleum. "Sally, can I use your computer? I gotta look up the number for the center they were heading toward. We'll see if they made it there last night."

Charlie pulled out his phone and tapped the screen. "I've heard tales of you trying to use a computer. What's the name of the center?"

"Sundance Hospital. Technically in Dripping Springs."

Charlie tapped a couple more screens and then handed the phone to Luke. It was already ringing.

"What an amazing modern world we live in," Luke said, admiring the sleek miniature computer that masqueraded as a phone. "Boy, I'm keeping you around." He winked at Sally and turned to pace nervously around the room while the phone rang.

Chapter Fifty-Five

The phone at Sundance Hospital rang twice, and the receptionist picked up. Luke asked if Kristin and the others had arrived the night before; they had. He asked if Kristin was still there, and he was on hold for a long time, listening to a static-ridden synthesizer version of "Don't Stand So Close to Me," before Kristin's gruff voice answered. She sounded like she was smoking, and Luke longed for a cigarette.

"Hey, Luke. I was going to give you guys a buzz before I headed back. I think everyone is settled here, finally."

"Cool," Luke said. "Listen, how is Brent? Is he—"

"Funny you should ask. He told me to drop him off at his house. Wouldn't come with us. I thought that odd, but he insisted. As far as I know he's there still."

Luke let out a big sigh of relief. "OK, thanks."

"Everything all right?"

"I'll fill you in later. Have a safe trip home." He hung up and handed the science fiction-age cell phone back to Charlie. "He's at his house. Thank God. Let's go ring his bell." After a cigarette, he added to himself.

Nothing in Fox Pass was far from much else in Fox Pass, given that there was only one major road, so it took them about fifteen minutes to get from Sally's house on the poor-but-comfy side of town to Brent's mobile home on the poor-and-scary side. Luke drove Charlie's Honda Accord, quietly marveling at the cleanliness of the car, and how everything worked on it. It was a shame, he thought, that such a comfortable vehicle would also be absolutely useless to his way of life. He resolved anew that once he had some money socked away, he was going to start saving for a really nice truck. An F-350 diesel, he thought, with a gooseneck hitch, crew cab, four-wheel drive, all power everything, truly massive tires, and a CD player. Multidisc CD player, he upgraded. Less than thirty thousand miles on her, bright blue with tan leather interior, he decided. He wouldn't even let people smoke in her. He could almost hear the throaty hum of her engine, revving ferociously. The fantasy was a pleasant distraction from the task at hand and kept Luke from freaking out.

At least, until Charlie leaned over Sally's shoulder from the back seat and asked, "So who is Brent again?"

"He's a tinker fae," Luke replied, reluctantly putting away the daydream of the truck, whom he had just named Artemis. "He builds stuff. He works for the same construction company I do. If he was responsible in the least he'd be in charge of his own team by now, but he's not, so he's lucky to have a job at all. We're friends of a sort—not close, but he's an OK guy." He paused, before adding, "Unless he really is behind some of this, in which case he's a son of a bitch who does a good impression of an OK guy."

"Luke wants to see the good side of everyone," Sally said, "so let me give you a different assessment of Brent. He's a lazy, entitled, creepy, selfish, immature brat."

"You're just mad," Luke said. They went over the railroad tracks, now officially on the wrong side.

"I have never liked that guy."

"Abundantly clear."

"With good reason!"

"I validate that."

"Thank you," Sally said, calming her hackles. "Here's what's up with me and Brent, Charlie. Some time ago he decided he liked me. So he started hanging out with me whenever he had the excuse, which was usually that there was a group gathering of myth-folk. A couple of times he volunteered to come help me out with something, since he had a truck and some DIY experience. I mean, I never asked, but he offered when I mentioned something that needed to get done around the farm. The last couple of times, when we were finished, he asked if I wanted to get dinner. I said no. I was polite and everything, but I didn't owe him a date for manual labor."

"So then Brent starts hanging out with me and Orson," Luke said, picking up the thread of the story. "Which was fine, if a little sudden. But he was always asking if we wanted to include Sally in our plans. Which I didn't, most of the time, because plans with Orson usually involved drinking beer and watching a football game, or hunting, which aren't things she's into, or doing some stupid guy thing."

"Sometimes I like stupid guy things, you know," Sally said, a sweet, affectionate tone in her voice that made Luke wonder if she was being serious or if he himself was the stupid guy thing she liked. He chose to take it the best way.

"Course you do. And I did call you when I thought you'd be interested. But would you have wanted to go turkey bowling at 1 a.m. at Walmart?"

Sally held up her hands. "Nope. I don't even want to know what turkey bowling is."

"It's where you get a frozen turkey—"

"I said—"

"And a bunch of those big bottles of soda—"

"Fine, thank you for not including me in all your shenanigans. Anyway, I figured out pretty quick that Brent was using my friends to finagle hanging with me. Not cool. So I sat down with him and explained that while I liked him as a friend, I wasn't interested in anything romantic with him. So he says that's fine, then goes around to anyone who will listen telling them how he got 'friend-zoned,' how he spent all this time and energy on me and I just led him on, how I talked big about how I wanted a good man but then I was really—" She stopped.

"Really into the bad boys?" Charlie supplied. "You gotta admit, August at least looks the part of bad boy. Motorcycle and everything."

"This was before August came into town. Actually, he said some unkind things about my virtue in regards to Luke. I'm sorry, honey, but he was rather unkind about your sexual habits."

Luke scowled and glared at the road over the steering wheel. Few things irked him like talking about people behind their backs.

Charlie whistled. "What a charmer."

"Yeah. Anyway, that's why I don't like Brent, and why I think his moral character is questionable enough to be a suspect, given all the other little bits of evidence."

"I still hope it's not him," Luke said. "I hope there's another explanation."

Sally put a hand on his knee. "I hope so too, baby."

Luke pulled over. They were across the street from Brent's mobile home. The car was in the drive. The lights behind the curtains were on.

Luke unbuckled his seat belt. "Time waits for no immortal being. Let's do this."

Chapter Fifty-Six

To Luke's surprise, Sally put a hand on his arm as he went to get out of the car, stilling him. Her hand was warm, and there was a not entirely friendly electricity to her touch that unnerved him. She was revved up and ready to rock and roll.

"Luke," she said, "I think you'd better stay in the car."

His brow furrowed, and his own stubbornness stirred to match hers. "I'm sorry, what? Maybe you had better stay in the car. You're here to accuse him, I'm here to hear his side of it."

"That's exactly why you should *both* stay here," Charlie said. "Luke's ready to defend this guy, Sally's ready to condemn him. Which speaks pretty fully of both your personalities."

"Hey," Sally said, a warning sharpness like a switchblade coming into her voice.

Charlie tipped his head toward her in deference. "I once promised you I would always tell you the truth, even when it was not what you wanted to hear."

Sally slumped in her seat and crossed her arms, glaring out the windshield. "You have a plan?"

Charlie nodded. "You guys and Allison stay in the car. I'll go talk to him first. Allison, if you see trouble coming on, you're the next one on the front line. Now, if he attacks me, I expect you all to come out with guns blazing. My devil form may be scary, but let's face it: I'm a computer tech from Austin, and this is my first rodeo."

"Sounds good to me," Luke said.

"Call me real quick, mute it, and keep your cell phone on," Sally said, "so we can hear Brent's side of it. I'll put it on speaker so we can hear."

Charlie did as she instructed, clipped his cell-serving-as-microphone to his belt, and approached the house.

It was eerie, watching the conversation on Brent's front steps and listening to it from Sally's phone. Brent crossed his arms and leaned against the door frame, casual but cross. The magical power difference between the two throbbed in the air, Brent bristling and intimidating, Charlie holding his ground impassively. They were parked far enough away, in a neighbor's driveway, that Brent had not glanced in their direction. It felt intrusive to Luke, dishonest, to listen in.

"Can I help you? I'm real busy," he drawled. "And I'd thank you to take a few steps back from my threshold." His accent was deeper South than Texas—Louisiana, or maybe Georgia. Luke only noticed it now that he was paying rapt attention to Brent's voice.

Charlie politely backed a few feet away from the bottom of the stairs. "I'm one of the myth-folk from Austin called in to help with the situation with the chupacabras and trolls," he said. Technically not a lie. "I wanted to offer you our support in pursuing justice against those who imprisoned you, and make you aware of the resources available for your recovery." Charlie's voice had hardly any accent at all, just a soft touch of roundness to his vowels that betrayed his Texan roots. Luke liked listening to him talk. He wondered briefly how much of his growing warmth toward Charlie was empathy and how much originated in his own heart.

"I'm fine," Brent said. "Most of the trolls involved are dead now anyway, right? Orson destroyed Alan's troll-self, Allison shot another—that just leaves the one Jeff took into custody, right? The senior, the one that tried to kill Luke."

Charlie shook his head. "It's more widespread than that, and moreover, the magic that the satyr unleashed is going to target a lot of people who were only peripherally involved. Whether or not he knew that is still under investigation. So we want to take everyone involved into custody, not only to uncover the truth—which tends to out one way or another—but for their own protection." Something about Charlie's stance changed, and the slight young man looked suddenly predatory. "I, for one, wouldn't want to wake up with a chupacabra at the end of my bed."

Brent shifted uncomfortably. "I don't know anything."

"Then why did the trolls kidnap you?"

"Hell if I know!"

"I think you do know, Mr. Parrings. And if you don't come willingly now, there will be little I can do for you later. You don't have to tell me anything. But do let us try to protect you until this blows over. Enough myth-folk have already died."

"Only three, Glenn and the trolls!"

"I think that's quite enough to warrant caution for the rest of us. With the unpredictable magic being thrown around, who knows who else might be targeted, or even possessed?"

Brent's pale, freckled face turned splotchy and ugly; he shifted from one foot to the other. Behind him, Luke heard Allison unbuckle her seatbelt. "That's just stupid, the trolls can't possess anyone else anymore, can they?"

Charlie took a half step forward, ducking his head sharply in an 'aha.' "Now Brent, just how did you know that?"

A frozen moment passed between them, in which Brent seemed to realize he'd been caught. Luke saw the realization written all over his face, even from that distance. A beat later, Brent whipped a gun out from the small of his back and fired. Charlie had only a few seconds to backpedal, and fell backward onto the dirt path, the force of the shot lifting him off his feet before dropping him. Sally leaped out of the car, with Luke and Allison on her heels. Brent slammed the door.

Sally ran to where Charlie lay sprawled on the ground. Allison drew a gun from the shoulder rig she wore and watched the windows, covering them. Luke hovered over Sally, wanting to haul her up off the ground and drag her back to the car, wanting to fall to his knees alongside her, wanting to charge in and throttle Brent with both hands—

Then Charlie sat up. He moaned piteously and pulled his T-shirt down to look at his chest. There was a light bulletproof vest beneath it. "Oh my God," he said, "I did not know how much that would hurt."

Luke huffed out a heavy breath, relief battling the adrenaline in his blood. "Shit," he said, "where did that come from?"

"Sally's father's closet."

"Daddy's been holding out on me," Sally said.

"Pity it wouldn't have fit you," Charlie said, "what with the boobs and all."

"Personally, I'm glad it was on you," Sally said. "Stand up, kid, back to the car and its illusion of cover."

They got Charlie into the backseat of the car, and Luke pulled the vest off of him. His heart ached as he saw the bruises already blossoming across Charlie's chest. The vest had stopped the bullet, but it could do nothing about the sheer amount of force a nearly point-blank shot delivered. Charlie would be lucky if his ribs weren't broken. If Brent had been using anything other than a dinky little pistol, he might have died anyway, just from internal damage. Luke cupped Charlie's cheek.

"Are you going to be all right?"

Charlie winced. "I think I'm done for the day," he said. He managed a small, reassuring smile through the pain. "But I strongly suspect I will be breathing when you come back."

Luke kissed him on the forehead. "Stay low, stay safe."

Charlie gave him an impertinent smirk. "I take a bullet, and I get a kiss on the forehead?"

If he could joke, he was going to be all right. Luke smiled down at him, and kissed his mouth. He felt so different from Sally, stronger and more needful. Charlie opened his mouth, a small sound shaking in his throat, and Luke pressed into him, touching lips and teeth and tongue. Charlie still tasted just a little like the blackberry jam they'd had on their biscuits at breakfast. And bacon. The satyr in Luke wanted to ignore the incredible danger of the situation, straddle the injured young man and... experience him. Behind him, he heard Sally take a deep breath and felt the mirrored stir in her. They needed a room.

It was Allison who jabbed Luke in the side with her shoe. "Hello, not the time, stop being a goddamn satyr, we have a bad guy! You *are* convinced he's a bad guy now?"

Luke felt a deep pang of regret. His eagerness to defend Brent might have easily killed Charlie. "Yes. Charlie, I'm so sor—"

"No, never mind, no apologies in war. Go kick his ass."

Luke stood up. "Now that, I can do."

Allison was already moving around the mobile home. "Luke!" she called. "He's gone out the back door." Two gunshots. "Shit he's fast!"

Sally took off to join her. Luke closed the car door with a pang of regret and ran after Sally and Allison. He reflected later that running toward gunshots was perhaps not the best move.

Chapter Fifty-Seven

Luke caught up to Sally and Allison behind Brent's house, and the three of them stopped, crouching, behind a pile of rust that was once a tractor. The backyard was a breathtaking field of chaos, full of cars, boats, bicycles, and parts for every mechanical thing ever made, all thrown haphazardly into the brush. Blackberry brambles crawled out from beneath a trio of old Triumph motorcycles, briars curtained off a stripped-down Volkswagen, and a holly bush was caught in a permanent act of exploding from within a propane gas grill, its red berries like bright embers. It looked like a mechanic's shop long after an apocalypse. For Luke, who was as delighted with machines as a child in a Toys"R"Us, it was a macabre scene.

"This," Luke said, "this yard—it's an atrocity. A mechanical holocaust."

"Focus, old man," Allison said. "Crimes against living things first."

"Oh God, is that a Mustang over there?"

Sally dragged Luke down behind an old Ford truck tilted onto its side. "Luke," she said, "look me in the eye, baby. There you go. Is Brent dangerous with access to all this?"

Luke thought about what he'd seen Brent do, magically speaking, over the years. Very little, really; the tinker fae had always kept to himself. "Well, most of his magic takes a lot of prep work."

"That's good."

"But for all I know, he's *done* the prep work and just had to come out here to get to it."

"That's bad," Allison said with a huff. She checked her phone. "Can you keep him here, keep him talking, for another ten minutes?"

"Maybe," Luke said. "What happens in ten minutes?"

Allison grinned. "I called for reinforcements."

"I fucking love reinforcements," Luke said. He stood most of the way up. "Brent! Hey man, it's Luke. What the hell's going on, man?"

"You tell me," Brent said. "You're the one who's come to take me in, apparently."

"Well, kinda, yeah. See, I took this pipe from Alan, and hell if it didn't look like your handiwork. Now, you know me well enough to know I'll hear your side of it. You want to tell me what happened?"

"You're politely ignoring Charlie getting shot in the chest," Sally snarled softly.

"Yes I am," he hissed back. "I'm stalling for time, remember?"

"I wish I had a good story for you," Brent called back. "I wish they'd tortured me, or misled me. But this time, it was all about the money, man. They offered me fifteen grand. Fifteen. Thousand. Dollars! For one job. I had to take it. Luke, you know what we make in construction. I was never going to make a good life for myself on that. Anyone in my position would have done the same thing."

Luke's blood boiled. "You knew what they were going to do with it? Call something up to go after me?"

"I didn't think they were going to try to kill you, or so many other folk. I thought they just wanted you preoccupied so you couldn't interfere."

Luke took several deep, steadying breaths. Time, he remembered. He was just stalling for time. "And here I thought we were friends," he said.

"You sure are naïve for being two thousand years old. We all got to do the best we can with what we got. It's not like you've always been Mr. Honorable, doing the right thing, looking out for everyone around him."

"Nobody's perfect. But I do my best."

"Oh, sure. Like with Sally, huh?"

Luke cast a look down at Sally. "What about Sally?" he called to Brent.

"You knew I liked her, and you boned her anyway!"

Allison rolled her eyes dramatically, and Sally signed, unmistakably, that she wanted to decapitate Brent. Luke drew in a deep breath and wincingly kept the conversation going.

"I'd really like to keep Sally out of it," he said. "What we got right now is kind of a standoff between you and me. You want to come talk to me face-to-face, or are we going to keep yelling across your backyard?"

Brent laughed. "You can come over here any time you like. But besides me to worry about, there are cottonmouths all through here."

"Shit!" Sally hissed, jumping away from the base of the truck, brushing at her pants and boots as if batting away invisible snakes. Allison was a little more controlled, but not by much.

"Who all you got over there with you, Luke?" Brent called. "Some friends? You got Sally with you now? You're a dumbass if you brought her with you."

"How's that?"

"Who's gonna protect her if you die? Not complaining, mind you. I'd love to get a good look at her titties."

Now all three of them wore matching homicidal expressions. Luke took a moment before answering, looking at Sally while he did so. "Brent, you are officially on my list. I'm gonna do whatever I can to bring you in. It would be nice if you were alive, but not necessary. And if it's not me taking you down, I assure you, the others will."

"Tell you what, man. You come blazing over here like the big billy goat gruff those trolls made you out to be, and you and me can rumble." Brent's voice turned to a snarl, and an ugliness came into it that Luke had never heard before. "And after I've put you down, I'm gonna have a good time with your girl. She might be a frigid bitch, but she'll learn how good it can be, how much she really wants it. I'm gonna rub my dick between her tits until I jizz on her face. I'm gonna turn her over a dirty workshop table and tie her to the vices, and I'm gonna fuck her till I come in her, then I'll fuck her with a vibrator till I'm ready to fuck her again. Maybe up her ass, too. I'm gonna make her like it, Luke. I'm gonna make you look like a bad prom lay."

As Brent spoke, the three myth-folk crouched behind the Ford reached a decision without exchanging a word. Anger drained away; such emotions were too reckless, too chaotic, for what they had to do. They turned cold, deliberate, as careful and deadly as spiders. This was not about vengeance, or betrayal, or outrage. This was putting down a threat, the pesky stray who'd taken a snap at a child, the garden snake who rose and struck with a spread hood, the beehive with an African queen. This was no longer an attack. This was extermination.

Allison checked her gun, made sure her spare clip was ready at hand, and looked up and down the yard for paths of cover. Luke took Sally's hand and squeezed it.

"Brent," Luke said, "I hope you have a better life next time around, because this one's over."

Chapter Fifty-Eight

Luke looked over the top of the rusted Ford, gauging how far away Brent was, obscured by multiple skeletal motorcycles and a contorted chassis. He put his hands on the ground. "Get ready," he said to Allison, and curled his back like a stretching cat. His magic roiled through him, a warm current in rivers of blood and muscle and bone. It washed out of him, into the ground, as if he were made of the same material as the earth. He focused it, sent it crashing toward Brent. The tinker fae shrieked as a jutting spire of rock threw him into the air. Allison fired, and Brent fell back to the ground.

"Damn," she said. "Just grazed him."

"Son of a bitch!" Brent yelled. "What the hell was that?"

"The power of sandstone compels you," Luke barked back at him. "Well, propels you, anyway. Give yourself up or we can continue playing Whack-a-Fae." He sat heavily, not wanting to admit how much raw energy it took for him to do that kind of earth magic outside of his home ground.

"I have a better idea," Brent said in a ferocious snarl.

Luke and Sally exchanged a dark look, and Allison checked her phone. She held up two fingers. Two minutes until reinforcements arrived.

There was a guttural, churning noise from where Brent hid. An engine choked and screamed to life. An enormous shape loomed up out of the junk, pulling itself together like a rust golem. It spread its great wings, patchwork canvas over metal spines, and engine-driven propellers lifted it rapidly into the air. It swooped skyward, its engines shrieking and smoking, like a terrible clockwork bat carrying a tinker fae in its skeletal belly. It gained speed and altitude with unbelievable swiftness and rode over the tops of the trees.

"OK," Allison said at last to the other two flabbergasted myth-folk, "how does he not know that he is a supervillain?"

"We are all the heroes of our own stories," Sally said.

"Oh shit," Luke said. "We're near the portal!"

Allison's face turned grave. "You think that's where he's headed?"

"It's where I would go if a bunch of myth-folk were after me. It's near impossible to track anyone through it. August is the only one I'd say has any chance of following him, and he's not here."

Allison nodded, tapped something into her phone, and then handed it and her gun to Luke. "We're also near the river. I'll beat him to the portal." She headed off in the direction of the river, skirting around the cottonmouth-infested junkyard to travel by a path more familiar to lawn mowers.

"Luke," Sally said as soon as Allison was gone, taking his face in her hands. "I have an idea. But I'll need your help. All the energy I've given you, that we've all given you in the past few days—you need to give me anything you have left to spare."

Luke frowned. "I—what? It doesn't really work like that, Sal. I get charged up, I can use it for my own magic, for grounding and earth magic and such. I can even give some of it back, like I did last night. Son of a bitch, was it only last night? But I can't give magical energy back the way I can take it, not to that extent. I'm not a car battery."

Sally huffed, frustrated. "You've done it before. You told me! Once a door is opened it can be passed through in either direction. Your words."

Luke shook his head, freeing himself of her hands. "I don't remember saying that. Doesn't sound like something I'd say."

"But it's something one of your first lives would have said. In one of our other lives, you told me about how you used magic from others to charge someone else. You may have hardly ever done it, but I know it's possible. You just have to be really careful, because it can kill you if you give *all* of it away."

"I'm sorry, which life? And I'm sorry, kill me?"

"The second one. In Greece."

Luke put his palm to his forehead, thinking hard. "I don't remember that."

She drew in a deep breath, eyes going wide. "The faerie chick.

In Tír na nÓg. She drained you of some of your memories. Well fuck." She grabbed him by his shirt collar and dragged him down into the tall grass. "OK, satyr, we're going to learn a new trick. I know for certain it can be done, you told me about it yourself. Work with me, baby. Charge the hell out of me, so that I can kick this guy's ass and we can go home. And, uh, don't die."

She kissed him hard, tongue and teeth and lips pressing against his with bruising intensity. He folded her into his arms and went on to her neck, biting just hard enough to hear her gasp. He rolled his tongue against the edge of her ear, and sucked the lobe into his mouth. She put her hands up his shirt and scraped her nails down his back; he shivered at the near-pain pleasure. She wrapped her legs around him, grinding against his erection through their jeans. He fell on the ground with her, groaning and rolling his hips against her. He was dizzy with want, aching to be inside her already, his heart driven to a frenzied rhythm with the sudden drowning lust.

She apparently was in a similar state, because she pushed him away to rapidly undo her jeans and push them down her legs and away, along with her panties, socks, and shoes. Luke undid his jeans and pushed them down. He just managed to get them and his boots off when Sally pulled him back down. His cock was achingly stiff and swollen and became even more so as she rubbed her clit up and down his shaft. Her juices coated him, and the heat of her pussy nearly burned. He tilted his hips back, to angle the tip of his cock against the folds of her pussy. She moaned, shivering, as he pressed the head of his cock inside her, then further in, then sank his cock into her to the hilt. She clenched around him, squeezing him, and it was almost too tight and too hot to stand. He held her down by her shoulders and began to move back and forth, fucking her with fierce, jutting thrusts.

Sally arched her back and spread her legs, asking for more of him. He pushed her shirt up past her pink bra, pushed the bra up too and exposed her breasts. He groped her roughly, bit her, and she cried out beneath him. She clawed at his shirt, pulled the shirt away from him. She bit him back. He drew his legs under him, and she straddled his lap. Luke drew gasping, rough breaths as she moved up and down on his cock, her breasts bouncing against him, her body spasming around his cock as she came.

Somewhere in his mind, he was aware that it was broad daylight, in an overgrown backyard, in full view of neighbors who potentially might be looking out their windows, especially with the gunshots. There was spear grass around them, and sharp little rocks under his thighs. He just didn't care. The suddenness of their encounter rocked his center, and he couldn't recover, couldn't think or reason. Sally pushed him down, riding up fast and down hard, pleasuring herself upon him, and he met her with equal vigor. She thrust a hand onto his stomach, just below his ribs, and it knocked the air out of him for a moment.

"Here," she said. "Gather your energy here, in the core of your body, like Allison told me to do. Remember that, when she taught me to charge you?"

Luke managed to nod, images of Sally in Allison's arms flickering across his mind. And he thought he couldn't be any more turned on. He imagined all his magical energy, every bit of lust and arousal he could gather, pouring into a tight, hot little ball under Sally's hand. It almost physically hurt, willing that much magic into one place. It seeped into him from the earth itself, like pulling up a plant by its roots.

She grabbed him by the horns and held him down. She rode him as hard as she could, a near frenzied rut. "Take all that," she panted, "and give it to me. Give it to me, baby. Thrust it into me and make me feel it. Come in me and send your magic along with it."

Luke cried out, a scream racking his throat, and came as hard as he could ever remember coming. His vision went white, little stars inside his mind, as sheer pleasure overtook him. He willed his magic into her, penetrating and saturating her with his energy, sending himself into her as surely as he sent his magic into the earth. She cried out too, and her body locked against his, rocking and clenching upon him, both of them nearly choked with the intensity of their orgasms.

Sally fell forward onto him and lay there, panting, spent. She pushed herself up on one elbow as soon as she could, dark eyes peering at him from under rumpled locks of equally dark hair. "You OK?" She was trembling all over.

"Yeah," Luke said. "It was hard to hold on to any energy at the end... but I think I did."

"Well, you're alive."

"You're sure blithe about that. And about asking me to risk my life."

Sally gave him a lopsided grin. "I have faith in you. I knew you could do it." She reluctantly pulled away from him, and their bodies parted. She gave a little moan and ran her hand down his chest. "I wish I could have you inside me a lot longer than this."

"Give me an hour or so and we'll see."

She stood up on quivering legs. "First, death and dismemberment. Then sex. Lots of sex."

He sat up on his elbows, watching her stand, naked and trembling. He was suddenly a little bit afraid of her; she was 100 percent serious. There was a murderous light in her distinctly avian eyes. She raised her arms, and called her storm out of a clear blue sky.

Chapter Fifty-Nine

Luke watched the storm coalesce out of nothing. The towering clouds swirled, swelling to greater and greater magnitude, and the wind blew around them in chaotic gusts. Lightning played around Sally, dancing through her fingertips and down her arms, to the brown-tipped mounds of her breasts, over her stomach, between her legs. She yelped and wriggled her body, black eyes wide.

"Oh," she said, "oh what the—oh!" She spread her legs farther apart, as if caught in the middle of a jumping jack. "I've never done this right after sex, when I'm aroused, when I'm so aware—holy shit!" Electric lights sparked across her legs, lighting up her skin, almost from the inside out. Luke reached out and touched her; he got a small jolt, not entirely unpleasant. He scooted forward to her and raised his mouth to her clit.

She almost buckled and fell on him but caught herself on his shoulders. She grabbed his horns and tilted her pelvis forward, giving him a better angle to suck and lick her. She tasted sweet, and musky, and her skin was burning hot to the touch. His mouth and hands buzzed with a faint electric hum, very nearly painful, but the sounds she was making were too delectable to even consider stopping. Besides, she was holding his horns, one of his favorite things ever. For that alone he would have endured much worse.

He ran his hand up the inside of her leg and pushed his fingers inside of her. The electric hum that buzzed through him followed, and he felt her muscles stiffen and swell with intense arousal. He had found a rhythm she liked, rubbing her clit roughly with his rolling tongue, and within minutes, it sent her over the edge again. She screamed, and it was far too like an eagle's cry for comfort. She tossed him away like a rag doll, end over end, several feet away. He watched as the lightning coalesced around her, and her myth-folk form manifested itself physically, completely in the mortal world. Dark brown feathers tinged with lighter penciling swept away from her swelling body; talons replaced legs and feet, and a cruel-looking, curved beak sang out the last of her cries. She raised her wings, and a hurricane-strength wind swept her into the air—and Luke against the wall of the trailer, narrowly missing a water spigot. She rose, screaming, into the storm, held aloft by the powerful winds she summoned around her. Luke watched her disappear over the tops of the trees.

He picked himself up out of the tall grass and stumbled toward the end of the trailer, intending to head for the car. A few steps from the corner he went back for his clothes. Pants and boots on, struggling to turn his shirt right side out and carry Sally's clothes too, he went for the car.

He half collapsed, panting, into the driver's seat and leaned over the steering wheel, trying to get his head to stop spinning and his eyes to focus as he turned the ignition.

From the back seat, Charlie said, "I see you managed to get your shirt off."

"I'm having a moment here, if you can't tell."

"Oh I imagine so. Let me frame this for you: you guys head off after the bad guy, there are gunshots and shouting, then a Da Vinci machine and a thunderbird fly off overhead. You come back alone, half naked. Gotta tell you, Luke, you lead one hell of an interesting life."

"Far too interesting at present. Let me get my head on straight."

"That's as likely to happen as me taking up competitive bass fishing." Charlie studied Luke in the rearview mirror, frowning. He got out of the car, moving slow and careful, and came around to the driver's seat. "Move over, incubus. I think of the two of us I'm in better shape. What the hell did you do, anyway?"

Luke slid over the center console and buckled himself into the passenger seat. "Not an incubus, those have no empathy. I gave Sally the magical oomph she needed to manifest her thunderbird self."

"That girl is repressed as hell if she needed so much help." Charlie started the car and pulled away from the drive. "Where are we going?"

"Back the way we came. Get as close to the mountain as you can, I'll tell you when we're near a trail." He leaned against the door, immensely tired and shivering. He had gone through withdrawal before, in other lives. That was what it felt like, he thought, like his body was lacking something it desperately needed to keep going. He ached all over; he felt faintly nauseous and dizzy. He couldn't stop trembling, and a clammy sweat broke out on his face and neck.

He wondered distantly what would happen to him if he'd given Sally too much of his own magic. Would he die? Eventually recover? Would his myth-folk self die, the way Alan's troll-self had died? Not for the first time, he wondered if there was an afterlife for myth-folk—or if, indeed, there was an afterlife for anyone. Life was cheap; he'd seen so many people die, including himself. It was very possible that this was all there was, and that in a few minutes, he might come to the end of his thousands of years. No eternal peace, no repose, no better life—just over. Not with a bang, he thought, but a whimper. He wished he could have remembered the rest of the poem.

Huddled into a corner of his own mind, chilled and feverish, contemplating death, Luke felt very small. Very alone. And not a little bit afraid.

Chapter Sixty

In the car rushing toward the portal at the edge of Fox Pass, Luke was having a quiet, queasy, possibly lethal existential crisis. Charlie watched him in his peripheral vision. "What's the matter?" he asked. "You're pale. And you're Mediterranean; it's wrong for you to be pale."

"I think I gave Sally too much energy," he said. "I have supposedly charged people before, the way I let them charge me, but I can't remember doing it. I didn't know when to hold back."

Charlie took one of Luke's hands and put it on his stomach. "Let me see if I can do anything useful while driving. I first saw you come out of a magical portal on an enormous black horse, carrying a spear from hell, with a pair of fully manifested horns on your head. That appealed to the devil in me like you wouldn't believe. Watching you and Sally, I can't help but be a little bit jealous. But just a tiny bit, because you guys are amazing together, and I can't be selfish enough to want to get in the way of that."

"This is a delightful conversation," Luke growled, "but satyrs don't run on adorable crushes tempered by respect and loyalty. We are creatures of earth magic, and we run on raw sexual energy." His voice was coming out clipped and snarled, like someone else's voice. "Being around horny people is a snack, being around horny people with a focus on myself is a small meal, sex with other myth-folk is satisfying, and an orgy with myself as a central point is a feast." This explanation taxed Luke of all his available willpower, and he curled against the door of the car, not caring that the seatbelt cut into his neck.

Charlie pulled the car over to the side of the road. "Criminy, I don't do lust very well," he said.

"Did you just say criminy?"

"I'm demonic! I'm not exactly wholesome."

Luke was too spent to develop a counterargument. So, he reached for the obvious. "What would Sally say to that?"

Charlie was quiet for a moment, thinking. Finally he said, "She would say that I wasn't really a demon, that I was one of the myth-folk, and I was closer to a mental construct of early colonial American folklore. That I existed because enough people told stories about me and believed in me. That I was formed out of the consolidated energy of belief and thought. Joseph Campbell, eat your heart out."

Luke wasn't sure he followed. Still, not being one to argue with a perfectly good overexplanation, he said, "Sounds about right."

"But it's people's beliefs in *demons*."

Luke made a rude noise in his throat. "I've met demons. Trust me, you're not one. You are stupidly, hilariously not one."

"How do you know?"

"I survived the encounter."

"Oh."

"Can this be about me now?" Luke said. "I feel shitty."

"Sorry!" Charlie said. He got out of the car and, in the slow, wincing walk of the injured, came around to Luke's side. He opened the passenger door, and Luke would have fallen on his feet if the seat belt weren't holding him in. There was no proper shoulder to the road, just a jagged edge where the asphalt faded into equally hard dirt and dirt-colored grass. Charlie knelt there and got as close to Luke as he could; he cracked his knuckles, preparing for battle.

"All right. Lust. Gotta be turned on while nursing a chest injury. Luckily, I had painkillers, so it's not so bad...." Luke got the distinct impression the boy was talking to himself. "OK. I've had a difficult time coming to grips with my sexuality. I tried really hard to change myself. But Luke, I look at you and I know the truth. I know that I like guys—no, not just guys. I like men." He said it the way some women might have said *chocolate*. "Muscular, sweaty, masculine men. Which is kind of unfortunate because not many of them are gay, but hey, problem for another time. You make me know myself—and I suspect you do the same to other people, like Sally and Allison. It's hard to hide from you. Sally managed it for so long just because she's so old. Me? I had no chance, I have to acknowledge my own feelings when you are around." He gritted his teeth, clearly reluctant to go full-on-lusty. "I look at you, and I want you to fuck me. I want your cock up my ass, pounding me like this was your last lay before the apocalypse. I want you merciless and demanding and dominant."

Luke felt a faint stirring outside himself, the now-familiar smell of forest, and rain, and moss that was Charlie's magical energy. His nausea eased, and he was almost able to catch his breath. Charlie was still talking; he tuned back in.

"I want to do things to you, too. I want to please you—I want to affect you, to stir you. I want to suck your cock until you almost come, then stop, then work you up to a climax again. And if Sally wants to watch, if that turns her on, the more the better. I—"

He faltered as Luke reached out and ran a hand down his chest, to his belly, and then reached between his legs. Charlie grabbed the frame of the car to steady himself. Luke found him already hard, from talking as dirty as he could muster. He gasped as Luke ran his hand back and forth, coaxing the lust in him to greater heights. The chill began to fade; things began to come back into focus. He undid Charlie's jeans and pushed them roughly aside. He needed the energy Charlie was giving off, desperately needed it. And he tasted so good, like earth magic mixed with water and air, and a hint of deep, ancient fires beneath it. Like so many young myth-folk, he had all the elements of magic in him, unlike the highly specialized older ones like Sally and himself.

He spit in his hand, grasped Charlie's cock and began stroking up and down expertly. Charlie cried out and stopped trying to talk altogether. Luke leaned farther out the door, grateful for the seat belt holding him in, and kissed Charlie roughly. He grasped the back of the boy's neck, pulling him closer, sucking at his mouth. Charlie rocked his hips in motion with Luke's strokes, making little sounds that were almost pained. His magic poured off him in a

steady stream, like water poured from an ever-full pitcher. It wasn't
the intermittent shocks of Sally's magic, or the waves of Allison's—
it was constant, thick and pure like cream. Luke liked the feel of
his cock, smooth and hot, the taste of his mouth, the strength of
his lips.

Suddenly Charlie pulled away. There was a decision sitting there
in his eyes, glaring out at Luke defiantly. It was an odd look. Charlie
reached over and undid Luke's pants, which had only a few
minutes ago been zipped back up. He grasped Luke's semi-hard
cock in his hand and began stroking him, coaxing him, looking
up at Luke with a wavering commitment to the moment.

"Sally's OK with it?"

"She better be, she put me in the state to need it." He was hard,
and looking at Charlie's archer's-bow mouth, he felt his own lust
answering the call to arms. His body stirred, blood and heat pooling
in his center, pleasure and hormones fueling what little strength
he had left. "Please. I really need this. Ordinarily just making out
would help a lot, but right now it's not enough. I need—"

That seemed to be all the encouragement Charlie needed. He
lowered his head and took Luke's cock into his mouth. Luke
gasped and arched against the seat, bucking his hips upward.
Charlie's mouth was hot and tight, and he was doing wonderful
things with his tongue. He stroked up the shaft, rubbing along the
tender vein underneath, vibrating over the very delicate bit of skin
below the head like a fiddler with a bow, sucking and resting,
sucking and resting in motion with his strokes. He was a true
prodigy at the art of the blow job.

And he knew it. The longer it went, the more energy came off
of him. Luke was saying things, but he wasn't really aware of them.
Encouraging, praising, cussing. Charlie was stroking himself too,
and the lust-magic he produced tasted sweet and dense, soaking
into Luke's spent soul. It was a massive relief, feeling that much
come back to him.

He came without much warning, and though he tried to say
something about it, Charlie didn't heed him, and kept sucking

through the duration. He felt it when Charlie came too, hitting him with a wave of lustful energy that left him breathless. He came hard, and it seemed to go on, and on, his body rocking with the pleasure of a second orgasm in such a short time. Charlie coaxed it on with his strong lips and hot tongue, and swallowed.

Charlie fell back against the car door, gasping and holding his chest. Luke stared unseeing out the windshield for a moment before he said, "Son of a bitch."

Charlie grinned. "So's all right?"

"That... has got to rank as the best blow job of my life."

"Of how many lives?"

"Don't push, boy, I was in France when it was sexy." He zipped up, unbuckled the seat belt and scooted clumsily across the center panel of the car. He was still dizzy, but in a very, very good way. Charlie climbed into the passenger seat, adjusting his glasses. Luke watched him with concern. "Still your chest, or did I take too much of your magic?"

Charlie shook his head. "Nope, just the massive torso trauma. My magic's fine." He turned to Luke with a lopsided grin that made him look younger and rakish. "I come from a spring, remember? That's what the Blue Hole is."

Luke returned the grin. "Splendid."

Charlie buckled up carefully; his brow furrowed as he did so. "There was a taste to you I couldn't quite place."

"Oh. That. Um. Well. See. Sally and I kind of had sex behind the trailer and I hadn't had a chance to really properly clean up yet." It came out all in a rush.

The blood drained out of Charlie's face. He looked like he wanted to say a lot of things, but in the end he pressed back against the seat and stared out the window. "I... now know what Sally's lady-bits taste like. I am deeply traumatized."

Luke put the car in gear. "C'mon, let's go see if my thunderbird girlfriend is done eviscerating the little fairy who threatened to rape her."

"I'm sorry, what?"

"I'll explain later. Right now, ass-kicking time."

Chapter Sixty-One

Luke drove up to the trail that would lead to the portal, enveloping the car in a cloud of red dust with a hard, sliding brake. He exited in a rush and started up the trail, leaving Charlie behind in the car. He glanced back as he ran, a little nervous about leaving the injured and exhausted Jersey Devil alone, but he had little other choice. He just had to hope Brent was the only baddie left.

The heavy scrub obscured his view until he was almost right on top of the portal. He stopped short of bursting into plain sight, peering through the last scrap of cover for an idea about the situation. The chill day had turned positively cold with the fierce thunderbird storm, the first truly cold day of fall. It was a wind that went right through the meager cotton of his T-shirt, almost alive in its aggression. Luke crossed his arms and searched the skies for Sally.

Up from the canyon beyond, a massive shape rose on feather-thin wings. The sheer size of the airborne predator shook Luke to the core. She dove briefly at something deeper in the canyon, then rose again, her talons empty.

"They've reached an impasse," a voice said, and Luke jumped. August stood, dead still, just inside the forest. It amazed Luke how completely invisible a half-ton horse and rider could be in darkness and cover. The horse's skin shuddered in anticipation, his ears swiveling like radar dishes to catch everything around him. August caught Luke's startle and shrugged. "Ghost magic." He gestured toward the canyon. "The fae is caught between them. Sally can't go much lower in the canyon without getting to where she can't go up again. Our mermaid friend is keeping the river too wild to land in, and the canyon widens out to Sally's advantage on either end. He's trapped—until Sally makes a mistake. If he can outmaneuver her, he can still get past her, up to the portal."

Luke nodded. "What can I do?"

"Can you fly?"

"No. What the hell kind of question is that? I'm a satyr."

"People around here have surprised me before. Does he want anything but to escape?"

Luke thought for a moment. "He's proud. And he'd like to see me dead."

August nodded. "Heckle him. Get his attention. Make him reckless. Annoy the shit out of him." He smirked as he looked down at Luke from, literally, his high horse. "You can do that, can't you?" He gathered the reins almost imperceptibly tighter and touched his heels to his horse's ribs. The enormous animal picked his way out of the thicket as if he moved through it every day. Luke looked at the fearsome creature and was glad it was August who was on its back this time. On cue, the horse gave Luke a sideways glance as it passed him and, Luke could have sworn, grinned with great malice. The pair crossed the open dirt between the forest and the portal in three strides, leaped, and disappeared into the portal. The air in the portal rippled as August went through it, like water into which a stone had been thrown. A big, black, snobby stone, Luke thought.

Luke stepped out from cover and hurried across the open ground to the edge of the cliff. The portal loomed large and threatening beside him, a natural stone arch of striated yellow sandstone. He looked down onto Sally's back and the top of Brent's flying machine. Below them, the Rio Grande roiled and frothed over its banks. Luke supposed he ought to have been thankful there was no one else around to see the man-sized bird with a wingspan like a pterosaur. He summoned up what he knew about Brent— his supposed friend, coworker, and fellow myth-folk, who had turned out to be far more deadly and treacherous than he could have imagined. Now what, he thought, would rile a man like that?

"Hey Brent!" Luke bellowed above the gusting wind. "You look a little busy down there, but I thought you ought to know—before my girlfriend knocks you out of the sky—what I'm going to do with your place. You know all your tools, your machines and supplies? I'm gonna donate them to the high school. I figure that way the dumb teenagers can use and abuse them, which is a better fate than throwing them all on the junk heap. Cuz that's really where they belong, I don't know if the school will even want that shit."

Brent answered back in a similar bellow, calling him names Luke wasn't sure were real words. The flying machine turned and pitched at a dangerous angle, nearly colliding with the wind-beaten wall of the canyon. Above him, Sally banked away early; she was big, and she turned more slowly. Having survived his error, Brent suddenly seemed to see the opportunity it had provided him. He braked and swept upward, propellers smoking. He ascended right behind the enormous raptor, who cried out in rage as her prey escaped. She swept up onto the plain with dizzying speed and banked around to come at him above the walls of the canyon.

Luke ducked as the flying machine swept over his head, dangerously close. Brent brought the machine around, heading for either Luke or the portal. Sally wouldn't be there soon enough to keep him from being mowed down by the propellers if Brent decided to take a pass at him. He closed his eyes against the whirling dust, hoping he would not be a tempting enough target, compared to the portal and escape.

August and his horse leaped out of the portal as Brent closed on it. The horse gave a monstrous scream as he came, and upon his back the headless horseman was a nightmarish specter licked with brilliant green ectoplasm like foxfire. As they landed, August drew back and threw the flaming skull he held in his hand. The fireball hit Brent in the chest as he tried to pull up and swerve away. White fire exploded out from the skull, and the thin canvas webbing upon the flying machine disintegrated with hardly a trace of smoke to mark its passing. Above them, Sally checked her attack, swooped away, and tucked her talons against her soft underbelly.

Brent fell to the ground in a heap of metal and soot and flame. He screamed, writhed, and whipped about, the spines of his machine threatening to impale anyone who ventured too close.

The horseman dismounted from his still-galloping horse, rolled his landing, and came up at a run. He grabbed one of the spines of the machine and flung Brent around, grappling for control.

Luke's mind buckled at the sight of August's undead form brought to light and flesh right in front of him. He thought he had seen it well enough, thought he was prepared for it, but the power of the headless horseman, the undead hunter of the Germanic forests, lay in the fear he summoned in those around him. Brent screamed, his mind cracking as well at the sight. Luke shook his head. If his rational mind wouldn't work, he'd have to fall back on instinct. He watched the motion of the fight and didn't think at all; he waited for his body to react, for two thousand years of fear and combat and rage to kick in.

The wings of the mangled machine swung wide. Luke's legs were already moving—he darted forward, as quick and sure as a mountain goat. Brent saw him coming and lashed out with an awkward backhanded fist. Luke checked himself for a beat, dodged the swing, grabbed Brent's arm, and lunged in to smack Brent in the face with all the force he could put into a crushing headbutt. He felt it even through his horns, which were made to absorb an awful lot of force. Brent crumpled to the ground, his hands on his face, blood leaking out between his fingers.

August appeared at Luke's side, and Luke nearly sucker punched him before August drew back his undead visage and threw up his hands. Luke stopped midair, his adrenaline-addled brain trying to make sense of how the headless ghost now had quite a nice-looking head on it. August dropped to his knees and cuffed Brent, hands and feet, with iron shackles. The tinker fae screamed, and no one gave a damn.

Chapter Sixty-Two

Luke felt Sally land behind him before he saw her. It wasn't her weight—even a massive bird like a thunderbird was relatively light—but the great gust of wind that nearly knocked him over, then abruptly died. The storm above them began to fall apart, dissipating back into the atmosphere. It was still cold. He raised his hand to touch her beak as she nudged his shoulder. He looked aside at her; alien eyes looked back, sharp and predatory. Her feathers were not soft, necessarily, but smooth. She moved with the rapid jerks and twitches native to birds and reptiles, and at the moment looked just about as forgiving.

August hauled Brent up onto the back of his horse and secured him there, having removed the mangled flying machine and tied it to drag behind the horse. August surprised Luke when he quieted Brent's screams by gently sliding a piece of cotton between the iron shackles and the tinker fae's wrists. As long as Brent stayed still, the iron didn't actually touch him. It was a small act of kindness, performed with an almost tender touch and the same low, murmuring voice he might have used to calm his horse.

Then again, he might've just wanted Brent to shut up.

August returned to where Luke and Sally stood watching. "I am taking him to New York," he said. "He needs medical attention, but we can't take him to a hospital. There is a witch up there who can fix him."

"Medical attention? For a broken nose?" Luke said.

August tried to suppress a smirk. "I think he may also have fractures in his cheekbones, maybe in his brow. You really smashed the hell out of him."

"Safe journey," Luke said, extending his hand. "Are we going to see you again?"

August gave Sally a quick sideways look, and she gave what

might have been a nod in return. He took Luke's hand and pulled
the satyr up against his chest. August kissed him, and somewhat to
his surprise, Luke found himself stirred. He'd warmed to the ghost
in the past few days; free of possession, August had proven himself
capable, compassionate, and powerful, and there was nothing like
adrenaline to kick-start a bond. Like before, he couldn't feel any
magic within August, the way he could in almost everyone else. It
was intriguing, kissing someone without feeling a rush of magical
energy, without knowing how turned on they were, like being
blindfolded. Sally's lust, even, was strangely tempered and unfamiliar,
seeing as how she was in her myth-folk form and not operating as a
human. For once, he knew that the excitement that made his gut
clench and his skin quake and his lips part was his and his alone.

It was pretty cool.

So he kissed August back, letting the ghost's tongue slide between
his teeth, tasting, testing. August was taller, stronger, and grew
demonstrably excited through his tight black jeans as they kissed. He
smelled of a sharp, tangy aftershave, a smoother cologne, saddle
leather and horse. Luke liked the curve of his spine and the swell of
his chest; images flashed in his mind of what August would look like
unclothed, and he was sure it would be a pleasant sight.

"Yeah," August said against his mouth as they parted, "I'll be
around."

Sally positively cackled. Or maybe, Luke thought, she was just
clearing her avian throat. Yeah right.

August gave Sally an affectionate pat and a kiss on her beak and
then swung up on the saddle in front of Brent, who was lashed to
the horse like a set of saddlebags.

Luke shuddered. "I think your horse just winked at me."

August grinned. "He might have. Don't worry, I'll keep a buffer
between you. Don't want a nightmare too interested in you." As Luke
choked and sputtered, August gave the horse—the nightmare,
apparently—a merry click of his tongue, and they trotted into the
portal, disappearing into the air.

In the silence that followed, Luke thought he heard a voice.

Frowning, he went to the lip of the cliff and looked down to the river. Allison was still in the river, treading water in the midst of the powerful current, screaming up at him. He cocked his head at Sally, who cocked her raptor-shaped head back at him.

"I think she's saying... did we get him."

Sally warbled her agreement.

"*Yes!*" Luke shouted back. "*Yes, we got him, he*—*what?* Oh, for crying out loud."

Sally held up one of her enormous talons and gave a thumbs up sign. Allison hooted and disappeared under the water, satisfied. Luke wanted to laugh but found all the energy seeping out of him, like water down a drain. It had been far too long a day.

"C'mon, Sal," he said. "Let's go back down the path, Charlie's got your clothes in the car. I figure that's why you're still all feathery." She walked beside him down the path, giving him affectionate nuzzles and biting his hair. She was far more graceful in the air, and it was slow going. "Cut it out," Luke muttered, playing grumpy as she pulled his hair. "You walk like a chicken. Bawk bawk bawk."

She might've laughed. Or it might have been a promise to kill him. With a thunderbird, it was hard to tell.

Chapter Sixty-Three

Luke sat in the passenger seat, exhausted but smiling, and Charlie sat braced and wincing in the back seat while Sally recounted her aerial battle with Brent and his flying machine. Her dark hair was a mess; she'd thrown on an old baseball cap of Charlie's from the depths of the trunk, drawing a ponytail through the hole in the back to keep it corralled. With every dramatic gesture she made, the ponytail flipped up or back or around, mimicking her excitement.

She finished her narration as they pulled up to the hospital. Luke helped Charlie out, and Sally followed in their wake. They went through the automatic doors into a blast of freezing cold air; no one had yet flipped it from AC to heat in the unexpected cold front. A woman sat with a boy holding a bandaged arm, both sullen and exhausted, and a heavily flushed young man lay across three of the orange plastic chairs, somehow asleep under a blanket despite how uncomfortable he must have been. They were the only other patients in the small town hospital, which also housed every medical professional in the county, save the veterinarian.

An iron-haired woman with a broad frown took Charlie's information. She looked up at him over the forms he'd filled out. "Kicked by a mule?"

Charlie had thrown on a T-shirt, also plundered from his trunk, to replace the one with the bullet hole. He tugged down the collar of the shirt to display the colorful bruise blossoming across his sternum. It reminded Luke of a watercolor painting he'd once seen of an exotic purple daylily.

The intake nurse whistled. "Lucky he didn't get you in the head."

No one said anything, but the three exchanged a dark look. Lucky, indeed. They got Charlie settled as comfortably as possible to wait for someone like a doctor to examine him and his "mule kick."

"Anything we could get for you?" Sally said.

"Actually," Charlie said, tapping his mouth, "something to eat would be great. It's past lunch, inching toward dinner, and I tremble to think what they serve here."

"It's not so bad," Luke insisted. "Least someone else is cooking."

"A real American cheeseburger?" Charlie said, looking at Luke with doe eyes.

"Aw shit he has wiles! It's not fair! Fine, pretty boy, I'll fetch you dinner." He leaned over and kissed Charlie's forehead, much to the interest of the intake nurse. "Anything else you want?"

"Inner peace."

"Anything for sale in Fox Pass."

"Naw," he said, settling back. "I have the internet in the palm of my hand. Thanks."

As Luke and Sally headed out the front door of the hospital, Luke looked back at Charlie. The lenses of his glasses were lit up by the light of his phone. Luke got the distinct impression that Charlie was a little relieved to be left to himself for a while.

Sally and Luke went to the only decent restaurant they knew of close to the hospital—which, by happy coincidence, was Allison's diner. Luke's face broke into a grin as he pushed open the glass door with its little chime. Cormick sat chatting animatedly with Allison in the back corner booth. He grinned and waved the newcomers over.

Allison's wet hair was pulled back into a ponytail and threatened to start frizzing if she didn't do something about it soon, but she, like Sally, appeared not to care too much about her hair at the moment. She beamed up at Luke, flushed with pride and excitement. She was wearing her work clothes, a skirt and collared shirt and apron over comfortable shoes, presumably the closest set of clean clothes she'd gotten her hands on after coming out of the river. She must have had a spare set at the diner. Luke was suddenly reminded of the time, not too terribly long ago, when she'd dragged him into her office and had her way with him. Despite having been run sexually ragged, he couldn't help but perk up and take interest. Inwardly he gave a little sigh; he might never get to fuck Allison again. That was a habit that was going to die hard. Long, slow, and hard. Unless Sally warmed to the idea of sharing him, which at the moment wasn't entirely out of the question, but he was not going to press his so-far astounding luck.

Cormick was talking, and Luke tuned back in as he tore his gaze from Allison. "I've just gotten off the phone with the council in New York," he said. "They're beside themselves that this went on as long as it did without their... management. And that it was a handful of rebellious, dare I say, secessionist hicks who solved it, not their own wayward representative. So they are making, uh, reparations, so that we don't raise a shitstorm and have them voted out of office."

"We could do that?" Sally mused.

"Well, if the whole nation got an earful of what happened here, and the council did nothing, yeah, I could actually see that happening. So they're throwing money at the problem until the problem goes away."

"I love being a problem," Allison sighed.

"Yes, honey, we know," Cormick said, patting her hand.

"How much money?" Luke said, eyes narrowed.

"Well, they're paying for the damage to Sally's folks' homestead, and to replace the car that got trashed. They're keeping tabs on every known troll, and especially every known bridge troll, in case a chupacabra shows up with the Wild Hunt on its heels. The trolls seem to be fine with that, considering what happened to Alan and what's-his-name. They're paying Luke's medical bills—"

"Oh Hallelujah!" Luke cried. "Bring on the copayments!"

"—and anyone else's who got caught up in it."

"Charlie will like the sound of that," Sally said.

"They're paying each one of us major players—that being everyone here, plus the kidnapped folk, minus Brent of course, plus Orson and Mae—a compensation package for 'endangerment,' whatever they mean by that. As for you...." He leveled his eyes and index finger at Luke. "They're paying you a field operative's salary for the past six months, since you kinda went and did a field operative's job for him."

"Ohhhh, man. I can't tell you how much that will help. What's a field operative make, anyway?"

"Ooh yes," Allison said, leaning on her elbows. "Tell us how much August is worth."

"You're getting seventy-five thousand."

Luke stood up abruptly, knocking his chair over backward. "Holy shit! Seventy-five? That dude makes a hundred and fifty thousand dollars a year?"

"Oh, now he is hot," Allison said. "Cormick, you have to marry him."

Cormick ignored Allison entirely and held up his hands. "I have no idea how much he makes. Feel free to ask him. I'm just the messenger." But he was smiling.

Luke beamed down at Sally and swept her up in an enormous hug. She hugged him back, squeezing hard. "This'll make getting started a whole lot easier."

"Getting what started?" she asked teasingly.

He pulled back and kissed her, touching her belly with his fingertips. "Everything."

In all the excitement, they almost forgot to bring Charlie his cheeseburger. Almost.

Chapter Sixty-Four

Sally's parents were waiting for them when Luke and Sally arrived at the house. The air was heavy with suspicion and alarm, which Sally disarmed with a hug around her father's middle. She said into his chest, "I'm sorry I can't tell you."

Wilson's eyes softened, and he kissed the top of his daughter's head. "I know you can't. I'm just glad you're OK."

Her mother, Georgia, got a hug next, though she was significantly less mollified. It took Luke asking what kind of new car she'd like as a replacement for the sedan to bolster her spirits. Wilson retrieved four beers from the refrigerator, and they sat out on the porch, talking about anything but what had actually happened, while the day wound down. Heavy in Luke's mind was the spot only a few feet away where Orson had impaled Alan with the black spear. The broken decking had been replaced with a new board that stood out in its newness, despite having been painted a nearly perfect match for color. The gravel in the drive where the chupacabras had danced to the mad music had been raked and filled. No matter what else one might say about them, the New York Council and the Fox Pass Council did not fool around when it came to covering up their activities. Luke reflected that even his parents would not have been so accepting of secrecy.

"Talked to your folks," Wilson said, as if reading his thoughts.

"Yeah?" Luke said, a little distantly.

"Your mama said she'd stopped by earlier, wanted to check that everything was OK."

"I'll give her a call," Luke said, and started to stand up.

"She'll be by in a little while, I asked them over for dinner," Georgia said.

"Oh," Luke said, a little mystified, and sat back down.

"I figured we might have some planning to do." She could not have been more plain.

"Yeah," Luke said, taking Sally's hand and grinning. "I guess we do."

"Thought you were gonna ask us about it first," Wilson said, "what with you having been so formal and all before."

"I haven't formally asked her," Luke said.

"Psh," Sally said, "formalities be damned. I'm marrying the man and that's that."

⁂

Charlie was released from the hospital within a few hours, and Luke's parents picked him up on their way over. Though he had three ribs with miniscule fractures, he had no internal damage to organs or tissues. Rest and relaxation were prescribed, which suited him very well. The doctor said he'd been lucky with his "mule kick" and released him, making it clear with a raised eyebrow and a disapproving grimace that he knew very well it hadn't been a mule that left the great stormcloud of a bruise on his chest.

Charlie walked in and declared to Luke as soon as he saw him, "This explains everything."

"Oh?"

"Your dad is crazy. But your mom seems cool. When she's not yelling at him."

"Was she driving?"

"No."

"Goddamn it, he's not supposed to drive! Dad!"

"Oops, I'm caught," Luke's dad, Donald Shepherdson, said. He was an enormous man with a magnificent mustache and a build of muscle and bone and gut beneath a layer of padding. He handed his homebrew beer to his much smaller and angular wife and prepared for a confrontation with his equally slender and wiry son.

"You don't have a license, you can't drive! Mom, why'd you let him drive?"

"I was tired. My blood sugar was all funny. I had a hard day yesterday." She gave him a pointed look.

"Son of a—you realize that if you get pulled over, you're going to jail, right?"

Donald shrugged. "I put a case of homebrew in the back. I figure if I get pulled over, I'll offer them some, as a special thank you for the great job they do as our protectors. Those boys, they really put it on the line, they deserve a relaxing beer more than most."

Luke rolled his eyes. "Of course. And since Alan is off the force, there's not a one of them would bat an eye. Fucking favoritism."

"Luke!"

"Alan's off the force?" Donald said. "Since when?"

"Yesterday," Luke answered. He narrowed his eyes, made sure Wilson and Georgia were out of earshot, and said, "Orson killed his troll soul with Cuchulainn's spear."

Donald shrugged. "Just like when you were a kid, ain't it? I don't understand half the things you say, weirdo." He retrieved his beer, made himself comfortable on the couch, and took no more notice of Luke's outrage or bizarre proclamations. Luke took a deep, steadying breath and pulled his mom aside for some whispering and hissing.

Dinner was as relaxed as a Shepherdson dinner ever was, interfused with bickering and "debate." The Wilson family was more sedate, but they were accustomed to the Shepherdsons. After the meal, they drank coffee as Georgia dug in the icebox for a thing of ice cream.

"So," Donald said to the room in general, "I take it we're going to have us a ceremony sometime soon."

"Dad," Luke said, "I haven't even bought her a ring yet."

The whole room couldn't help but smile.

"June's always nice for weddings," Georgia said.

"But it's so hot," Agatha said. "How about April or May?"

"Or October," Sally said. "That'd give us about a year to plan."

Luke almost said something about how there might be a baby born before then but decided he'd best keep his big mouth shut.

He put his arm over Sally's shoulders. "Personally," he said, "I don't see why we need a big ceremony. Why not just something simple, in about a month? We could have it up on my mountain. There's a big field of Johnny-jump-ups and wild violets will be in bloom then, right next to the sunflower patch, which will still look good. Say, our folks, my brothers—least, the ones who aren't in jail—and our closest friends. It'd be easy, and we could get on with the business of married life, instead of focusing on the wedding."

"David could officiate," Wilson said, referring to their long-time Methodist pastor.

"Could put Cormick in charge of the food," Luke said.

"And I'll bring the booze," Donald chimed in.

"There. Planned." Luke sat back with a satisfied air.

Sally shook her head and looked at her mother and future mother-in-law. "Men."

Agatha guffawed. "We'll get together later and change their plans. But really, it doesn't sound half bad."

Georgia sighed. "It sounds lovely. But I was kind of looking forward to planning my daughter's wedding."

Sally kissed her mother's cheek. "S'okay, Mama. You can help us build and decorate a nursery. For a theoretical baby," she added, holding up her hands as the whole room looked at her. Georgia looked more than mollified.

Wilson slumped in his seat. "My stars, that was five hundred times easier than I thought it would be." He clapped Luke on the shoulder. "Thank goodness it's you, boy."

Luke smiled genuinely. "That is perhaps the best compliment I've ever received, sir."

Chapter Sixty-Five

It threatened to storm the morning of the wedding. Sally took care of that. It took another couple of fae spells to turn it warm before three, when Sally met Luke by the sunflower patch.

She let her father give her away. Her dress was simple, new white satin to her bare feet. She wore her grandmother's gray shawl, the one piece of weaving the impoverished Navajo woman had kept for herself, hand spun from a favorite ewe's last fleece. It represented the grand sum of all Sally knew about her grandmother. She borrowed Allison's mother-of-pearl butterfly hair clips, and a small stone of turquoise in a silver pendant. Luke wore a white shirt, black slacks, and suspenders under a dark red vest. His hair behaved. They each thought the other resplendent.

Luke couldn't help but smile at their friends, seated beyond the mass of parents, grandparents, brothers, nieces, nephews, cousins, aunts, and uncles. A lot of them were members of the Fox Pass council, and one from New York in black motorcycle leathers had slipped in at the last minute. Luke's brother Matt, Orson, and Cormick were beside him; Sally's cousin Nell, Charlie, and Allison were on Sally's side.

A Methodist minister read familiar vows. Luke hardly heard the words; he could only gaze at Sally's smiling face. He put a ring on her finger, a small band of silver and turquoise, and she put one on him. He raised her veil, and they kissed. Their assembled loved ones clapped, congratulated them, and put the folding chairs away. There was eating to be done, and dancing, and celebrating. Luke barely remembered any of it; all he could recall, later, was his beautiful and radiant and happy bride.

As the light and the warmth of the day failed, family and friends left, in ascending order of importance. Allison took Charlie back to her house, and everyone kissed everyone else good-bye, promises of lives lived close hanging unspoken among them. Sootie chased the familiar taillights down the driveway and then ran back with her tongue lolling, scattering offended chickens. Luke fed the goats, sleeves rolled past his elbows, and Sally turned off the outside lights. She waited for him on the front porch, a vision in white with the gray wool shawl now wrapped close around her. Luke joined her on the porch and wrapped his arms around her waist. They kissed, long and slow and deep, and went into the house together.

In years to come, the house would expand. Luke's tiny bedroom became the nursery when they built on a larger master bedroom; they added a third bedroom when the nursery was needed again in a few years. The kitchen expanded, as did the living room, and then another bedroom appeared, and a mudroom off the kitchen. More land fenced in, more garden space plowed, a proper workshop built for Luke and an office for Sally. A swing set and a tree house went up, and a rotating cast of bikes, toys, sporting equipment, and, finally, far too many cars full of teenagers littered the front yard. The flower patch where they'd married came to house a pair of ponies with a small red barn and a wall full of ribbons, and a stall was added on for an enormous palomino quarter horse, where one little girl or another could almost always be found. A stone in the front garden stayed undisturbed for Saul, and many long years later, another for Sootie.

But none of that was even a scribble on paper yet, that first night. They went to the little bedroom with the door Sally and her father had fixed, to the little twin-sized bed. Luke lay down beneath Sally; he swept her hair from her face, studying her smile. "I'm yours," he said. "You got me. No matter what happens from here on out, I'm yours."

"I know," she said. "I know it bone-deep. And that's why I can stand to share you, when I have to, even enjoy it. I know you're always coming home to me."

Their bodies moved together as the moon blazed cold, blue light through the time-frosted windowpanes. He drank in her magic, and gave it back to her in equal measure. They did not stifle their cries—who else was there to hear? They wore out the words "I love you" and "Oh God." They slept in each other's arms, as late into the morning as the animals would allow.

Their myth-folks selves might live forever, or at least as long as any of them could perceive. But for Luke and Sally, one lifetime would have to be enough.

Chapter Sixty-Six

If it hadn't been for the horns, she wouldn't have recognized him as a satyr at all. The only thing Greek she could tell about the young man was his Roman nose. The rest of him was generic European—blond hair, gray eyes, and pale skin. His hooves were not visible, clad as he was in loose cargos and hiking boots. Her hair was dark; like his nose, it was the last vestige of her myth's native people, the dying notes of the Navajo in her blood. He sat a little ways apart from the other myth-folk, arms around his knees, practically screaming "introvert." Trish stopped a few feet away from him, waiting to be noticed. Her bare toes dug into the sand, and she kicked a little at him.

"Hey," she said.

He looked down at the sand, then up at her. A little wrinkle appeared between his eyes as he studied her, wary. "Yes? Can I help you?"

"You're a satyr."

"Well spotted."

"I knew a satyr in a past life."

"Lots of people knew a satyr in a past life."

She made a face at him, waiting out his bullshit. Finally he huffed, "All right, how long ago was it, and what was your satyr like. I'll tell you if it was me. To my knowledge there isn't a warrant out for any of my past lives' deeds."

She plopped down beside him in the sand. Here, near the bonfire, it was still warm. Farther down the beach, the sun-drenched sand was cooling rapidly. Her hands were chilled, and she dug them into the warm grit.

"His name was Luke Shepherdson. He lived in the early twenty-first century, married to a thunderbird named Sally."

"Sounds familiar," he said. "Had five kids, lived in Texas?

Carved pan pipes and other flutes, and his wife sold them online?"

She grinned. "Yes, that's him!"

He smiled back at last and offered her his hand. "That was me. My name's Elliot. You, ah... you look a little avian." He squinted at her.

She gripped his hand. He had nice hands. "Trish. And yeah— I'm a thunderbird, I was Sally. Man, I've been hoping to run into you since that life! I've had four since then, on my fifth now." She grinned, wide and goofy.

"I'm on my fourth," Elliot said. "Two of mine were really short, and the last I was up on Mars."

"Well how awesome to finally find Luke's reincarnated soul again! Not that we're the same folk by any means," she added.

"No, of course not, but that was a really nice life," Elliot said. "I agree, it's great to find someone who remembers that time."

They eyed each other, their thoughts mirrored in the other's eyes. But it was too early, their association too new. They spent the rest of the evening talking. The bonfire blazed into the night, and the other myth-folk all around them hardly seemed to even exist. Trish's sisters tried to pull her away to join the dancing, but to no avail. The more they talked, the more they remembered—about the lives Luke and Sally had lived, about the myth-folk they had known, about their children and grandchildren, and the vast lineage that followed.

"Shame Charlie died so young."

"Fuck cancer," Trish answered. "I ran into him last life."

"How was he?"

"A she. And much better adjusted. Especially since she had the full benefit of myth-folk magic, unlike Charlie."

"Shame what happened to August."

Trish shook her head, sobering. "The sucky part was that they never found the body."

"I guess he knew what kind of dangers he was getting into, being a field operative for the New York Council. I just wish Cormick hadn't been with him at the time."

"True that. Allison wasn't the same after, and since last life she was a confirmed bachelor, I'd say the shadows of the loss are still with her." Trish raised the beer in her hand, which was beginning to turn warm. "To old friends, long recycled."

Elliot raised his plastic water bottle and tapped it against her beer bottle. "To old friends."

"So," Trish said, "whatcha got going this time around?"

"I'm moving to Australia in a few months. I have an opportunity to work in a research lab, where I won't have to deal with people much. It will be better for me than dealing with the general public."

"Get out!" Trish said. "My mom lives in Australia!"

"Big country. Where at?"

"Victoria."

"Now that is a coincidence. The research lab is in the Murray region. Your mom wouldn't happen to raise sheep, does she?"

Trish nodded vigorously. "One of the only big Merino flocks left, after synthetic protein fiber production displaced the wool industry. There's still a niche market for people who want the real thing." She narrowed her eyes. "What are you doing in that area? It's almost all rural now. Not weapons testing, right? You don't strike me as an animal person."

"Oh ho," Elliot said. "I'm not an animal person, she says. Birdie, you're going to be hearing about that one for ages."

Trish couldn't help but smile at the implied promise that they would know each other long enough to have history, and that this was the start of it. "Did I just step in it? What?"

He grinned wide. "I'm a veterinarian."

"Well shit. But hey, I bet my mom will like you."

"As I recall, sheep were integral to your background in Luke and Sally's life too."

"Sheep is life. That's a Navajo saying. They're important."

"But the Merino flocks aren't Churros," Elliot pointed out.

"Meh," Trish said, "we're all mutts now. It's a fuzzy heritage."

"Especially with sheep."

Trish snorted and elbowed him. "Go get me another beer, satyr-boy. Get yourself one too. You're letting me talk too much."

Elliot fetched beers. As he handed her one, he said, "You're really more like Allison, you know. Sally was never so forward. She was cautious, almost suspicious. Allison was the one to go after what she wanted."

Trish smirked. "And Luke would have made at least three passes already," she said. "Maybe it's because after Luke died, Allison moved in with Sally and they had a lovely eight years living as cranky widows, chasing chickens and grandchildren. She had a big influence, especially there at the end."

"Is that what happened? Nice. Allison and Sally were hot together, once Sally loosened up some."

"See? The beer's working already. So, Mr. Satyr Veterinarian. Luke had Sally, and a trio of other long-term lovers to feed off of. What do you do to keep charged up?"

Elliot cleared his throat. "I don't do a whole lot of magic."

"Seriously?" She felt a little disappointed.

"It's complicated."

"You don't have to tell me now," she said. She slipped her hand into his. "We're old souls. We can take our time."

Elliot and Trish were not Luke and Sally. But somewhere in their souls, a shadow of their former selves remained, with enough love between them to know that no matter what troubles arose, they would be on the same side, for each other's sake, in this life and in many lives to come.

About the Author

Julie Cox lives in Texas with her husband, children, and ever-expanding menagerie of animals on their farm. She runs a small online yarn business and teaches yarn spinning. She has numerous stories published with Circlet Press and elsewhere. For her full list of published works, see her website at www.lazypifarm.com.

www.ingramcontent.com/pod-product-compliance
Lightning Source LLC
Chambersburg PA
CBHW022022240626
47154CB00007B/2224